Chemmeen

THAKAZHI SIVASANKARA PILLAI (1912–1999) was a Malayali novelist and short story writer whose work focussed on the oppressed classes. He has written several novels and over 600 short stories. His best-known works include *Kayar* and *Chemmeen*. He won the Kendra Sahitya Academy award in 1958 and the Jnanpith award in 1984.

ANITA NAIR is the bestselling author of *The Better Man*, *Ladies Coupé*, *Mistress* and *Lessons in Forgetting*. Her books have been translated into over thirty languages. This is her first work of translation.

Chemmeen

THAKAZHI SIVASANKARA PILLAI

Translated by

ANITA NAIR

HARPER PERENNIAL

First published in India in 2011 by Harper Perennial
An imprint of HarperCollins *Publishers*
a joint venture with
The India Today Group

Copyright © DC Books
Translation copyright © Anita Nair 2011

ISBN: 978-93-5029-086-6

2 4 6 8 10 9 7 5 3

HarperCollins *Publishers*
A-53, Sector 57, Noida, Uttar Pradesh 201301, India
77-85 Fulham Palace Road, London W6 8JB, United Kingdom
Hazelton Lanes, 55 Avenue Road, Suite 2900, Toronto, Ontario M5R 3L2
and 1995 Markham Road, Scarborough, Ontario M1B 5M8, Canada
25 Ryde Road, Pymble, Sydney, NSW 2073, Australia
31 View Road, Glenfield, Auckland 10, New Zealand
10 East 53rd Street, New York NY 10022, USA

Typeset in 10.5/14 Adobe Caslon Pro
Jojy Philip New Delhi 110 015

Printed and bound at
Thomson Press (India) Ltd.

Part One

One

'That father of mine talks of buying a boat and nets.'

'What a lucky girl you are, Karuthamma!'

Karuthamma didn't know what to say. More to fill the silence than anything else, she blurted, 'But there isn't enough money. Do you think you could give us some?'

'But where do I have the money?' Pareekutty spread his palms out in front of her.

Karuthamma laughed. 'So why then do you strut around calling yourself Little Boss?'

'Why do you call me Little Boss, Karuthamma?'

'So what should I call you?'

'You must call me Pareekutty.'

Karuthamma trilled 'Paree'… and then she burst into laughter.

He insisted that she say his full name. Karuthamma stopped laughing. Suddenly grave, she shook her head. 'No.' Then she said, 'I can't.'

'Well, I won't call you Karuthamma either!'

'What would you call me then?'

'I'll call you the Big Momma Fisherwoman.'

Karuthamma burst into laughter. Pareekutty too laughed.

Long peals of drawn-out laughter! What, indeed, were they laughing about? Who knows! But there was to that laughter much unfettered joy!

'Well, when you have bought your boat and nets, will the Big Momma Fisherwoman tell her father to sell us your catch?'

Karuthamma replied, 'If you give us a good price, of course, we will.'

More laughter!

What was so hilarious about this conversation? Was there a joke in there somewhere? Could people go off into paroxysms of laughter just like that?

All that laughing brought tears to Karuthamma's eyes. Her bosom heaved. 'Oh, don't make me laugh like this, my Bossman!'

Don't make me laugh too, Pareekutty retorted.

'Oh! You are so … so … you are such a Bossman!'

They laughed again as if they had tickled each other. Now it is a given in the law of tickles that laughter dwindles eventually into a solemnity that dissolves into tears. And so Karuthamma's face took on a ruddy hue. Her smile faded. A complaint emerged. She fumed. No, it was actually indignation. 'Don't look at me like this!'

He had committed a crime without knowing it. Pareekutty said, 'But you are the one who made me laugh, Karuthamma.'

'Oh! What shall I say, my Bossman?' Contrite, Karuthamma crossed her bosom with her hands and turned her back to him. Suddenly she flushed at the thought that she was wearing only a thin mundu.

Just then someone called for Karuthamma from her home. Chakki who had gone to sell fish in the east had come home. Karuthamma fled.

Pareekutty felt a sense of unease. He worried that she was offended.

As for Karuthamma, she too felt as if she had stung him with her reproof. He must be hurt, she fretted.

And yet, when had she ever laughed like she had? Never before and never with anyone. It was most extraordinary. All that laughter had made her breathless, almost as if her lungs would burst ... and strangely, it left Karuthamma feeling naked. She wished she could disappear. She had never known anything like this before. So was it then in that peculiar state of mind, disconcerted and perturbed, that Karuthamma felt something strike deep within her?

Her breasts heaved. They seemed to burgeon by the moment. His wandering gaze had fixed there on her breasts where a pulse fluttered. Was that how that laugh had shaken itself free? ... And she had been wearing only a sheer mundu. Beneath which she was naked.

Had his gaze offended her? Pareekutty anguished. Was that what made her leave? Would Karuthamma ever come back?

He would apologize to her. He wouldn't ever be so uncouth or so disrespectful again.

It seemed that the two of them needed to seek redemption in each other's eyes.

Once upon a time a little girl of four years had wandered along this seaside. A little girl who collected shells from the beach and ran to gather the silvery minnows that flew off the nets the men flung out of their boats. In those days she had a little boy companion. Pareekutty. Wearing a pair of trousers and a yellow shirt, with a silk handkerchief knotted around his throat and a tasselled cap, and clinging to his father's hand. Karuthamma remembered her first glimpse of him very well.

Pareekutty and his father built a trading shack to the southern side of her hut. It still stood. And young Pareekutty was now its owner–trader.

And so on that seaside they grew up as neighbours.

Karuthamma's mind wandered as she stoked and poked the fire in the kitchen. Embers flew and burnt outside the stove. Her mother who came into the kitchen stood there taking in Karuthamma's vacant gaze and the untended fire.

Chakki nudged Karuthamma with her foot, shattering her reverie rudely. Chakki demanded furiously, 'Who are you thinking of?'

Anyone looking at Karuthamma would have asked that of her. So you mustn't censure Chakki. It was obvious Karuthamma wasn't in this world.

'Ammachi, ichechi was on the far side of the shore with the Little Boss. They were standing behind a boat and giggling,' Karuthamma's younger sister Panchami reported.

Karuthamma quivered. Her secret crime. What should have stayed undiscovered now lay revealed.

But Panchami wouldn't pause even then. 'You should have seen how they were laughing, Ammachi!'

This is what happens if you mess around with me, Panchami waggled a warning finger at Karuthamma and ran from the room.

Karuthamma had left Panchami at home when she had stepped out. Panchami hadn't been able to go out to play with the neighbourhood children. Chembankunju was insistent that the house be never left vacant. In its confines he was hoarding money in the hope of someday buying a boat and nets. Panchami had been forced to stay indoors. This was her revenge.

How could any mother not be perturbed by such news?

Chakki demanded of Karuthamma, 'What is this I hear?'

Karuthamma didn't have an answer.

'Girl, what were you thinking of?'

And now Karuthamma had to speak. She didn't have an option. So she stumbled to find an explanation. 'I was just out … wandering on the beach…'

'And on the beach?'

'Little Boss was seated in a boat.'

'So what's so funny about that?'

Karuthamma tried to explain, 'I was merely asking him for the money we needed to buy the boat and nets.'

'So who asked you to go around cadging for cash?'

Karuthamma stuck to her story. 'I heard you and Accha talking the other day. You were saying that you were going to ask Little Boss for money.'

It wasn't a valid explanation. She was merely trying to justify what she had done.

Chakki scrutinized Karuthamma from head to toe.

Chakki too had been that age once. Or, was it that Chakki remembered a time when she was as old as Karuthamma was now? Then as well there were several shacks on that seaside, and in those shacks Little Bosses. And in the shadows of beached boats those Little Bosses too had been willing enough to tickle Chakki into peals of laughter. Who knows?

But what was certain was that Chakki was a fisherwoman born and bred on the seaside. And an inheritor of a long tradition of sea lore.

On a mere plank of wood, the first fisherman had rowed through waves and currents to a point beyond the horizon. While on the shore his faithful wife had stood facing the west, waiting. A storm blew up and churned the sea. Whales with their mouths gaping open gathered. Sharks beat the water into a frenzy with their tails. The undertow dragged the boat into a whirlpool. But he miraculously survived all these dangers. Not just that, he returned to the shore with a huge fish.

So how did he escape that tempest? Why wasn't he swallowed by the whale? How was it that his boat didn't shatter to bits despite being battered by the shark's tail? The whirlpool dissipated; the boat moved on ... How did all of this happen? Only because a chaste wife had stood on the seaside, praying and waiting for her husband's safe return. And that was the lode of hope the women of the seaside clung to. The nugget of faith that Chakki melded into her everyday life and made it her very own.

Or perhaps, when Chakki's bosom too had ripened into fecundity, a Little Boss had let his gaze rest upon them. And that day, Chakki's mother too must have told her about the traditions of the sea; the demands it made on its women.

Chakki, who was impervious to what Karuthamma may or may not have been guilty of, said, 'My daughter isn't a little girl any more. You are a fisherwoman now.'

In her ears, Karuthamma heard the echo of Pareekutty's teasing: Big Momma Fisherwoman.

Chakki continued, 'In this vast sea, there is much to fear, my daughter, my magale. All of which determines whether a man who goes out to sea will return. And the only thing we can do as women is keep them safe with true minds and bodies. Otherwise, they and their boats will be swallowed up by the undertow. The life of the man who goes out to sea rests in the hands of his woman on the shore.'

It wasn't the first time that Karuthamma had heard this cautionary admonishment. Each time a few fisherwomen got together, you heard this being said.

And yet, what was wrong with sharing a laugh with Pareekutty? She had not yet been entrusted with the life of a man going out to sea. And if such a life was in her hands, she would cherish it. She knew how to care for it. No one needed to tell her, a fisherwoman, that.

Chakki continued to speak, 'Do you know why the sea cries at times? The sea knows that if the sea mother gets angry, all will be ruined. But if she is pleased, she will give you everything, my child. There is gold in the sea, my daughter, gold!'

Chakki imparted a great truth to her daughter then. 'Virtue is the most important thing, my daughter. Purity of the body and mind! A fisherman's wealth is his fisherwoman's virtue.

'There will be Little Bosses who, with scant respect for our traditions, will defile our seaside. There are these sluts who come from the south to peel shrimp and help hang out fish to dry. They sully our seaside. What do they know of the seaside's propriety? They are not children of the sea. But we are the ones who have to bear the brunt of their doings.

'Be wary of shored boats and thickets on this shore.'

It was with a grave face Chakki continued forewarning her daughter. 'Look at you! All breasts and buttocks. Little Bosses and other such feckless men will want to keep looking at your breast and bum.'

Karuthamma shivered. In the shadows of the shored boat, that was precisely how it had happened. And the resentment she had felt at that moment – she could have acquired it only congenitally. When a man stares at your breasts and bum, it is disrespectful to a child of the sea.

'Magale, you shouldn't be the reason why this shore turns barren or be the reason why the mouths of its people are filled with mud!'

Karuthamma now grew frightened. Chakki went on with the aplomb of one who knew her words had struck a chord. 'He is not one of us. A Muslim. And he probably doesn't realize any of this.'

That night Karuthamma couldn't sleep. She wasn't angry with Panchami who had let her secret out. She didn't even feel any resentment. How could she? Was that because she felt guilty? An age-old moral code of that community was vested in her too. And perhaps that was why she was scared of straying. As long as the fear resided in her, how could she be angry with Panchami?

Just then the strains of a song wafted in from the seashore filling Karuthamma's ears and trailing her, wrenching the very earth from under her feet.

Karuthamma listened.

The singer was Pareekutty. He wasn't a musician. But he sat in the boat singing. How else could he let her know that he was there?

And she heard.

It struck her where it was meant to.

Karuthamma became restless. Should she slip out unnoticed? But he would again look at her breasts and bum ... She would have to go to the shadow of the shored boat. And that was a place fraught with dangerous temptations ... And he was a Muslim.

It was the chorus of the people who went out to sea. Karuthamma knew fear then. If she were to hear it for a little while longer, it would tempt her to go to him. She had known a certain pleasure at the piercing intensity of his gaze on her bosom. Weren't breasts made of flesh after all?

Karuthamma lay on her stomach pressing her breasts down. She stuffed her fingers into her ears. And yet, the song found its way in.

Karuthamma wept.

She knew that the flimsy door to the room of her heart could be opened with ease. Or it could be stormed open.

But thereafter were walls that were inviolable. A strong and enduring wall made of an ancient and sacred moral code of the children of the sea. It had neither doors nor windows. It was here she lived.

But even those walls could crumble when called by flesh and blood. Hadn't such walls fallen before?

Pareekutty's song spread across the lonely seaside. It wasn't meant to tempt a fisherwoman to stealthily open her door and step out on her own. It had neither a beat nor a rhythm. Nor was the singer's voice even fine. Yet, it had a life of its own. For it reverberated with his need to let her know he was there, so he could make his apologies to her.

Like she was consumed by her need to offer penitence.

Pareekutty continued to sing. His voice cracked.

Karuthamma pulled her fingers out from her ears. She heard her parents speaking in the adjoining room. No, they were squabbling. Karuthamma listened. They were talking about her.

Chembankunju said, 'I know all that, woman. You don't have to tell me. I am a father too!'

Chakki reproved, 'You are a father, are you? I am glad that you remember that! Your daughter will be led astray.'

'Go go, woman! I will have her married before that happens.'

'And how are you going to manage that? Who is going to marry her without money?'

'Listen to me,' Chembankunju laid out his life plans before her. Karuthamma was hearing it for the hundredth time.

In anger as much as in grief, Chakki said, 'In that case, all you will have is your boat and nets.'

Chembankunju retorted decisively, 'No matter what, I won't touch a coin from that money I have put aside. So don't even think of that!'

Chakki snapped, 'A Muslim man will end up seducing your daughter. That's what's going to happen.'

Chembankunju didn't speak. Didn't he understand the gravity of her words?

A little later, he said, 'I'll find someone.'

'Without paying any cash?'

He grunted reaffirming it.

Chakki asked, 'Then he must be a moron or a deaf-mute!'

'Wait till you see, woman. Wait, will you?'

Unconvinced Chakki said, 'Why don't you just drown your daughter in the sea?'

Chembankunju snorted.

Chakki asked abruptly, 'Tell me, whom are you buying this boat and nets for?'

Chembankunju was silent. The boat and nets were his life's ambition. He had never asked himself whom it was for.

Chakki made a suggestion, 'Why don't we consider that Vellamanalil Velayudhan?'

'No, he won't do.'

'Why not? What's wrong with him?'

'He is a fisherman. A mere fisherman.'

'If not a fisherman, whom do you plan to find for your daughter?'

There was no answer to that.

Karuthamma's ears echoed with 'A Muslim man will seduce your daughter'.

Her father hadn't perhaps understood the import of it completely. In her chest her heart drummed as if it would burst. Hadn't the Muslim already seduced her?

In the distance Pareekutty continued to sing.

Two

The next day Karuthamma didn't step out of her home. There was much hustle and bustle on that day in Pareekutty's fishing shacks. From the east many women had come to help. Heaps of dried fish lay on braided palm-leaf mats.

In those listless hours, a furtive thought shot through her like a streak of lightning: would Pareekutty stare at the breasts and bums of those women too?

Just after it turned noon the boats that had gone out to sea began returning. Chakki took her basket and went to the seashore. On her way out, Chakki said in a tight voice, 'Girl, don't forget what Ammachi told you.'

Karuthamma knew what she wasn't supposed to forget.

A little later Chembankunju arrived. Karuthamma served him his lunch. Unusually for him, he looked at her carefully. He saw her every day. So what was the significance of that look that day? Had her father discovered her transgression? Karuthamma worried. In that case, wouldn't that look have borne the mark of censure? However it wasn't so.

Chakki had reminded him last night that they had a grown-up daughter at home. From the time he could remember, he had been struggling to acquire a boat and nets. And now this: a grown-up daughter! Some unsuitable man would have his way with her, Chakki had said. So that was why he had appraised her.

To this day Chembankunju was a hired hand. Taking a share for the work he does in other people's boats. First he worked as a rows man. Now he was the helmsman. Owning a boat was his life's purpose and so he clung to the money he had made. He had accumulated much money over the years. Yet it wouldn't suffice for a boat and nets.

The girl was of age. An age where slips could happen. Chakki was right. Her anxiety had reason. Should he buy the boat and nets or get his daughter married off? This was his dilemma. Chembankunju too had a word of caution to offer, 'Girl, you need to look out for yourself!'

So her father too had now counselled her.

Karuthamma didn't answer. Neither did Chembankunju expect her to.

In the evening, after having disbanded his workers, Pareekutty was perched on the boat. Perhaps he hoped that Karuthamma would come that way, as she had yesterday.

Chembankunju walked towards Pareekutty. Karuthamma watched them converse for a long while. What could they be talking about? she wondered. Perhaps her father was asking for a loan.

That night the husband and wife talked for a long time in stealthy whispers. Karuthamma wished she could find out what they were talking about.

Pareekutty sang that night too. Karuthamma lay within her hovel and listened to it. Once, she had only one thing to tell Pareekutty, 'My Bossman, you mustn't stare at my breasts so...'

Now she had one more thing to tell him. He mustn't sing!

Until two days ago, she had flitted around carefree as a butterfly. In two days so much had changed! Now she had reasons to lose herself in thought. So she began to fathom herself. And with it began an understanding of the gravity of life. She would have to watch out for herself. Each step had to be carefully considered. In which case, would she ever be able to skip and run without a care? As she used to.

A man looked at her bosom. And just like that she became a woman.

The next night she didn't hear Pareekutty's song. That night too the moonlight washed the seashore in its silvery light. The mysterious song of the sea beat its way through the coconut fronds and wafted to the east.

Pareekutty's song. When it didn't fill her ears, Karuthamma felt a great unease. Wouldn't he sing again?

After supper, Chembankunju stepped out. Chakki stayed awake. Why wasn't she sleeping? Karuthamma asked her mother.

Chakki told her to go to sleep.

And so Karuthamma drifted off into a light sleep.

Suddenly she woke up with a start. Someone was demanding, 'Is Karuthamma awake?'

It was a voice she knew. A voice she recognized only because of the faint tremor it bore. It was Pareekutty.

Chakki said, 'She's asleep.'

Karuthamma heard the embarrassment in her mother's tone. Karuthamma broke out in a sweat. She rose and peered through a slat of the makeshift door. Chembankunju and Pareekutty were heaving in something heavy. Not one or two but seven laden palm-leaf baskets. Dry fish.

Karuthamma felt as if a fist had reached in and grabbed her insides. She saw Pareekutty, Chembankunju and Chakki stand in the front yard deep in a whispered conversation.

The next day Karuthamma questioned Chakki about the

baskets. Chakki didn't meet her eye when she said carelessly, 'That Little Boss kept it here.'

Karuthamma wouldn't let it be. 'Why? Can't he keep it in his shack?'

'What's your problem if it's here?'

In a little while Chakki demanded furiously, 'Who is he to you anyway? Watch yourself, girl!'

There was so much Karuthamma wanted to say and ask. He was no one to her. But what they had done was still thievery. Weren't they becoming beholden to him? Her father had said, 'Girl, you need to look out for yourself.' How could she if they put themselves in his debt? But Karuthamma didn't speak.

The next day the dried fish was sold. And the day after, the sea flung its bounty into the nets. Having brought back the catch to the shore, Chembankunju went out in the boat again. And Chakki went to the east to sell fish. Panchami wasn't at home either. Karuthamma was all by herself.

Pareekutty came there then.

Karuthamma fled and huddled inside the hovel. He stood in the yard. Silent. Waiting.

There was a certain consternation in him. His mouth was dry. He said aloud, 'I have given the money for the boat and nets!'

There was no answer.

So he continued, 'Now will you sell us your fish?'

'If you give us a good price, we'll give you the fish' should have been the retort. That was what Karuthamma had said once. But no words were spoken now. It was after that conversation conducted in the shadow of the boats that the uncontrollable laughing fit had emerged. Pareekutty must have expected a repetition of that episode. But it didn't happen. Silence.

Pareekutty asked, 'Karuthamma, why aren't you talking to me? Are you angry with me?'

He thought he heard her sob from within.

'Are you crying, Karuthamma?'

Pareekutty then offered, 'If you didn't like my coming here, I'll leave…'

There was no answer to that either. And so from a dry painful throat, Pareekutty squeezed out the words, 'Shall I go, Karuthamma?'

It was as if that query flung itself onto her heart. And yet all Karuthamma could say was, 'My Bossman, you are a Muslim!'

Pareekutty didn't understand the relevance. 'So?'

There wasn't an answer for that. So what if he was a Muslim? And then Karuthamma too asked herself that.

Suddenly she said furiously, 'Bossman, go stare at the breasts and bums of the women who work in your shack!'

She was accusing him of a roving eye, Pareekutty realized. She must assume that he seduced all the women who worked for him. How was he to prove his innocence to her? He wished he knew. He hadn't ever looked at any woman as he had at her.

With all the sincerity he could muster, he pleaded, 'I swear by Allah, I haven't ever!'

It was precisely what she wanted to hear. An affirmation of goodness. She wasn't suspicious. But refraining from merely looking at other women wasn't what she wanted of him.

She wished she knew how to tell him what she expected of him. For which she would have to tell him of the traditions of the sea that bound her; the dictates that governed her life. She didn't know how to; nor did she have the courage.

There was a long silence. Neither of them spoke. As if conscious of that silence and that it would only grow, Karuthamma said, 'My mother will be here soon.'

'So what?'

She quivered in fright. 'It's wrong! It is a sin!'

'Karuthamma, you are inside the house. And I am outside here. So what is the problem then?'

Should she explain this as well to him? But how? If she were to begin explaining, there was so much to say!

Pareekutty asked, 'Karuthamma, do you like me?'

She replied abruptly, 'Yes, I do!'

It was his desire for her that made him demand, 'Why then, Karuthamma, are you not stepping out?'

'No, I won't!'

'Listen, I won't make you laugh. All I want is to look at you … and then I will leave.'

Helplessly, she cried, 'No, no … how can you?'

A little later Pareekutty said, 'Well, I am going …'

As if in response to that, there was a sound from within the hovel. 'I will always like you …'

What more could be said to pledge a troth?

Pareekutty left. And only then it occurred to Karuthamma that she hadn't spoken any of what she had meant to say. All she had done was voice the unspeakable.

That night she saw Chembankunju and Chakki sit in the light of a kerosene lamp and count money. However, it seemed it wasn't enough. But there was a certain sense of relief in Chembankunju.

He said, 'Thank god, we manage to accumulate this much without getting involved with Ousep or one of those cut-throat fellows!'

Chakki too was relieved. Imagine their plight if they had borrowed from one of those moneylenders who walked around with cash only to net gullible fisherfolk.

In which case there would be neither boat nor nets; nor the money sunk in the deal.

Only recently both Ousep and Govindan had offered to lend

them money. But Chembankunju had refused it. If he got involved with them, he knew he would be ensnared in their eternal debt. And soon, they would take away his boat and nets and make it theirs. That was how it had always happened on this shore.

But the money he had wasn't enough. So what was to be done?

Chembankunju said, 'Let the Little Boss give us the rest too. What?'

For the first time in her life Karuthamma felt hatred for her parents.

She despised her mother more because her mother wasn't even protesting.

In the next few days, Pareekutty's shack was busy. Fish were dried and put away in baskets. Karuthamma knew the reason for the frenzy. In a few days Karuthamma had learnt the measure of the world.

With the elation of someone who senses a change for the better in their lives, Chakki told Karuthamma, 'Magale, we too are going to own a boat and nets!'

Karuthamma didn't speak. She was unable to share her mother's excitement. A change had come upon her.

Chakki said to herself, 'The sea mother has blessed us.'

The pent-up ire in Karuthamma spilled over. 'Won't the sea mother be angry if you cheat people?'

Chakki peered into Karuthamma's face. She didn't flinch. And she had more to ask of her mother.

'Ammachi, why cheat that naive man to buy a boat and nets? It is cruel ...'

'What are you saying? Cheating?'

Boldly, Karuthamma stood her place. 'Yes.'

'Who?'

Karuthamma answered with a stony silence.

Chakki said, 'If we borrowed money from Ousep, he'll soon make the boat and nets his.'

'That's not it, Ammachi. If you borrow money from Ousep, you will have to pay it back and the interest you owe.'

'Don't we have to pay this back?'

'This ... this, do you mean to really pay this back?' She flung the question at Chakki's face.

Chakki tried to defend what they had done. That the dried fish bought from Pareekutty was merely a business deal. All Chembankunju did was ask, Chakki argued. He didn't insist. He didn't lie or deceive. They would return the money; that much was certain.

Karuthamma asked, 'If your intentions were so honest, why bring the dried fish in at midnight? Why not do it during the day?'

'Look, the sea's crying,' she said abruptly.

It was as if she meant that her parent's deception had made the sea cry. Chakki was furious. 'What are you saying? That your father stole the money?'

Karuthamma didn't speak.

With the power vested in a mother, Chakki demanded, 'Who is that Muslim boy to you? Why do you care so much?'

Her tongue curled to say he was no one to her. But the words were not uttered. Why should she insist that he meant nothing to her? The silence was an act of courage. Was Pareekutty no one to her? He was her everything, Karuthamma realized then.

Chakki repeated her question and then added, 'Will this girl bring doom upon the seashore and the fisherfolk?'

Karuthamma protested fearlessly, 'I won't break any rules.'

'So why are you so bothered about his welfare?'

'You will ruin him. He will have to tear down his fishing shack and leave.'

Chakki fell upon Karuthamma in a torrent of abuse. She stood there listening. It didn't irk her one bit. Chakki was merely blabbering. When the abuse began to veer towards the vulgar, Karuthamma asked her mother quietly, 'Do you think he gave the money because he trusted my father?'

'Why else?'

Suddenly Chakki remembered that Karuthamma had asked Pareekutty for money. That perhaps was why Karuthamma had so many questions.

'Or, do you think it's because you asked him for it?' Chakki asked.

Yes. That's why. That's only why – But Karuthamma couldn't say it. Even though she knew that Pareekutty was in love with her.

Karuthamma said, 'Don't make me say things, Ammachi!'

'What?' Chakki paused and then asked, 'Why, did I flirt with him to get the cash? What's there for you to talk about?'

Karuthamma broke down. She cried, 'Why, Ammachi, did you take money from him? You are the one who advised me on how to behave and now you have placed us in his debt…' Karuthamma's throat constricted.

Chakki realized what Karuthamma meant. She was right. For a while Chakki was disturbed. Had they put themselves in peril?

Chakki asked, 'What happened, child?'

Karuthamma wept.

'Did he come here, child?'

Karuthamma uttered a big lie, 'No!'

'Then what is it, child?'

'What will I do if he comes here?'

Chakki hastened to prove the innocence of that transaction. She hadn't weighed its implications. All she had done was ask

Pareekutty a favour; and he had complied. They meant to return the borrowed money.

Karuthamma was right to doubt it. One thing was certain. Little Boss was a decent man. However, he was young.

Chakki suddenly felt disturbed. Perhaps they shouldn't have taken that money, she thought. But Chembankunju wouldn't understand any of this.

Chakki began nagging Chembankunju once again about Karuthamma's marriage. 'You must talk to that Velayudhan. That's the first thing to be done. After that we can consider buying the boat and nets.'

But Chembankunju wouldn't agree. He had made up his mind.

How could she reveal everything? Frustrated and furious, Chakki said, 'All these years I roamed the countryside selling fish from my basket to help you buy your boat and nets. Henceforth don't expect this of me ...'

Chembankunju threw her a challenging look.

'What senseless talk is this?' he demanded.

Chakki was petulant. 'That's exactly what I mean.'

'What?'

'I need to watch out for my daughter.'

'And that means?'

'She's a grown-up girl – with tits and a bum. I can't leave her here alone at home and go away all day.'

Chakki had made up her mind. And so she continued, 'Or, get her married off!'

Chembankunju was silent as though he had understood what Chakki meant. If Chakki didn't go to the east to sell fish, it would be a great loss. He asked, 'Is anything wrong?'

'Nothing as of now. But what if something happens?'

They had to be careful. But Chembankunju had faith in his daughter. Karuthamma was a sound girl; not given to reckless impulses. Even if she was left alone, she wouldn't succumb …

Chakki demanded, 'Have you heard of momentary lapses?'

Chembankunju didn't speak.

The next day Chakki didn't go east to sell fish. And Chembankunju didn't force her either.

That night they were planning to bring in more baskets of dried fish. But that night Chakki too protested. 'We don't need this.'

Chembankunju asked, 'Why not?'

'Why are you cheating that boy?'

'Who said I am cheating him?'

'What else? Do you really intend to return the money?'

Chembankunju insisted he would.

Karuthamma thought she must inform Pareekutty that he wouldn't get his money back. She sought a chance to meet him in stealth. But it didn't happen.

That night Pareekutty came laden with several baskets of dried fish again. And Chembankunju took it from him without any hesitation. He didn't even mention when he would return the money.

At that point Karuthamma felt that she would even dare confront her father. However, it was Chakki she held responsible.

Karuthamma knew this would be a burden that would weigh her down forever.

Three

Chembankunju now had enough money. So he set forth in search of a boat and nets.

The seashore rumbled with this news. It was rumoured that he had found an ingot of gold. One day, they said, he found a chunk of black rock that had washed ashore. When he picked it up, it was a gold ingot.

Others claimed that he had accumulated the cash by virtue of his thrift. However, that didn't seem all that plausible. All of them were hired help like him. There would be nothing left to save up after meeting everyday expenses. So how could he have found the extra money to put aside?

Achakunju was Chembankunju's peer. And his house was adjacent to Chembankunju's. To the north, in fact. They were childhood friends. And so, soon everyone began questioning Achakunju: How much money did Chembankunju take with him? Once he bought the boat, whom would he hire to work for him? Where did he find the money from? Questions teeming with such curiosity.

Achakunju didn't have a clue. But he pretended as if he knew every single detail. Chembankunju had suddenly become an important man. So shouldn't his best friend too have a share of that eminence? And so Achakunju answered the questions as best as he could. Thus, Achakunju too became a man of some consequence.

Kochuvelu asked him a question, 'I heard Achakunju chettan has a share in it …'

A question that threw Achakunju into a tizzy. However, he wasn't going to give himself away to anyone. 'Maybe. Or maybe not!'

It was a question meant to deflate Achakunju's put-on importance. On hearing Achakunju's retort, everyone burst into laughter. Achakunju blanched.

'Why are you laughing?' someone taunted. 'Can't Achakunju chettan buy a boat and nets on his own? Why does he need to be only a part owner?'

Embarrassed, Achakunju retorted, 'If everyone started buying boats and nets, who is going to man them?'

Kochuvelu muffled his laughter and said, 'Yes, that's why Achakunju chettan isn't buying a boat and nets …'

That was when Achakunju realized that his friends were mocking him. Thereafter, when anyone spoke to him about Chembankunju's boat, he would snub him. Soon the people found his snubbing hilarious and began provoking him with pointless queries.

One day the catch was poor. Achakunju got three rupees. He owed some money to Ahmed Kutty who ran the tea shop. It was an old debt. That day Ahmed Kutty pounced on Achakunju and prised it out of him. And so Achakunju reached home empty-handed. Meanwhile, Nallapennu, who had no provisions for cooking supper, was waiting for Achakunju to come home with some money. A great quarrel ensued between the fisherman and his wife. She accused him of squandering his earnings on drink, tea or snuff. She refused to believe Achakunju's version of what had happened.

He opened his mouth and blew his breath into her face so she would know that he hadn't drunk away the day's earnings. But she wouldn't still believe him.

Nallapennu said, 'You spend everything on drink ... which is why we can't even manage for a day without your earnings.'

'Did I drink today? Don't you dare accuse me!'

'You probably didn't drink today? But isn't that what you do on the days you have money?' It was the wail of a woman who didn't know how she was to provide supper that night.

But Achakunju reprimanded her in a terse voice, 'Don't you dare be arrogant!'

'Am I being arrogant? Your playmate is buying a boat and nets and here we don't even have enough for supper tonight. Am I being arrogant?'

Achakunju's answer: Two blows on her back.

What kind of a bloody ill fortune was this? He was being scoffed and teased by everyone on the shore because Chembankunju was buying a boat and nets. And he was not to have any peace at home either.

'If someone is buying a boat and nets, why are you taking it out on me? Why am I being made to pay for it?'

Chembankunju accumulated the money by starving himself. Neither Achakunju nor anyone else there would be able to do the same.

From the northern end of their hovel, Chakki and Karuthamma eavesdropped on the quarrel.

Chakki called out, 'Achakunju chetta, did we ever come begging to your house during the days we were starving ourselves?'

Achakunju turned towards Chakki. 'Don't ... don't you dare ... I have known Chembankunju since we were boys.'

But Chakki wouldn't stop. 'What do you know? If a fire has not been lit in your hovel this evening, that's your wife's fault.'

When the conversation veered towards her, Nallapennu bristled. She said, 'Don't you dare insinuate things about this fisherwoman…'

'Ha … And what will the fisherwoman do?'

Achakunju demanded of Chakki, 'Do tell me what is our fault?'

'Jealousy!'

'Of whom? Your fisherman?' Achakunju showed his disgust by hawking and spitting out a huge gob of saliva. 'Which man's going to be jealous of that lowly piece of riff-raff?'

Chakki was furious. 'Do you think you can get away saying anything you want?'

Achakunju retorted, 'What will you do?'

'What will I do?'

'All this conceit because you suddenly have some money!'

Karuthamma grew perturbed as she watched the argument turn into a squall. She tried to gag Chakki by placing her palm on her mother's mouth. But as Achakunju wouldn't stop, Chakki's wrath too grew. In the end Karuthamma dragged her mother away.

When his anger had subsided, Achakunju began to ponder. The quarrel troubled him more than the fact that no food had been cooked that night in his home. It was customary for the women to squabble. But he had never got into a row with either Chembankunju or Chakki. And it had happened now. Achakunju couldn't sleep.

The next morning, before he went out to sea, he borrowed two rupees from the boat owner and gave it to his wife. And that afternoon he handed over to Nallapennu his entire earnings for the day. Then he proclaimed that he was setting a pattern for the future.

'Listen, Nallapennu, I am going to give you all that I earn. Keep it safe. Let us see if we too can put some money away.'

Nallapennu was delighted by this turn of events. She said, 'Even if we don't buy a boat and nets, we won't at least go to bed hungry.'

'Who says we won't have a boat and nets of our own? Don't be so dismissive. It may just happen, you know.'

That's true. Nallapennu thought with a surge of hope. She said, 'Look at what has happened to our neighbours ... they were like us once ... now they won't even talk to us!'

Achakunju didn't like that. He said, 'Why talk about other people? Let us just mind our own business.'

'No ... I just mentioned it. But I must say Chakki has become such a conceited so and so. That's what she is now.'

Achakunju reprimanded her, 'Hold your tongue, woman.'

'I am not saying a word.'

'That's best. Let us see what we can do with our lives.'

Nallapennu had only one complaint. 'If only you had thought of this earlier.'

Achakunju grunted. She was right. But more to assuage himself, he said, 'Woman, why does a fisherman have to hoard anything? His wealth lies to the west; a whole expanse of it. And do you know what the ancients said – a boat and nets are for the people on the shore. Never mind all that! If a fisherman makes up his mind, who can stop him from owning a boat and nets.'

'All that's fine ... but can't you see that a playmate of yours is now the owner of a boat and nets.'

Achakunju said, 'Chembankunju is a smart man. A real smartie! All he thought about was buying his boat.' Achakunju grunted again as if affirming what he had deduced. 'Let us see!'

And so a decision was made.

In the evening, he had to go to the boatyard to mend the nets. That day several fish had escaped through the gaping holes in the nets. By the time Achakunju got there, the other fishermen too had gathered and had begun their work. Once again the conversation steered towards Chembankunju.

Achakunju asked, 'Don't you have anything else to do, you lot! Why gossip? Go on, go on, say and finish it and let the poor man rest thereafter…'

Ayankunju demanded, 'What are you so upset about?'

Achakunju replied quietly, 'Why? Did I say anything wrong?'

Raman Moopan put on the countenance of a judge. 'Why? Don't we have the right to discuss Chembankunju?'

'What right do you have?'

Raman Moopan was astounded. 'That's wonderful, Achakunju. If one of the young boys were to say it, I would let it pass. But you … you are an experienced fisherman.'

Achakunju didn't understand the implication. All he had meant was that they shouldn't gossip. And wasn't that expected of a mature man? Wasn't that a good thing?

Achakunju asked, 'Why Moopan … what do you mean?'

Raman Moopan put down the string and flung a question into Achakunju's face. 'Achakunju, don't you know the dictates of the shore?'

Achakunju knew that indeed. Nevertheless…

Raman Moopan continued, 'Do you think that Chembankunju has followed those decrees?'

Achakunju couldn't understand where all of this was leading to.

Raman Moopan elaborated, 'Have you heard of anything like this on our shores? Not just in the past, but even in recent times … has it ever happened that a grown-up girl is left unmarried?'

Ayankunju filled in the pause. 'In the past, the shores had a protector.'

Raman Moopan added, 'Listen, when you have a marriageable

girl in the house, what kind of a man buys a boat and nets instead?'

In ancient times, the Shore Master wouldn't allow it. Those were laws that couldn't be defied. And the fisherman, who was protector of the shores, would make sure that the laws were followed. For those laws had a purpose. It was for the well-being of the fisherman that these laws were made.

Ayankunju asked, 'So what does the law say? What age should the girl be married off at?'

Raman Moopan was an old-timer. So he said, 'Ten years!'

Vellamanalil Velayudhan asked, 'And what happens if the girl is unmarried after she has turned ten?'

The rhetorical query carried the tinge of insolence. Seeking to question the dictates of the shore.

Raman Moopan pounced on it: 'What happens if she is not married off? It cannot be. It is not meant to happen.'

Velayudhan allowed himself to reveal his mind. 'What can the other fishermen of the shore do?'

'The family will be excommunicated. They won't be able to live on this shore any more.'

Another young man Punyan commented, 'But all that was in the past...'

Ayankunju's retort was fiery, 'No, no, it holds good even now. Do you want to test it? We will show you ... we will show you how we make that big man Chembankunju run around in circles.'

Raman Moopan exhibited his tacit approval. Then he brought forth another decree. 'Is everyone meant to own a boat and nets, Ayankunju?'

Ayankunju responded, 'No, of course not!'

Raman Moopan now elaborated this dictate further.

The children of the sea are the inheritors of countless riches. It is customary for their palms to brim. So it is quite possible for each one of them to acquire his own boat and nets. If every man on the shore has a boat and nets of his own, who will go out to the sea?

He demanded, 'If one of us on the shores here wanted to buy a boat and nets, don't you think it is possible?'

That was true!

Ayankunju threw up a question loaded with gravitas now. 'In which case, why is it that not everyone has a boat and nets of his own?'

There is a reason for that as well. The children of the sea are of five kinds: Arayan, Valakkaran, Mukkavan, Marakkan, and a fifth caste of no particular name. And then in the east there are some subsects of men who man the boats.

Only the Valakkaran is allowed to own boats and nets. In fact, in the east the protector of the shore, the Shore Master, would permit only the Valakkaran to buy the boat and nets. And that too based on his judgement.'

Velayudhan asked, 'So which kind is Chembankunju Uncle?'

Punyan smirked.

Raman Moopan said, 'Mukkavan!'

Punyan sneered, 'He now wants to know Chembankunju's caste!'

Achakunju asked, 'Why is that, Punyan?'

'They made him a marriage offer. To marry that girl.'

'That's good,' Achakunju said. 'She is a good girl.'

Ayankunju didn't like that though. He said, 'For you, Achakunju, everything about Chembankunju is good.'

Then Ayankunju turned to Velayudhan with a piece of advice. 'You are not going to get anything from that skinflint. Remember that ... and as for the girl, she is not what you think she is.'

Achakunju was annoyed now. 'What are you saying? How

can you thwart that girl's marriage proposal? Is that any way for a fisherman to behave?'

Ayankunju replied, 'I am merely speaking the truth.'

Aandi who was silent until then spoke up now, steering the conversation in another direction. 'What happens if a man unauthorized to buy a boat and nets buys one? Has anything like this ever happened before?'

'Yes. But he didn't enjoy the benefits of having a boat and nets for too long!'

Then Ayankunju wanted to know who in their community were of Valakkaran caste.

Raman Moopan said, 'Cherthala Pallikunnath are the Valakkaran kind; Alapuzha Paruthikavalakkaran, and here Ramankunju's family, Kunnale etc…'

'What are the offerings one must make to the Shore Master before buying a boat and nets?' Punyan wanted to know.

'Seven shags of tobacco and fifteen rupees. And the Valakkaran too have to do it.'

Next, the conversation moved to the protector of the shores and his jurisdiction. 'The Shore Master has a great deal of power.'

Blowing a whiff of rebellion against that power, Velayudhan demanded, 'One's buying a boat and nets with one's own money. So why should one make an offering to the Shore Master?'

Punyan pounced on that. 'Look at that! He's already behaving like Chembankunju's son-in-law!'

Ayankunju added his two bit to that. And then some more. 'Go on, why don't you and your prospective father-in-law oppose the Shore Master when you bring your boat and nets here. You'll find out for yourself what happens then…'

That was a challenge. For without the Shore Master's permission, Chembankunju wouldn't be able to put his boat and nets out to sea. It just wouldn't happen, Ayankunju proclaimed.

It was a challenge Velayudhan wanted to take up. But what right did he have? Nevertheless, Velayudhan protested. 'You are jealous.'

'A fisherman, jealous?'

'Of course!'

Achakunju saw that it was leading to a quarrel and so he intervened. 'Hold your tongue son,' he advised Velayudhan.

For a little while, no one spoke.

And while such gossip and arguments heated up the shore, Chakki sat weaving daydreams. In a few days, she would be the wife of a boat owner. The dream of a lifetime was coming true. And how they had worked for it – her fisherman and she! It was only because she was better than all the women around. And once they had a boat and nets, it was quite possible that they would find a better alliance for Karuthamma too.

The mother spoke to the daughter. 'Daughter! Your father has big ideas. With the big catch this year, he will buy land and a house of our own. And then he'll get you married off.'

Karuthamma didn't respond. Chakki continued to speak aloud to herself, 'The sea mother has blessed us. We don't have any debts. And if the big catch doesn't happen, no one will demand anything of us...' But before Chakki could finish, Karuthamma demanded, 'Are you claiming that we have no debts, Ammachi?'

Chakki understood then that Karuthamma was referring to the debt they owed Pareekutty.

Chakki squirmed. She scrambled around and found an answer. 'No, you don't have to consider that as a debt.'

Karuthamma asked a trifle brusquely, 'No, you don't think so?'

'That's not it. If we don't pay it, he's not going to seize the boat and nets.'

'That's because the Little Boss is a gullible soul.'

Chakki feigned anger and asked, 'What is this? When you talk of that Little Boss, your words drip a sweetness?'

Karuthamma didn't speak. Neither did she blanch under her mother's questioning.

Chakki continued to query her. 'If you stay unsullied, you'll find a good, able-bodied young man ... it is up to you to decide your fate!'

Karuthamma was unruffled. And she felt a certain courage gather in her. She asked, 'Am I the one who is tainted?'

As if she hadn't heard Karuthamma's retort, Chakki demanded, 'Who is the Little Boss to you?'

Karuthamma didn't say he was nothing to her. But her eyes filled. What crime had she committed?

Chakki too knew that she was innocent. And that she hadn't transgressed. That she is still the girl she was.

It was wrong to have borrowed money from Pareekutty. Was it a crime for Karuthamma to ask that they pay the loan back? Yet ... and yet, she had a certain tenderness for Pareekutty. And she was troubled by the thought that he would have to suffer such a loss. They should have married her off a long time ago. Chembankunju didn't seem to realize this.

'It is for you, darling, that father's working so hard,' Chakki continued. 'My dear, will you be the reason we lose all of this...'

Karuthamma didn't speak.

Chakki asked, 'Can Ammachi ask you something? You must speak the truth? Do you like that Muslim boy?'

Karuthamma who should have said 'No' didn't speak. That stony silence frightened her mother.

Chakki felt her peace of mind collapse. She wailed, 'Oh my sea mother, that scoundrel has seduced my daughter!'

Karuthamma clapped shut Chakki's mouth with her palm. 'What rubbish is this, Ammachi?'

Chakki turned a pleading gaze to her daughter and implored, 'My daughter, don't betray us!'

And yet Karuthamma wouldn't say that she felt nothing for that Muslim boy.

That evening Achakunju came to Chembankunju's home. He told Chakki all about the discussion on the beach. 'The people of the shore are planning to instigate trouble. Ayankunju and Raman Moopan are the main troublemakers,' he said. 'When Chembankunju comes home, the first thing he needs to do is find a solution for this. Chembankunju and I are playmates. I can't agree with what the others say about him. Nor will I go along with it.'

And so Chakki's new-found fragile peace was destroyed once again.

Chakki knew what it meant to have the shore go against them. What crime had they committed to warrant this? That they hadn't married their daughter off yet?

Four

Ayankunju, Raman Moopan and two other men of the older generation went to meet the Shore Master, taking it upon themselves to represent the interests of the entire fishing community. They took with them an offering as a mark of respect. After all, they were the bearers of ill tidings. The news they carried with them would ruin the entire shore and the fisherfolk. This was their petition of sorrow and prime complaint: Chembankunju has a grown-up daughter. He hasn't yet married her off. She frolics on this shore.

The Shore Master listened to them carefully. He would look into it, he promised.

However, somewhere within Ayankunju a thought rankled. Their complaint hadn't been viewed with the importance it deserved. The Shore Master hadn't given it its due weightage.

The petitioners continued to wait even after the Shore Master had spoken. He asked, 'What are you continuing to stand here for?'

Ayankunju had one more charge to make. 'While the girl is determined to ruin our shores, Chembankunju has gone off to buy a boat and nets.'

Now that was news to the Shore Master. 'But where did Chembankunju get the money from?'

The older men didn't have an answer.

Ayankunju voiced a suspicion with great humility, 'He is a fisherman after all. So has he taken permission to buy a boat and nets?'

'No! No! He didn't!'

'Well, what should we, the people of the shore, do?'

The Shore Master thought for a while and said, 'He seems to think that times have changed.'

Ayankunju grunted 'Yes'.

The Shore Master issued a command, 'Let him bring his boat. However, no one is to go to work in it without letting me know first.'

'Yes, of course, that's how it will be,' Ayankunju said. 'However, there are some brash young men. I can't speak for them!' Ayankunju was thinking of Velayudhan.

The Shore Master dismissed that of no consequence. He knew for a fact that no one would dare to oppose him publicly. Not yet.

'I'll take care of that. Tell the rest of the fisherfolk that he doesn't have my permission to buy a boat.'

Triumphant Raman Moopan and Ayankunju returned. They went from home to home announcing the Shore Master's decree. However, Ayankunju was quite certain that Velayudhan alone wouldn't comply. Anyway, how much can a pup's bite hurt? He would discover it the hard way.

Chakki came to know of what had happened.

She had heard stories of how the Shore Master's wrath had ruined lives. Of families who had to flee the shores and who didn't even have the solace of knowing that they could be fisherfolk on other distant shores. Malicious gossip had feet that would reach any shore they went to. Then the only recourse left was to convert to another religion.

These days the power of such decrees didn't hold. Hadn't times changed? Nevertheless, if the Shore Master willed it, there would be no one to work their boat. No one would cross their threshold at a birth or death. Such ostracization could happen even these days.

They should have made an offering and sought permission before setting out to buy the boat and nets.

And yet, what crime had they committed?

The entire shore was abuzz with the news of the Shore Master's ban. They were being punished for not marrying off a grown-up girl, the women said.

And Karuthamma wished she hadn't been born. She was the cause of such troubles and sorrow for her parents. She hadn't wanted to grow into adulthood, feel her breasts blossom. She hadn't defiled the seashore. What harm was she doing by being as she was? However, none of these arguments, logical as they were, was any good.

Both mother and daughter awaited Chembankunju's arrival with much trepidation.

A few women were at Kalikunju's house. Chakki eavesdropped on their gossiping. One woman said that Karuthamma had a relationship with Pareekutty. She had seen them talking and laughing standing in the shadows of a beached boat. That's why they were not marrying Karuthamma off.

Could any mother listen to such slander about her child? Chakki leapt out of her hiding place with the ferocity of a tiger to defend her daughter. And thus the long-slithering tongues of the women gathered there ran amok.

In Chakki's youth, she too had ruined the shore, they claimed. In which case, who was the father of one of Kalikunju's children, Chakki demanded. Wasn't it one of those Muslim traders? The one who dealt in dry fish and went from home to home offering an advance for what he would buy. It seemed then that all the women gathered there and their mothers had secret stories of their own.

It was a battle – Chakki on one side and the rest of the women together against her. But Chakki fought fiercely.

Karuthamma stood by the fence, listening. She was astounded by the allegations. Had her mother too been in love in her youth? Have these women defiled the shores? Wasn't there any sanctity to all the traditions mooted? Was it all just talk?

The western sea lay quiet and vast despite these women and their sordid pasts. To this day the boats went out to sea. The rains fell and fish were spawned. The fisherfolk lived and thrived. So what was the meaning of all those old dictates?

As the quarrel grew noisier, they began talking about Karuthamma again. Karuthamma clapped her ears shut. All tittle-tattle! She was Pareekutty's mistress! Only someone like him, a brawny Muslim, could control and keep a lusty warhorse like her satiated. They were not marrying her off only because they were terrified of losing the income she brought in. Such gossip could only mean one thing: what the women had slandered her mother with and what her mother had thrown back into their faces were all falsehoods.

Unable to stem the flow of abuse from Chakki's tongue, Kalikunju declared, 'That's it! You had it! Wait and see what's going to happen! The Shore Master has decided what to do with you!'

Chakki wouldn't budge. She was ready for battle. In fact, the need to combat only grew. The need to combat everything.

'What is there to decide? What is the Shore Master going to do?'

At that point, Karuthapennu spoke, 'The Shore Master knows how to deal with scum who have no respect for traditions!'

Chakki defended herself stoutly, 'What can he do to us? We'll become Muslims if need be or convert to another religion ... What will the Shore Master do then?'

Another woman said, 'Say it, say it, will you? That you set up your daughter with that Muslim man.'

Yet another woman said, 'That's probably what the mother and daughter wanted!'

Chakki asked, 'So what's wrong with that?'

Karuthamma experienced something that she had never known until then. Was it an ache? She wasn't sure. Was it a great relief? She wasn't sure of that either.

Karuthamma called out to her in a forlorn voice. Perhaps her tongue was beginning to weaken and so Chakki turned towards her daughter and went to her.

But Chakki kept muttering to herself even after reaching their hovel.

Karuthamma felt the need to ask her mother countless questions. But she didn't have the courage. All she could hear was the throbbing echo of her mother's claim: we will convert to Islam if need be. Her nerves quickened. An unbearable kindling of feelings. Wasn't it but natural? Her heart had been abducted.

Since chaos and danger were part of their lives, her heritage had her locked in a fortress where traditional rules and dictates determined every breath. And here was someone actually pointing the way out of that fortress. All that was needed was a decision. And everything would fall into place.

Become a Muslim. What would happen then? She saw herself dressed in a tunic and heavy mundu with the curve of her ears pierced and adorned with gold and wearing a head scarf. Pareekutty would be delighted if she were to go to him dressed like that! And then he could gaze at her bosom as much as he wanted. Look at her bum. Even if she didn't comprehend it entirely, this perhaps was the only means of escaping the tangled mess of their lives. She wouldn't have to be a fisherman's wife. If Pareekutty were to come there at that point, she would have said, 'We are going to convert to Islam.'

And Pareekutty would leap with joy.

But had her mother meant it in all seriousness? She probably spoke it on the spur of the moment driven by her rage. And she was afraid to ask her mother if she had really meant it.

If she did so, her mother would assume that she wanted it to be true.

And so Karuthamma lived contained within her tormented thoughts.

Some representatives of the Shore Master arrived there. But Chembankunju wasn't back yet.

A few days later, Chembankunju's newly acquired boat docked at the shore. And it had nets.

It used to belong to Pallikunnath Kandankoran, a netsman. It wasn't new any more but it used to be a rather celebrated boat once. During the season of the big catch at the Cherthala seashore even the people of this shore had seen it in its unvanquished glory.

So what if it was a little old. How did the Kandankoran netsman let go of the boat? He must really be in dire straits. And everyone knew that he was as big a spendthrift as he was famous.

All of them came to look at the boat. But not one of them said a thing. It was obvious that all of them were struck by the same thought – Chembankunju was fortunate to have acquired this splendid boat.

Achakunju said to a group, 'It looks as if Pallikunnath's prosperity has come away in the boat with Chembankunju.'

Ayankunju dismissed it airily, 'Rubbish! How could that Kudummakaran's prosperity attach itself to a mere fisherman?

Haven't you seen Pallikunnath Kandankoran when he stands next to the boat? That golden complexion and the slope of his pot belly. Have you seen how he dresses? In a white mundu and a black-lined cloth draped on his shoulder. So how can you even compare the two?

Raman Moopan had his own titbit to add. 'In which case, that skinny black Chakki will soon resemble Kandankoran's wife! Have you seen her?'

Ayankunju said, 'Ah ... you can't look at her without a secret sigh! She is such a beauty...'

When Chembankunju returned home, he felt his head would explode. He had sailed into their shore with much excitement. He had been very fortunate to acquire this particular boat. And he had been to the Pallikunnath Kandankoran mansion, dined there – all of which he was aching to tell his wife about. And then there was Kandankoran's wife...

He had come home wanting to share all of this and now it seemed as if someone had trampled all over him. He had never felt so downcast. Once, all he had was a dream. Now, even as it was shaping into reality, the dream was falling apart.

And his crime? That he hadn't been to see the Shore Master before he set out to buy his boat and nets. Fine. He could understand that. After all he had violated an ancient code. But he had eked out the money for the boat and nets with great difficulty. And there just wasn't enough to keep aside twenty-five rupees for this purpose. How could he have known that it would be considered such a great wrong?

Chembankunju asked his wife helplessly, 'What did we do wrong? How have we hurt anyone?'

Chakki said, 'Do we have to do anything? This is just envy!'

'That's true. But ... if we had about twenty-five rupees to spare, all of this could be sorted out. And how are we to find that? We have to make some more money to stock the boat. All there is now is a mere mackerel net.'

Chembankunju voiced a list of his troubles. Who else could he express this to? And who else would listen to him?

Instead of comforting him, Chakki only railed at him, 'Why did you have to drag this bloody bane onto our heads?'

Chembankunju didn't speak. He too must have felt weighed down by the burden. All that he had was spent. And the community was against them.

Chakki continued, 'If we had married the girl off with the money we had, would we have been punished so?'

But Chembankunju wouldn't still speak. If you have big desires, you seldom find peace. Does that mean one has to be content with what one has?

It should have been a day of celebration. The day when his life's greatest desire had been fulfilled. But that day the house was sunk in gloom.

Late in the night, Chembankunju spoke to his wife, 'If we had thirty-five rupees, we could sort everything out!'

How is that possible, Chakki asked.

And so he laid his plan out to her.

'Tomorrow morning I shall call on the Shore Master. All of this will be sorted out then.'

'What about the sardine nets and support nets?'

'That will happen too!'

Chakki had already raided her nest egg. Given him the money she had secreted away in a bamboo piece and buried in the ground. Now Chakki blamed Chembankunju.

'Do you see the state we are in? If only we had put some money away in a piece of gold. We could have at least hawked that. But you dismissed my plea then!'

Chembankunju agreed. 'There is a way, Chakki.'

'And what's that?'

'That…' Chembankunju was reluctant to voice his thought.

Chakki demanded again to know what it was.

Chembankunju said, 'Well, if we approach that boy once again, things will happen.'

Chakki clapped Chembankunju's mouth shut hastily. She wasn't sure if Karuthamma was asleep or awake.

Chembankunju removed his wife's palm from his mouth and asked, 'Why? What's wrong?'

'Speak softly.'

'Hmm? Why?'

There was much that Chembankunju didn't know. Perhaps what no father should ever know. But words had to be spoken.

Chembankunju asked again. And so Chakki whispered in his ear, 'Karuthamma says it isn't seemly. If she discovers this, she will start a quarrel.'

'What else can we do?'

'That's what I am thinking about too!'

A little later Chembankunju asked, 'Is he there?'

'Should be!'

'I think I'll go and check.'

Chakki didn't speak. Chembankunju opened the door and stepped out.

Karuthamma was asleep. She didn't know any of what was happening. Much later Chembankunju returned. His face had cleared up. It was evident that he had accomplished what he had set out to do!

'He's such a simple boy. A good boy though! He had thirty rupees with him and he gave it all to me.'

Even if Chakki was relieved, she felt a sense of unease. Tainted money! Chakki heard Karuthamma speak in her head.

Yes. Why had he always given them the money when they had asked for it? Was that even a moot question? Only because of Karuthamma. Why else?

The next morning, Chembankunju went to see the Shore Master. At first, the Shore Master was belligerent. Then he settled down. However, he was insistent that the girl be married off as early as possible. And demanded that his share of takings be sent to him on a daily basis.

Now it was Chembankunju's turn. He voiced his protest at the clamour of envy he had to put up with.

The Shore Master promised to find a solution. And so troubles were alleviated, at least, for the moment.

But he needed five hundred rupees to be able to launch the boat with all its accessories. That too would happen.

But how? Chakki wanted to know.

Chembankunju said, 'Pareekutty will give it to us.'

Chakki was astounded. Without Karuthamma's knowledge, yet another battle took place there.

With the power vested in him as the husband, Chembankunju commanded, 'You must ask him.'

'I can't…'

'In which case, the boat won't go out to sea.'

'Good.'

But Chakki didn't have the heart to stand her ground. And Chembankunju wouldn't budge. It was as if he wouldn't do anything more, Chakki thought.

And that was precisely what Chembankunju had hoped would happen.

Chakki asked, 'Tell me, will you return all the money?'

'Of course,' Chembankunju said. And he would pay him interest, he claimed.

So this time Chakki was the one who approached Pareekutty.

In the dead of the night, dried fish was sold to make money to buy the accessories for Chembankunju's boat.

All was ready. Now what were left were the men to be hired.

The Shore Master quelled the protests of the older fishermen and made the arrangements. It had only been a minor obstacle, after all.

Once they had seen the boat, everyone longed to work in it. Achakunju had thought that Chembankunju would seek his counsel and invite him to work in the boat. In fact, they had quarrelled about this in his home. Achakunju had been even prepared to oppose the Shore Master's dictates. They were childhood friends after all.

But Chembankunju hadn't spoken to him despite running into him a couple of times.

Chembankunju chose twelve men. Achakunju wasn't one of them.

There was to be a small ritual the day before the boat was put out to sea. They had to organize a feast. Chembankunju arranged to buy the provisions for it from trader Hassan Kutty. His guest list included a few relatives who lived at Kakkazhath and Punnapra. Chembankunju sent Karuthamma to invite them for the ceremony.

Karuthamma walked along the shore immersed in thought.

'Will you sell your fish to us?'

That gentle query made Karuthamma halt in her tracks. Pareekutty stood before her. How? Where? How had he sprung up there from the middle of nowhere?

Karuthamma didn't speak. She didn't even say what she once had – if you give us a good price, we will.

She wasn't that Karuthamma any more.

Pareekutty asked this new Karuthamma who stood with her head bowed, 'Are you angry with me, Karuthamma?'

She didn't speak. She felt as if her heart would burst.

'If you don't want me to, I won't speak any more.'

In truth, she had so much to say. So much to ask. In fact, she would even have liked to ask – shall I convert to Islam?

She stood silently in the shadows of a boat pulled onto the shore. She felt his gaze on her firm high breasts. But she couldn't say either – Don't stare at me so, my Bossman.

She raised her face to him, 'I have to go, my Bossman.'

She needed his consent to leave. She couldn't just walk away.

Suddenly, a frightened Karuthamma said, 'Someone will see us!'

She walked on. She had walked only a few feet when she heard him call. 'Karuthamma!'

There was something strange in that call, in his voice. A strangeness which she had never known or heard before.

She jerked back as if she had been snagged by a fishing line. He didn't walk towards her. Perhaps she had paused expecting him to go to her.

Neither of them knew how long they stood like that. What could have been the emotions that churned in her?

The sea wasn't angry; the wind didn't rise. Little waves rose and broke into a froth of foam. The sea smiled. Had such a love story ever been played out on these shores?

All that Pareekutty had to say and ask emerged in one question. 'Do you like me, Karuthamma?'

Unable to help herself, Karuthamma said, 'Yes!'

Such greed to know more. 'Do you like only me?'

And Pareekutty got his answer almost instantly.

'Only you.'

Her own voice quaked in her like a clap of thunder. It was perhaps then she became conscious of what she had done. Of her admission. Her words appeared before her, frowning with censure. She looked at Pareekutty's face. Their eyes met. All that had to be spoken was said. Their thoughts and desires revealed to each other.

She walked on.

Five

In the wee hours of the following day, almost everyone gathered on the waterfront. Chembankunju's boat was being put out to sea. Since there was a new boat, all other boats too had to be put out to sea at the same time. Chakki, Karuthamma and Panchami were at the shore too. Pareekutty too stood there but a little away. Panchami pointed out Pareekutty to Karuthamma. And Karuthamma pinched Panchami in return.

Raman Moopan whooped loudly to call in the latecomers. Ayankunju chastised them. 'How can they be late when they know there's a new boat?'

Chembankunju's boatsmen were prepared. One of them began singing Pareekutty's song. It was a song that throbbed with grief.

Over the coconut palms in the east, the moon peeped to see Chembankunju's boat being launched. The sea mother was happy. People gathered around each one of the boats. The first boat to be put out to sea would be Chembankunju's.

Ayankunju called out fluttering his palm on his open mouth to produce a series of sounds. Everyone else took up that auspicious cry as well. The seashore echoed with that cry.

Raman Moopan said, 'Take the oar, Chembankunju.'

Chembankunju raised the oar and laid it on top of his head

in an act of supplication. Then he prayed to all his family deities, asking for their blessings and support.

All of them began pushing the boat. The boat slid through the sand, cut across the water and was soon bobbing on the sea.

Chakki and Karuthamma stood praying, their hands folded like a blossom in bud. When they opened their eyes, the boat was rising above the waves and dipping into the trough and heading towards the western horizon. There were omens to be read.

Raman Moopan and Ayankunju stood on the shore, casting portents. Raman Moopan asked, 'What do you think, Ayankunju?'

Ayankunju answered with a question. 'Don't you think the keel favours the west?'

'Yes. The slant is to the south.'

Chakki went towards them eagerly. She wanted to know their predictions. She asked, 'What do you think, Ayankunju chetta? Will it be good?'

With the gravity of the wise man, Ayankunju said, 'It is good, woman. You will never know hard times again!'

Chakki once again folded her palms in a gesture of invocation and called out her prayers to the all-powerful mother of the sea.

The boat was racing to the heart of the ocean. It raced as if it knew victory was in sight.

Karuthamma said, 'Our boat has a certain grandeur to it, don't you think, Ammachi?'

Her eyes followed the boat as she spoke, 'And look at the way it moves.'

Ayankunju said, 'Do you even have to wonder about it, sister? It may be yours now. But do you know whom it belonged to once? Pallikunnath Kandankoran was its owner. Has there ever been a boat like this on the shores? So full of felicity, but everything that is his is like that. He has a wife; she glistens like molten gold. There isn't a woman like that amongst the fisherfolk. She is so beautiful. As for the house, that's the kind of man he is. And now the boat is yours. That's your good fortune, sister!'

All the other boats too went out to sea. Soon the only people left on the shore were the mother and daughters. And Pareekutty. As the cold breeze blew, Pareekutty shivered. Far in the high seas, the boats spread. They were casting the nets.

Pareekutty walked slowly towards Chakki. Karuthamma moved behind her mother. Panchami stood gaping at Pareekutty's face.

Pareekutty asked his usual question; only this time it was addressed to the mother. Whether it was in seriousness or in jest, it was the only question he could ask, 'Would you sell the fish to us?'

Chakki replied, 'Who else would we sell it to, child? Who else?'

Chakki didn't understand the hidden nuance of that query. How would she? It wasn't a mere query. There was an entire ocean of feelings trapped within it. Karuthamma who stood behind her mother said, 'I am cold, Ammachi.'

It was the day the boat had been put out to sea. So Chakki couldn't leave without saying the words she knew she ought to. 'It's because of you, child, that we could put this boat out to sea. It wouldn't have happened without you.'

Pareekutty didn't respond.

Karuthamma knew a sense of relief. At least her mother had said as much. Acknowledged their debt.

Chakki continued, 'When the big catch season is over, we'll pay you back.'

'No, don't. What if I don't want it back?'

'How can you not want it back? But why?'

Pareekutty said, 'I didn't give it to you to take it back…'

Chakki couldn't understand this. Not that Karuthamma

understood it either. But she felt suffused by a heat. Chakki felt a suspicion wriggle into her.

'What is it, child?'

Pareekutty said firmly, 'No, I don't want it back.'

A moment later, Pareekutty continued, 'Karuthamma asked my help to buy a boat and nets. And I offered you money. Now I don't want it back.'

Karuthamma felt darkness swamp her eyes. Her head reeled.

Chakki spoke brusquely, 'Why would you offer money to Karuthamma? Who is she to you?'

Then in a harsh voice she stated, 'That is not possible. It isn't right. You have to take the money back.'

Pareekutty sensed the sternness in Chakki. He didn't speak.

In the manner of a mother addressing her child on the good and evils of life, Chakki continued. 'Child, you are a Muslim. And we are fisherfolk. You were childhood playmates and once you may have played together on these shores. But that was then. We will marry her off to a suitable fisherman. And you must marry a good Muslim girl.'

After a moment, Chakki went on, 'You are children. You don't understand the gravity of the situation. You mustn't ruin our reputation. If someone were to see us standing here like this, they would start slandering us. That's how people are!'

Chakki asked her girls to go with her. She then turned and spoke to Pareekutty with a careful gentleness, 'Listen to me, my son, you must take that money back.'

The mother walked away. Karuthamma and Panchami followed. Pareekutty stood there watching them go.

Everything that Chakki said was right. And it had to be spoken with such firmness. But those words had rent Karuthamma's heart.

When they had walked some distance, Karuthamma turned

to look back. It wasn't done consciously; but how could she not look back?

When they reached home, the song that had pierced her wafted in from the seashore.

Chakki said to no one in particular. 'Doesn't he ever sleep?'

Chakki turned to Karuthamma, 'We have to send you away from this place as soon as possible…'

There was an allegation in her mother's statement. That she was a great burden to them; the cause of why none of them had any peace. Unable to contain the sorrow and anger in her, Karuthamma protested, 'What did I do?'

Chakki didn't speak.

In the light of the dawn, Chakki and her children went to the seashore to see the boats return. All the boats were in the high seas. From the look of the sea, it seemed as if they had had a good catch.

'What do you think they got? What fish would it be?' Karuthamma asked her mother.

From the signs, it should be mackerel.

Karuthamma spoke with great enthusiasm, 'Oh, what an auspicious beginning!'

'The mother of the sea has been good to us, daughter.'

Like a little child lisping its desire to its mother, Karuthamma said, 'Ammachi, we must give our catch to the Little Boss!'

Chakki didn't show any displeasure. Neither did she demand who the Little Boss was to her. Chakki too wanted it to be so. But Chakki had doubts of her own. 'I wonder if that greedy father of yours will do it!'

Karuthamma had a solution. 'When the boat approaches, we must go and wait there. And you must tell father.'

Chakki agreed to that. It was necessary. Something that needed to be done.

Panchami stood vigil on the shore so that she could call them over when the boat was spotted. That was when another obstacle popped up. The women from the neighbourhood – Nallapennu, Kalikunju, Kunjipennu and Lakshmi – arrived there. They had a favour to ask for. Kunjipennu wanted to know if they were going to sell the fish by lot to the big shacks or to the petty traders. To sell as a lot to the big shacks had become an established practice on that shore. And so the women who went to sell fish in the east had to beg and plead for fish from the big shack owners.

Kunjipennu said, 'But we don't need to tell you this, Chakki chedathi, you already know about it.'

Chakki could empathize with their need. There was no profit to be made by buying fish from the big shack owners. It wasn't just that they had to pay the demanded price but they also had to endure their abuse.

'What do you want me to do?' Chakki asked.

Nallapennu spoke with a certain authority, 'You must sell the fish from your boat to us fisherwomen.'

Chakki didn't know how to answer. They were all neighbours, after all. And what they said couldn't be disputed. But how could she make promises? She had her own doubts if Chembankunju would agree to any of their schemes. And Pareekutty had asked for the fish. But how could she tell them any of this?

Kalikunju asked, 'Chakki chedathi, why don't you say something? Are you wondering if Chembankunju chettan will agree? Chakki chedathi, you must insist. The boat and nets after all came from some of your earnings too. The money you made by lugging fish around in a basket!'

Chakki very well knew their observation was grounded in truth.

Lakshmi said, 'Would you still continue to come to the east with us to sell fish?'

'Why do you even ask? Even if we have a fishing fleet, Chakki will always be Chakki,' Chakki said.

Lakshmi apologized, 'I didn't mean it like that. I just thought we could buy the lot and divide it amongst us.'

Chakki gestured her helplessness. 'I really don't know if that man will agree.'

Nallapennu said, 'You must insist. Then it will happen!'

Kalikunju turned to Karuthamma, 'You must tell your father too!'

Karuthamma retorted with firmness, 'No, I won't!'

But Panchami agreed to do so. When the boat was in, before the shack owners staked their claim, she would speak to her father. She had her own plan. When the boat was in, she wanted to grab a basket of fish, dry it and start building her own store of dried fish. To make that happen, it was imperative that her father didn't sell the catch to the shack owners.

'Let me see,' Chakki said, trying to extricate herself from an awkward situation. But she knew it wouldn't happen. She could see much trouble ensuing from this.

As the sun rose in the sky, the shore began to fill with the shack owners, women with baskets and children. In the outer seas, seagulls circled in the air. The men in the boats were either pulling the nets in or shaking out the catch. Each one tried to guess what fish it would be.

Khadar thought it must be small fry. Whatever it was, there seemed to be plenty of it. Suddenly, two seagulls came flying in from the west towards them. One had a fish in its bill. All of them looked skywards at it. And a single call emerged: 'Sardine! It's sardines!'

It seemed that the boats had begun moving in. The boats turned east. Panchami ran home.

'Ammachi, ammachi, it's sardine. The catch is sardines!'

Karuthamma and Chakki ran out eagerly. And again at that point, Chakki called out her thanks to the mother of the sea.

Mother and daughter rushed to the shore. They wanted to see their boat return laden with its mighty catch. From the high seas, the boats vaulted in on the waves. Mother and daughter argued about which one was theirs.

Ever since they had discovered that the catch was sardines, there was much hustle and bustle on the shore. Kunjipennu, Nallapennu, Kalikunju, Lakshmi had all gathered around Chakki. Panchami had a basket ready. As they stood there, they saw one boat move ahead with the speed of a bird, bounding from the crest of one wave to next. It seemed laden.

Panchami spoke without thinking, 'There seems to be just one man aboard!'

The arrival of the boat was like a hero's triumph. Above were seagulls hovering. Behind, the other boats. And there seemed to be a great noise of celebration coming in from the seas.

And standing at the stern of that triumphant boat was Chembankunju. He wasn't standing. He was leaping and bounding as he flung the oars in and out, rowing the boat homeward. He wasn't in the water but floating in the air. And his oar created ripples in the sky with great speed. Such was the power of his rowing that the boat sliced through the waves. There was much grandeur in that arrival.

Kalikunju said, 'Look at him! The way he's coming in – isn't that something?'

Everyone agreed that the boat was indeed a handsome one. Chakki pleaded, 'Don't tempt fate, people!'

The boat came in closer. Chembankunju had undergone a transformation. And what a change it was!

Chakki said, 'What grace!'

The grace of a man fostered by the sea.

And then someone dragged the boat onto the shore. The oarsmen put down their oars, jumped out and pulled the boat higher onto the shore.

Children gathered around the boat. Panchami was one of them.

Chembankunju glowered and leapt from the stern onto the shore in one bound. The children shrieked and scattered in all four directions. Panchami stood her ground. Why should she be scared?

Chembankunju hollered, 'I don't want anyone picking any fry from my boat!' And then he grabbed Panchami and hurled her away.

The girl fell to the ground screaming, 'Ammachi!'

Chakki and Karuthamma called out in anguish. One of the woman said, 'Heartless creature! What kind of a man is he? An ogre!'

Just as Chembankunju had, Panchami too had a dream. To pick the small fry, dry and hoard them. One day it would fetch a sizable income. So she had gone to her father's boat vested with the authority of a daughter. But Chembankunju couldn't see any of that. He was so drunk by pride and self-importance.

What lay in the boat was spawned by the sea. No one had sown it. Or reared it. So a portion of it – the fry at least – was for the poor and the destitute; that was the rule of the sea.

'What's with you? Are you an ogre?' Chakki screamed and gathered Panchami into her arms. Mother and daughter rubbed Panchami's chest. She was hurt rather than in pain. It was her feelings that were hurt rather than her body.

The shack owners pushed and jostled around the boat. Pareekutty was ahead of all the others. Chembankunju didn't seem to know anyone.

Khadar Boss asked, 'So what's on sale, Chembankunju?'

Kunjipennu, Lakshmi and the other women ran around the boat in circles. Panchami, who had promised to buy them fish from the boat, lay stunned and breathless on the ground. And Chakki was at her side.

The shack owners were finalizing the sale. Kunjipennu told the others, 'Let us ask him anyway.'

Nallapennu retorted, 'What can one ask that ogre?'

The other boats began to draw closer. Chembankunju wanted to close the deal before that.

Pareekutty asked, 'Will you sell the fish to me?'

Chembankunju pretended to not see Pareekutty. Instead, he said aloud, 'I want to be paid in full. Do you have the cash? I want cash!'

Khadar Boss thrust a sheaf of hundred-rupee notes into Chembankunju's palm; the sale was done.

Pareekutty ran towards the other boats. But the fish had already been sold.

When Panchami's cries had subsided, Karuthamma saw Pareekutty walk away with a downcast expression. He didn't have enough cash.

Karuthamma told her mother, 'The Little Boss didn't get any fish!'

Chakki walked towards Pareekutty. 'Didn't you bid for the fish, Little Boss?'

'I did.'

'What happened?'

Pareekutty didn't speak. He hadn't been able to buy any fish that day. There hadn't been such a sardine catch in the near season.

Chakki understood it all now. She had seen Chembankunju transform into someone else.

She said, 'The sight of all that abundance has turned him into an ogre, Little Boss.'

'I had some money with me and I would have paid the rest later.'

'Is that why the sale didn't happen?'

'Probably.'

Pareekutty walked away. Karuthamma yearned to talk to him. But how could she?

His query and her retort to it had come true. Those words boomed in her ears:

'When you have a boat and nets, will you sell us the fish?'

'If you give us a good price, we will.'

Kalikunju and Nallapennu were grumbling. They had to buy fish from the shack owners. Chembankunju gave the workers the share. The nets were washed and laid out to dry. Then he went home. He had a great deal of money in his hands. Life had a whole new radiance. He was treading a new path.

Since the early hours, he had been toiling hard. But he wasn't tired even as he headed home.

But the house was unhappy. He showed Chakki the fistful of cash. Chakki however showed no interest. 'For whom is all this money?'

'What a question, woman!'

'Look at Panchami's chest.'

Chembankunju picked up the still whimpering Panchami and examined her. There were bruises on her chest. He asked, 'Why did you come there, child?'

Chakki explained Panchami's purpose. Suddenly Chembankunju felt a great swell of love for his daughter. She had wished to make money. He liked that. He promised to give her a basket of fish thereafter.

Chakki then moved onto Pareekutty. 'That was unpardonable. Without him, there would have been neither boat nor nets.'

Chembankunju couldn't understand what was wrong. 'Why? What do you mean, woman?'

'Why didn't you sell him the fish?'

'How would I have managed then? Don't I have to pay the fishermen who came with me?' Chembankunju continued, 'And there is a problem if I sell him the fish; he will want to deduct the money I owe him from the price.'

'Are you saying that his helping you is now to be held against him?'

Karuthamma too was furious. From her room she called out, 'There's nothing left in his shack.'

That evening there was a quarrel in Achakunju's home.

The wife said, 'You kept saying that he was your childhood friend. What happened to your dream of working in his boat?'

Achakunju retorted, 'And you? You went chasing after Chakki. What happened to that?'

Achakunju continued, 'When people get a coin or two in the hands, they forget the past.'

Nallapennu agreed.

Achakunju reiterated his dream once again. 'Well, let me see if I can acquire a boat and nets too.'

Nallapennu however wasn't all that convinced about his resolve.

Six

Chembankunju was a fortunate man. Seldom was his catch matched by anyone else on the shore. In fact, his catch was always twice as much as the others'. When he flung the net, it would rise to the surface laden. A wonder indeed!

Every night when he counted the day's earnings, Chakki would say, 'We need to get the girl married.'

And Chembankunju would pretend that he hadn't heard her speak.

But Chakki too could be adamant. She would continue, 'What's on your mind? That she stay here forever?'

Chembankunju wouldn't speak. He probably didn't think it as important as making money. When it was to happen, it would.

Chembankunju had put together all the accessories required for a boat. He could go to sea any time now. He was all set.

Pareekutty's shack seemed to have shut down. Nothing seemed to be happening there. He had no money either. His Vaapa chastised him a great deal. Abdullah Boss said that he knew Pareekutty had given all his money away to a fisherwoman.

Karuthamma heard this from across the fence. She turned to her mother and insisted that they repay Pareekutty his money back right away. She flung into her mother's face what Abdullah Boss had told his son. Could there be anything more shameful?

For hadn't Pareekutty dipped into his capital and given it all away to a fisherwoman?

'We'll pay it back. In time,' was Chembankunju's retort, his usual one as always.

For Chembankunju had a new dream. Several new dreams. He wanted to acquire two more boats and nets. Then a piece of land on which he would build a house. And plenty of money in his hand.

'Haven't I slaved all my life? ... Now like that man Pallikunnath, I too want to enjoy life! Enjoy! Enjoy! Enjoy it to the fullest!'

He had also decided that he wanted to fatten Chakki up.

Chakki said wrily, 'As if I will ever fatten up now ... at this age!'

'Why not? Of course, you too will become plump.'

Chakki had never ever heard Chembankunju talk about wanting to enjoy life. Pleasure had acquired a whole new dimension for him.

She asked, 'What pleasure do you want in this old age? Where do you get such ideas from?'

'Listen, who said you can't enjoy your life in old age too? You must take a look at that Pallikunnath man ... you should see how he relishes life.'

Chakki looked at him wondering if she ought to advise him. Was he going astray?

Was it wrong to want to pleasure in one's old age?

Chembankunju said, 'Let me tell you something. His wife's your age. But she's always dressed up ... with her hair finely combed, a pottu on her forehead and her lips a fiery red ... and her skin has the sheen of gold. You should see them. They are like a young fisher couple.'

Chakki asked, 'So is that what you want? For me to doll up and flit around like a young girl?'

'What's wrong with that?'

'I would be so embarrassed.'

'Why would you be embarrassed?'

'I can't … I just can't!' Chakki confessed with a bashful expression.

Chembankunju continued to describe the multitude of delights that Kandankoran's life was blessed with. He hadn't eaten as well as he had in the Pallikunnath house. The curries there had a unique flavour. Like a young couple, they squeezed the most out of every moment of their life.

'Do you want to hear something else? It was quite embarrassing … one day when I went there, I found them together. Kissing and fondling each other, like young lovers…'

'Oh oh, such goings-on … rubbish!' Chakki remarked.

Chembankunju asked, 'What's wrong with it? I told you they are like newly-weds, the way they are with each other.'

'Don't they have children?'

'One boy.'

Chembankunju appraised Chakki carefully and said, 'We must fatten you up like Papikunju. And then we have to indulge in some of that youthful delight…'

In her heart Chakki too wished for the same. To be held and kissed. But she wouldn't ever speak it. 'First, you need to sort yourself out.'

'Yes, of course. I need to sort myself out and then the rest will follow…' Chembankunju smiled. The thought of his soon to be joys glimmered in his eye.

Chakki grumbled, 'You seem to be bedazzled by that woman…'

'That's true. Anyone would be!'

A little later Chembankunju said, 'He's a lucky man.'

'Let's hope we too are blessed by the mother of the sea. Once we have land and a house of our own and enough money to live on even if we don't go out to work, we too would be as carefree as a young couple,' Chakki declared. 'And by that time, we would have married the girls off too.'

That was what Chembankunju had in mind too.

'But I am not pretty,' Chakki said.

'But you would be pretty when the time came,' Chembankunju asserted.

'What if I am dead then?'

'Rubbish! Don't say such things.'

All of a sudden the colour of the sea changed. A denseness. The waters of the sea were tainted red. It was that time of the year for the mother of the sea. For sometime hereafter she would be unable to bless them. The sea would be barren.

A couple of days passed. Chembankunju couldn't stay idle. What if he went out into the deep seas? He would find fish there.

He called his boatmen and consulted them. But none of them would give him a clear confirmation of intent. Very seldom had anyone from that shore gone deep-sea fishing. And during this month of murky waters, no one ever went to sea.

Chembankunju was stern. 'Let me tell you something. If you can't be bothered to go with me, you will starve. I can't give you an advance.'

The starvation continued. And continued. The little money people had were all spent. A few tried going out to sea. But they couldn't find even a fish scale.

This was the time when hunger troubled everyone. The workers and the boat owners. The boat owners too had little money to spare.

The neighbourhood was sunk in penury. Everywhere everyone

starved. Achakunju, who had decided to acquire a boat and nets of his own, was the worst hit. He had children to worry about.

One day they hit rock bottom. The previous day, they had shaken out the flakes of dry fish clinging to the baskets, sold it for a pittance and bought tapioca for a meal. However, there was nothing for this day. Achakunju and his wife began squabbling. Achakunju slapped his impudent wife and walked away in a huff. It is the lot of the woman to bear the burden of her wailing children. So how could she walk away?

Instead, Nallapennu cursed Achakunju. 'I know what this walking away in a rage is all about. You will go fill your belly at the tea shop while we…'

However, Achakunju pretended not to hear the accusation and walked on. Perhaps he was only looking for the means to alleviate the problem.

She waited until evening. Finally, Nallapennu took a bronze tumbler and went seeking Chakki. She was willing to hawk or sell it but she desperately needed a rupee. Chakki accepted it as collateral and lent her a rupee.

Lakshmi, who heard about this, came with a pair of little gold studs that had adorned her daughter's ear lobes. Soon everyone was at her doorstep and Chakki began finding it a terrible nuisance. She didn't have all that money to loan. But no one would believe her when she said so.

Kalikunju went with a cauldron to Chakki. She had scrounged and saved to buy the uruli from Mannarshala the previous year. But Chakki said, 'Where am I to find the money if each one of you come here? I don't exactly dig the cash out of the ground…'

Kalikunju had been driven there by her children's hunger. And she hadn't expected such a curt dismissal.

Chakki continued, 'Everyone wants Chembankunju's cash.

But when we needed help, there was no one ... then each one of you were willing to betray us.'

Kalikunju demanded, 'What did we do?'

'No, you didn't do anything. But there's no money here.'

'How can you be like this? As if you don't know me?'

'I have to watch out for myself too...'

Kalikunju lost her temper. 'Just because you are rich now...'

'Ah, now she becomes rude...'

Soon it became an argument. Karuthamma intervened. She was scared. As the argument got more vicious, she knew she would be discussed.

Karuthamma fell at Kalikunju's feet and pleaded. Finally Kalikunju took her uruli and left.

Karuthamma turned to her mother. 'What's wrong with you?'

'What do you expect me to do?'

'Ever since we got the boat and nets, the two of you have changed.'

That evening as Chembankunju ate his supper, Chakki sat by his side telling him the gossip. The story of hunger on their shore. A fire hadn't been lit in any of the homes there.

Chembankunju said, 'Let them starve! Let them all be ruined!'

Karuthamma was shaken.

Chembankunju continued, 'Let them all burn! That will be useful for us...'

Karuthamma couldn't understand the reason for his venom. But she felt a great disgust for her father then.

Chakki asked, 'Why would it be useful for us?'

'Let them suffer ... when they have money in their hands, they caper around. Then they need to go to Alapuzha to fill their bellies with shop-bought food. And if the fisherwoman doesn't have clothes, they buy the most expensive kasavu sari. They behave as if they don't walk on the ground. So let them count the stars now...'

Karuthamma couldn't still understand the reason for her father's diatribe. Chakki then brought up the old theory, 'A fisherman doesn't set aside anything ever.'

'Let them not! Which is why they are suffering now. You better tell your daughter all this else she too would end up starving.'

Chakki said with a little smile, 'Ah, what a sensible fisherman you are!'

'Yes, I am a sensible man! Which is why I have money in my hands!'

'Don't tell me about that! That Muslim boy has had to shut down his shack. And our girl is here getting long in the tooth...'

Karuthamma wanted to snap: He too ought to suffer, right, Accha!

Chakki and Chembankunju took advantage of that fallow time on the shore. They acquired several bronze vessels, gold ornaments and other valuables for almost next to nothing. When they married their daughter off, they wouldn't have to spend as much as they may have needed to.

One day, they acquired a sturdy bed. When her husband came home, Chakki had a bashful grin. 'I bought a bed!'

Chembankunju leered, 'Why?'

'What's a bed for? To sleep on!'

'Who's going to sleep on it?'

'When the girl's married, her husband and she...'

'Really?'

'What else? Did you think it was for us oldies?'

Chembankunju seemed to accept that. Then he said, 'But I'm going to get a mattress made. Just like the one I saw at Kandankoran's.'

'In which case, you will need to find a woman to match ... to sleep with you...'

'I'll turn you into that woman.'

A slightly more elaborate plan had sprung in Chembankunju's mind. Or, perhaps it was just another dimension of his dream to live life to the hilt. He made plans to acquire one more boat of his own.

Almost all the money he had was sunk in movables. However, he still didn't see it as an impossible task.

One day when Chembankunju woke up, it was to find Ramankunju Valakkaran hovering around. Chembankunju welcomed him with much fanfare and ceremony. Ramankunju was a netsman of the shore. He had two boats of his own. For some time Chembankunju had worked in Ramankunju's boat. But all his immovable wealth had to be sold off one by one.

Ramankunju needed money. In these times of penury, he had to pay an advance to his workers. He usually borrowed money from Ousep. However, he already owed Ousep a great deal. So how could he approach Ousep again?

Ramankunju said, 'They have been with me for a long long time ... and they are starving now. There isn't any fish in the sea. How can I close my eyes to their plight?'

Chembankunju agreed. 'Yes, of course. You must do so. Especially someone like you...'

He offered to lend money. 'So how much would you need?'

'One hundred and fifty will do!'

Chembankunju counted out the cash. Ramankunju asked, 'Aren't you paying your workers an advance?'

Chembankunju scratched his head and said, 'How can I? I am only a worker like them. Can a squirrel open its mouth as wide as an elephant's?'

Ramankunju laughed.

Chembankunju explained his stance once again.

When Ramankunju left, Chembankunju went to Chakki and pranced around her in glee like a lunatic. Chakki had never seen him like this.

Chakki asked, 'What is all this madness?'

'What do you know, you creature! His Chinese fishing nets and boat will be mine in a month's time.'

Then he added, 'Now you see why you need to have cash in hand.'

Chembankunju's workers began demanding an advance. He asked them, 'Are you willing to work?'

They said yes.

Chembankunju said, 'In which case, let's go deep-sea fishing…'

'But how can we? In this evil time?'

Chembankunju came up with a new ploy. He said he would hire new workers. And they would be his permanent employees. 'I have put all my money into the boat and accessories. Do you expect me to sit around doing nothing? It breaks my heart…'

Chakki and Karuthamma discovered this only when one morning they saw Chembankunju's boat race into the western horizon. He was standing at the stern.

That day thirteen families waited on the shores. Wives and children pleading with the gods to spare the men. The older men said that the undertow was treacherous. There would be whirlpools in the outer seas.

By dusk, the boat hadn't yet returned. The seashore resounded with wails. By night, the entire fishing village was gathered on the shore. They all stood waiting, staring at the western horizon. The night sky was clear. The stars were all out. The sea was quiet. In the distance, someone thought they spotted a speck. Could it be the boat?

But the boat didn't arrive.

Kochan's old mother beat her chest and demanded that Chakki give her back her only son. Vava's pregnant wife didn't blame anyone. But she stood there sobbing. The seashore filled with waves of loud grief.

Closer to midnight, an uproar rang through: 'The boat's coming!'

The boat sped through the waves like a bird. There was a shark in the boat. They had got one more. But as they couldn't fit both into the boat, one of the sharks had been slaughtered to pieces.

Chembankunju divided the cut-up shark amongst the women so they could sell it in the east. It was enough, he said, if they gave him the money after the sale. Kalikunju, Lakshmi, all of them got a share. And so that day the hearth was lit in many homes.

Two days later, the baits were sprung again. That day as well Chembankunju was triumphant. Even when the sea was barren, Chembankunju was flush with funds. The elders were silent in their failure. 'It's because of Chembankunju that our bellies are full,' the women said.

Some other boats people also decided to go out to sea. That there would be an abundance after this starvation was how they consoled themselves. Last year, the chakara had happened to the north of Alapuzha. Hence, in all probability, the big catch should happen on this shore this year. And by ill fortune, if it wasn't so, they ought to be prepared to trail it with their nets. Which meant the boats and nets had to be repaired and ready. And it had to be done in these penurious times, the boat owners worried.

Ousep and Govindan arrived on the seashore with laden money bags. Everyone was in need of money. And would agree to any terms and conditions. Shack owners sucked up to the managers of big shrimp exporters in Alapuzha, Kollam and Kochi. Thus the seashore was muddied with borrowed monies.

The strong nets needed to be repaired. Several small traders called on various homes offering loans to the women. They were paying in advance for the dry fish the women and children would gather and keep. Meanwhile, it was rumoured that a young Muslim man was stabbed by Kochutty's husband when he found him in his hovel.

Chembankunju began seeing a great deal of Ramankunju. The latter was scared that he would have to pay back the borrowed money. But Chembankunju didn't ask for it back and instead offered small sums as temporary loan.

Pareekutty made no preparation to trade during the big catch. His Vaapa had asked him to shut down the shack. Abdullah insisted that Pareekutty give up trading in fish and do something else. But Pareekutty wouldn't have any of it. 'I can't!' Pareekutty said.

He hadn't decided to leave the shore yet, he stated brusquely.

Abdullah was astounded. His son had never before spoken to him in that manner. Abdullah demanded, 'Why is that?'

Pareekutty said, 'You took me to the shores when I was a boy and turned me into a trader of fish. I can't trade in anything else. I don't know how to.'

'But you lost even the principal; all that we invested in it!'

Pareekutty had his justification for even that. 'But don't you see Vaapa, there will be both profit and loss in any trade! And sometimes even the principal would be lost!'

'And what if there are more losses?'

Pareekutty had only one answer to that. 'Why don't you give me my share of the inheritance? You don't have to give me anything thereafter!'

'But what is left for me to give you? A plot of land is all there is!'

Abdullah has many troubles. Once he was a man of wealth. But all of it was gone now. And he had a daughter to wed. She was betrothed. Abdullah described his predicament. But Pareekutty wouldn't change his mind.

Karuthamma noticed that in Pareekutty's shack there was none of the hustle and bustle that happened before the chakara. He wasn't buying the mats or the baskets with handles. The cauldrons were not mended either. Nor was he building the hearth. She told her mother that now was the time to give Pareekutty what they owed him. If they felt any gratitude for what he had done for them, now was the time to help him out.

Chakki began pestering Chembankunju. It was of no use; worse, it only seemed to irritate him. That was when Karuthamma knew for certain that her father would never return Pareekutty's money. That was when she arrived at a few decisions of her own.

One day, she told her mother, 'My body can't bear this burden any more.'

At first, her mother didn't comprehend. 'What burden is your body having to lug?'

Karuthamma wept. Chakki consoled her. But Karuthamma was insistent, 'I am going to tell Achan – everything and all – I know then that money will be found.'

Chakki was shaken. 'My daughter! You mustn't!'

Chakki feared Chembankunju's wrath if he were to know what she had done. She didn't even dare think about it. And from Karuthamma's tone of voice and choice of words, she worried that there was so much she didn't know.

In a solitary moment, Karuthamma's mind wandered. She loved Pareekutty. There would be no place for another man in her heart. She wished she could forget him, their relationship for just one moment. For she was born a fisherwoman. And she would have to die as a fisherman's wife. That was how it should be, she knew. So shouldn't she have to forget Pareekutty?

If they could pay the money back, free themselves from that debt, she believed she would be able to forget Pareekutty. She couldn't bear to see him desolate and ruined because of her. In fact, it was this image of him that haunted her.

As the days went by, nothing changed. Chembankunju didn't return the money.

Seven

The fisherfolk waited with much eagerness. Every day in every home as people survived on boiled tapioca and gruel, all of them turned their eyes seawards with the same question. Oh mother of the sea, when will we be able to eat a proper meal? When will we be able to shape little balls of rice for each mouthful?

They knew the answer themselves: when the chakara season arrives! It had been so long since they had eaten a fillet of fish.

When the tea-shop owner stopped giving credit, the fisherman confronted him with a, 'One day, soon, the big catch will happen!'

The women wore faded, tattered, much patched clothes. And when they complained, they were told: 'Let the big catch happen, and I'll buy you the finest of mal-mal cloth!'

All needs and desires would be fulfilled then.

Karuthamma too had a desire. Or, was it a need? She told her mother about it. There would be much money made during the big catch season. Apart from that, they ought to set aside a big share from their everyday takings. And with that they would be able to repay Pareekutty. Chakki too would like to build a capital. But with that, she hoped to do something else. Buy gold.

Karuthamma said, 'I don't want gold or baubles! I just want you to repay the loan.'

Chakki said, 'But isn't that debt your father's responsibility?'

'But he won't repay it!'

Chakki agreed. And so Karuthamma made her plans. Panchami too had a plan. She would pick the small fry from the nets. Besides that her father had promised her a basket of fish from each catch.

Pareekutty too made some decisions. Abdullah mortgaged his house and land to a moneylender, the setu, for two thousand rupees. If he were to plan the big catch sale well that year, they would be able to pay off the debt and get his sister married off. That was his resolve.

Achakunju too would like to profit from this big catch. He hoped to become a boat owner as well. The sea's long drawn-out barenness had been unexpected. And they had starved during that time.

Achakunju approached Ousep. He too wanted to buy a boat and nets. He was ready for any kind of arrangement. 'I too want to stand at the helm of a boat and go to sea. And my wife too must come to shore waiting for me to return.'

Ousep asked, 'What do you have in hand, Achakunju?'

'Nothing,' Achakunju replied.

'So how do you expect to do it?'

In the end Ousep came up with a plan. He would save the money Achakunju made during the big catch. When the season was over, the boat could be bought. And Ousep would subsidize what was needed.

'But there's one thing! The boat and nets will be in my name. I will only give you a share of the takings, Achakunju. The share due to the boat owner will be mine. But you will receive the captain's share. So will you make over to me the money you make during the big catch season? I'll safeguard it!'

Achakunju agreed. That was customary on the seaside. He

went home and told Nallapennu about it. 'You must also give me your earnings from your sale in the east,' he said.

'But why? You give me your share.'

'You stupid cow, I intend to give both our earnings to Ousepachan.'

Nallapennu wasn't too happy about this. She asked, 'How did Chembankunju chettan buy his boat and nets? He gave everything to Chakki.'

However, in the end, they decided to entrust everything to Ousepachan.

Achakunju told everyone that he too was going to buy a boat and nets.

And as they waited with much expectations, the fallow season came to an end. The head of the storm broke. The ensuing currents made them decide that this year the big catch would be on their shores. The eyes of the fishermen lit up with the radiance of hope. Soon, the shore bustled with activity. It had transformed into a little city. Little huts popped up on either side. Tea shops, tailor shops, textile shops, jewellery shops – all of it was there. That year, they were even going to harness power using a generator. So there would be electric lights as well!

The second storm too broke. The sea turned and tossed. Everyone leapt in joy. Dreams burst into bud. When the churning seas settled, it would give rise to their prosperity.

The sea became calm. Boats arrived from distant shores. It was the season of rains. Winds rose, dense grey clouds gathered. But the sea lay tranquil as a pond.

Chembankunju's workers were quick. He had honed their skills even better. Chembankunju rode the stern with a great vigour. It was always a sight to watch and marvel at.

On the first day, the catch wasn't much. The fish were still waiting for the seas to temper down. Nevertheless, all the boats were out at sea. That day Chembankunju had the best catch.

Ayankunju opined that it was because Chembankunju had set out earlier than anyone else. However, Raman Moopan was of a different point of view. 'He's bought with the boat Pallikunnath's good fortune as well!'

All the other boat owners swore that even if they couldn't better their catch significantly, it would have to at least match Chembankunju's. In truth, he was an inspiration to them.

Ayankunju spurred his men on. 'Don't make me holler for you. You must be here before dawn breaks. Hey, don't you have any pride?'

Each one of them felt a competitive sap leap in them. They would try and match Chembankunju's catch.

Contrary to custom, people gathered on the shores earlier than ever. But some of them still had to be shouted awake and urged to come. The tea shops too began their business earlier than usual. That day Chembankunju's boat set out late. He hadn't known about the others leaving ahead.

From the movement of the boats, it was quite evident that it was a good catch day. Traders and vendors went to the shores. Pareekutty was restless. He seemed to be expecting someone. He had only a little cash in hand. The setu's manager had promised to come with the money. But he hadn't arrived yet. Pareekutty was waiting for him.

In every way, it was a day of fortuitous events. The sea was bustling with fish and apart from that it was a bright and sunny day. If shrimps were steamed, it would dry quickly enough. He would be able to make some money that day.

Time sped. The setu's manager Pachupillai didn't come. Pareekutty began to worry that he wouldn't be able to profit from the big catch. The boats turned back to shore. Pareekutty became even more anxious. Others stood there with the necessary sums of cash. The shore rang with boisterous cries of celebration. In the restaurants, they laid out the banana leaves and began serving lunch onto them. When the boats drew closer to the shore, the people on the shore would rush to drag them onto the sand. In little hovels, fires were lit and tin-coated iron vessels were put on them. Not a moment could be wasted. Pareekutty's workers also got ready.

The first boat to draw closer was Chembankunju's. As always it rode the seas. Khadar Boss said, 'Don't even think of winning against him!'

Maideenkunju agreed.

One old fisherman said, 'That is a god riding the stern!'

The boat drew closer to the shore. Shrimp. In all sizes.

Pareekutty leapt towards Chembankunju. What had happened the previous time had escaped his memory. But then anyone would forget in such a moment of excitement! Pareekutty requested, 'Chembankunju, give me your catch!'

Without a trace of pity Chembankunju looked at Pareekutty's face and retorted, 'Do you have the money? Or scram!'

That too was customary behaviour from this fisherman when the boat reached the shore. But even before Pareekutty could find an answer, Khadar drew closer. Pareekutty knew for sure then that he wouldn't get Chembankunju's catch. Pareekutty ran seeking other boats.

As usual, Chembankunju was the one who decided the price of the fish for the day. The catch was good that day. And he had the biggest haul of them all. Pareekutty managed to buy one-third of the catch from another boat. That was all he could afford to buy.

Setting aside money for the expenses, Chembankunju divided the income between the workers. Suddenly he had a thought. He said, 'Look, we had a really good day at sea; and look at the water ... it's shimmering in the sun. It is a perfect day. And the price is good!'

The men didn't understand what he implied.

'You asses, what I mean is you have to winnow when the wind is right. It is a good time to make money. What's the point in stuffing your faces with rice and lying on your backs? I am ready to go back to sea for another haul!'

Achakunju who stood nearby heard what was being said. Even though Chembankunju hadn't spoken to him, he said, 'I can't help but say this. Just because you can make money, you don't empty the sea out.'

Besides, it wasn't the accepted norm to go to sea twice a day. It wasn't allowed.

Chembankunju said, 'Think about it!'

The shore was resplendent with prosperity. It seemed as if gold had been flung around the hovels. Steamed shrimp was laid out to dry.

That day Achakunju didn't go to the restaurant to eat. Hadn't he made a decision on what his life would be like henceforth? He went home. That was the agreement. Nallapennu asked, 'How come you are here? Haven't you eaten your lunch?'

Achakunju was furious. 'You won't amount to much ever. You will never own a boat and nets.'

Achakunju turned and walked away. Even though she felt guilty, Nallapennu said, 'Why didn't you tell me when you left at dawn?'

'Didn't we clasp hands and agree upon this?'

That was the truth. As Achakunju walked away, Nallapennu said, 'Take what you need for lunch and give me the rest. I'll keep it. We can give it to Ousepachan later.'

Achakunju flung several notes and coins at her.

After he had eaten his lunch, Chembankunju returned to the shore. But none of his men came. So his dreams of making even more money that day came to nothing.

In the evening, boats came from Cheriazhikal, Trikunnapuzha and other such places. It rained heavily that night. The next day the boats set out only after dawn had broken.

Chembankunju scolded his men for not putting the boat out to sea earlier. That day too Chembankunju was ahead of everyone else. But there was another boat that was surging ahead, the boatman rowing strongly without pausing for breath. Everyone began asking whose boat it was. The boat was from Trikunnapuzha. The boatman's name was Palani. A young man.

Chembankunju's and Palani's boats stood neck to neck. It seemed as if they were competing with each other to race ahead. With a determination veering towards doggedness, the two of them rowed powerfully; the steersmen prodding them on. It was a splendid sight.

It looked as if Chembankunju's boat had fallen back a bit. Who would get the greater catch this day? It was difficult to decide based on where the boats were anchored and how the nets were flung.

On their way back to the shore, too, the boats raced each other. If the helms drew any closer, it would end in a tussle. When the helms brushed, everyone quailed in fright.

Karuthamma asked, 'Ammachi, why is Achan so stubborn?'

Chakki too was anxious.

Let the catch be over and done with. But why be stubborn about it? Chembankunju wasn't young. If the helms crashed, anything could happen. Each one of those moments stretched like an epoch. Whew! The boats were finally nearing the shore.

There was much jubilation on the shore. No one won. Nor

had anyone lost. They were on par. There was enough fish in both boats.

The boats drew closer. Karuthamma looked carefully at a bandana-wearing Palani who jumped onto the sands holding a huge oar in his hand. He was a young man of splendid and sturdy proportions. Chembankunju embraced Palani. He said, 'You are the sea's prince, my boy!'

Palani didn't speak.

That day it was Palani's catch which fetched the best price. And so Chembankunju suffered a small loss.

Chembankunju asked Palani, 'What's your name, my boy?'

The sturdy young man was shy. The man who stood before Chembankunju wasn't the young god who had lorded the stern with such vigour. He wasn't the young man who stood holding an oar larger than Chembankunju's and with his eye fixed on the horizon. Now he was a bashful boy. Where did all that dignity disappear?

The young man said, 'Palani.'

'You know your job, my boy! It isn't enough if you are born a fisherman, you must know how to fish the waters.'

Palani continued to be silent.

Chembankunju asked, 'What's your father's name?'

'Velu. He's dead!'

'And your mother?'

'She's also dead!'

'So who else do you have?'

'No one.'

Chembankunju asked in surprise, 'No one?'

Palani was quiet.

When Chembankunju went home, Chakki asked him, 'You may think you are young but is this any way to behave?'

Chembankunju didn't seem to hear her. A new big thought

had entered his head. The oblivion he felt when he rode the stern of his boat at sea was something he could talk to her about. But that wasn't what he wanted to tell her. He had an important subject to bring up with his wife.

Chembankunju told his wife quietly, 'Did you see that boy who stood at the stern of the boat?'

'I did.'

'He's a smart boy, isn't he?'

Chakki too was drawn towards him. Not just her, everyone else on that shore felt the same about the young man.

Chakki asked, 'What is it?'

'It would be good if we can get him.'

Chakki didn't speak.

Chembankunju continued, 'I asked him. He says he is all alone. Nothing wrong with that. Probably it's even good.'

Chakki asked, 'So why didn't you invite him home to eat with us?'

'I didn't think of it.'

In fact, Chakki felt relief course through her. Chembankunju had found a boy for their girl. It meant he hadn't forgotten his duty as a father.

That young man was a prize. Someone would snatch him away. Chembankunju too was worried about that. After lunch, Chembankunju went back to the shore.

Palani and others were asleep under a coconut palm. Chembankunju wasn't able to talk to him that day.

The next day, too, the competition raged at sea. Chembankunju lost. Palani had the greater catch.

Chembankunju's workers grew even more aggressive. Karuthakunju said, 'Let them not come to our shore and show off.'

Kunjuvava would have liked to have challenged their boat. But it would end in a squabble.

Chembankunju intervened. 'What's this? Are you jealous when you see men who know how to work well? What's it for? If you want to win, try working harder.'

At that point, Chembankunju's workers had another thought. If not at sea, they would have to take on the outsiders on land. Velutha protested. 'If they are here on our shore now; tomorrow we'll be on theirs.'

That didn't matter. Something had to be done. It was a time when money brimmed their palms. If it ended in a police case, so be it. That was their attitude. It was a state of mind Chembankunju was familiar with – and which was the reason for his anguish. It wasn't just Chembankunju's workers. All the other men on the shore too were jealous. No one ought to be that smart! they said. Nevertheless, there were many people who opposed this as well.

In the ensuing days, there was a fight at the beach between the boatsmen of the shore. Two or three were hurt on their heads. That day and the next, none of the boats from that shore went out to sea. Everyone was in hiding. The policemen arrived on the shore and took away a few men. The Shore Master intervened and got them released.

One by one, they went to meet him with an offering of thanks. Then there was a collection taken. And thus the police case was hushed up. All this kerfuffle meant that all the money made from the big catch was spent.

Velayudhan alone didn't go to meet the Shore Master. He knew that the Shore Master had singled him out. The man had him arrested by the police. Velayudhan was in jail for a week. When he got out, he said, 'I don't care. I am not going to kow-tow to him.'

Chembankunju lost a week's takings. In that season of plenty, it was a huge loss.

They began working the sea again. Everyday Chakki would ask Chembankunju to invite Palani home. One day all the workers of the boat took a day off and went to Trikunnapuzha. But Palani didn't go. Chembankunju asked Palani, 'Why didn't you go, my son?'

'Where do I go to?'

That was the fact. Whom did he have at Trikunnapuzha to visit? Chembankunju invited Palani, 'Then, why don't you come to my house to eat some lunch?'

Palani accepted the invitation. In Chembankunju's house, they put together a feast of many, many dishes.

Palani wasn't the child of a family. He was the child of the Trikunnapuzha shore itself. He had no memory of either his father or mother. If you were to ask him how he had managed to survive, he would say he did precisely that – survive! Who brought him up? No one did. No one ever made any effort for him. He worked for just himself. When he was a little boy, he was flung out to sea to hold the string of the nets. A sea in which stingray and porpoises gambolled. No creature ever had an anxious moment about him. When he was old enough, he began working the boats and so began earning money. When he had money, he spent it. And when he didn't, he managed. Did he have dreams? Perhaps. No one ever desired that he eat, that his belly be full. And neither had he ever spared such a thought for anyone.

This afternoon for the first time someone had cooked a meal for him. And a woman stood at his side to ensure that he was served, that he ate well. It was an overwhelming moment.

Chakki found out his favourite among the curries. She served it onto his plate again and again.

Did Palani ever wonder what all this was in aid of?

Chakki asked, 'How old are you, son?'

'Ahh...' A shrug.

He didn't know.

Chakki's enthusiasm quelled. How could he not know how old he was. All questions hereafter would have to be carefully worded. What was his caste? Whatever it be, they had to know.

'Where do you live, son?'

'I have a little hovel.'

'What do you with all the money you make?'

'What do I do? I spend it.'

Taking it upon herself to play his mother, Chakki advised him. 'Son, you have no one. How can you spend all you earn? If you fall ill tomorrow, what will you do?'

Palani mumbled an 'Oh!' as if he had thought about it and arrived at a conclusion.

How easily he dismissed it! That he had survived and stayed alive this long was a miracle. So how did it matter if he was laid up in old age?

Chakki retreated into a silence. She had nothing left to ask. He was an able man. Not a bad sort. He drifted along with no one to share his joys or sorrows. No one had ever considered the passage of his life before. A little later Chakki asked once again in a motherly manner, 'Is it enough to live like this?'

'Why not?'

That meant he had no goals in life. Was that proper? And yet, what else could one think. His snappy retort, neither faltering nor stumbling, prompted one to assume so. He had never set a goal for himself in life. No one had ever wanted that of him.

Chakki said, 'Well, that isn't enough then!'

Palani didn't speak.

Chakki continued, 'Son, you are alone. And you are a hard worker. But all this will change. You won't be so fit one day. And a man has to have some possessions in his life. You need someone to take care of you. You need that too. Son, think about it, someone to cook for you, and if you have the place, a home – won't that be something?'

Palani continued to be silent.

'Son you must marry.'

'Well!'

'Shall I go ahead and decide it for you?'

Palani consented with yet another 'well'.

Chakki continued to ask, 'Don't you want to know who the girl will be?'

'Who?'

'My daughter.'

Palani agreed to that as well. Even though the proposal had progressed that far, Chakki saw many shortcomings in it. And only a few virtues. Palani had neither family nor roots. When you gave your daughter to a man like that, what do you do if he turned out to be a rascal? Whom do you ask to intervene?

Chembankunju said, 'But he is a good man.'

'If someone asked you, where have you got your daughter married off, what do you say?'

'He'll build a house.'

But above all else, something else disturbed Chakki.

'What is his caste?'

'He is human. And a worker of the sea.'

'Our relatives will be upset.'

'Let them be!'

'Then we'll be all alone.'

'So?'

Chembankunju continued with steely resolve. 'I'll give her to him.'

Eight

It continued to pour. The rains wouldn't pause. There was plenty of shrimp in the sea. But no boats could set out. For, after all, it is a man who must work the boat. And it was bone-chillingly damp. Then one morning the sun rose in a clear sky. The boats were launched. There was a good catch. The boats came back to shore and brisk trade happened.

But once again the skies darkened and the rains began. There had never been such a heavy downpour. It continued the whole day.

In the sheds, the fully dried shrimp lay. There were also semi-dried ones. And steamed shrimp. And rotting heaps of fresh shrimp. All the sheds were in a mess. And showed every sign of a huge impending loss.

In the first part of the season, there had been adequate sunshine. And each day's catch was well used. The big traders continued to hover. But this ill fortune had descended upon them.

Pareekutty had yet another trouble to deal with. The first consignment he sold had been good! The next consignment had not been dry enough. That's what the setu had claimed.

The setu said, 'We don't want your business. Just give me back my money and take your goods away!'

The setu wouldn't agree no matter what he said. Pareekutty went to each and every shop in Alapuzha. But no one wanted his shrimp. The godowns were full, they said.

Pareekutty fell at Pachupillai's feet and begged for clemency. He needed a huge loan from the setu. And he would offer Pachupillai a commission from it. Pachupillai promised to do his best. With that Pareekutty hoped to salvage his losses and use the money to buy more fish. But then the wind and rain began.

Pareekutty's investment began to rot and stink. In a day's time, all that was left to do was to bury it in the sand.

The seashore was sunk in gloom. The boats were going out to sea. And they were bringing back big catches. They were able to sell shrimp to the homes nearby. And there were lorries that came in once in a while. But that was all. They were not able to quote their prices any more. They had to sell at whatever price they were being offered by the traders.

There was no business in the restaurants. Not a soul entered the textile shops. The peanut sellers couldn't even find children to sell their peanuts to.

When would all of this change? Even eking out a daily livelihood was difficult.

All the boat owners on that shore were devastated. Especially Ramankunju. His business that year hadn't taken off. Ousep began demanding his money. He had begun eyeing Ramankunju's Chinese fishing nets.

One day they had a bitter disagreement on the shore. Chembankunju fluttered in his thoughts as Ramankunju swore to return Ousep's money in a week's time, no matter what.

Ramankunju asked Chembankunju for the money. But this time Chembankunju wasn't ready to hand over the money. Ramankunju sensed the unwillingness.

'What is it, Chembankunju? Tell me, what's on your mind?'

Pretending to be embarrassed, Chembankunju said, 'How can I without any surety?'

'What do you want as surety?'

'That … what do I say?'

In the end Chembankunju told him what was on his mind. He wanted the loan of Ramankunju's Chinese nets as surety.

And so Chembankunju managed to acquire the Chinese fishing nets.

That day too there was a little feud in Achakunju's house. Chembankunju had not one but two boats now. Nallapennu prodded Achakunju, 'What's the point in calling yourself a man?'

'Listen, you need to pitch in too. Where is the money that we were to have given Ousepachan?'

'Do you expect me to walk around naked? Or, is it possible to drink water without vessels?'

'Now if it had been with me…'

'You would have spent it on drink!'

Achakunju reached out and gave her two tight slaps.

Chakki was excited about having one more boat. But she was also distressed at not having settled Pareekutty's dues. And Karuthamma wouldn't stop reminding her about it.

On the day the Chinese nets and boat was brought in as surety, Chakki told Chembankunju, 'This is disgraceful.'

'What?'

'You made him bring his stock across to us at midnight and now you are pretending it didn't happen.'

Chembankunju snapped at her to keep quiet.

'There's no point in snapping at me. That boy is in deep trouble. If you don't help him now, there's no point…'

'Where is the money?'

Karuthamma, who was overhearing this exchange, spoke up, 'You have to give that money back, Accha!'

Chembankunju frowned. 'How does it concern you?'

She was not afraid to answer him back. And she had plenty to say. She decided to tell him that she had been the one who had asked him for the money first. And which was why, even though they had no money to pay for it, he had given them all of his stock. There was a hidden warning there. The richer they got, the more she was indebted to that Muslim man.

Chakki paled at the thought of Karuthamma speaking out. That would be disastrous.

Chakki took on Chembankunju. 'What's there so much to rave and rant about? She's only speaking the truth!'

'How does it concern her is what I would like to know. Did she take it from him? Is he demanding his money from her?'

In some consternation, Chakki replied, 'Just because he didn't ask her, can't she tell us what's bothering her?'

Chembankunju spoke in a grave censorious manner, 'Let me make this clear. This is men's business. You have nothing to do with that. You are to be married off.'

That bit of advice was right. It was a lesson Karuthamma had to remember.

Chembankunju now directed his ire towards Chakki, 'It's all your fault. She's picked up all this from you.'

Chakki was silent.

Later when the mother and daughter were alone, the mother asked the daughter, 'How could you forget yourself? You were going to tell your father everything, weren't you? Didn't you hear the tittle-tattle in the neighbourhood? If any of that reaches your father's ear – oh mother of the sea!'

She understood. However, she still couldn't help herself. 'We have to give that money back.'

'That's what I want to do too.'

'Ammachi, you keep saying this. But you haven't still paid back the money. I told you all the things we could do. But you didn't do any of it.'

A moment later, she continued, 'Everything can wait till that loan has been paid back...' She paused mid-sentence.

Chakki understood where it was leading to.

'You are right. It's the correct thing to do.'

Chakki had tried to fathom Karuthamma's feelings about marrying Palani. But she refused to reveal her true feelings, saying neither yes nor no. Perhaps it was because she was shy, Chakki told herself. After all she was a young girl. But she was also worried about Karuthamma's relationship with Pareekutty.

If she were to ask Karuthamma's friends to probe her mind, soon the entire shore would sing with gossip. And it was at that point that Karuthamma declared, 'Only after you pay off that debt...'

Whew! That was a relief! Chakki's face lit up with a radiant smile. She asked, 'So my daughter, you are agreeable to this marriage, aren't you?'

Karuthamma didn't respond. Chakki continued with the same elation, 'He is a good boy, my daughter, a very good boy!'

Chakki continued to praise Palani. There were enough reasons to sing his praises. And as she heard him being praised, Karuthamma sensed a certain resentment wiggle its way into her. She felt a slow rage gather in her. Besides, there were enough reasons to contradict all of what Chakki said. How old was Palani? Didn't she have a right to know? Who were his family? And most importantly, had Palani found a place in her heart?

Chakki felt a huge relief. She continued to talk about him. Karuthamma felt breathless. She felt she would explode if she didn't speak. She burst out, 'Oh, keep quiet, Ammachi!'

And then she mumbled through clenched teeth. Chakki couldn't make out what she said. But Chakki went on, 'I'll sort the debt out before you are married.'

With a great deal of anger and bitterness, Karuthamma said, 'Of course, you will. So why didn't you do it all these days?'

'I'll keep a tight control!'

With utter hopelessness, Karuthamma said, 'You know it won't happen! The wedding will take place and that will be the end of it.'

Chakki said firmly, 'Wait and watch!'

All her chaotic thoughts tussled and turned into a firm resolve in Karuthamma. 'Unless you pay that money back, I won't agree. Or, I will kill myself … that's for sure!'

Chakki grew anxious. 'Don't talk rubbish, my child!'

Karuthamma burst into tears. 'What else can I do? He is ruined. If we didn't have the money, I would understand that … but it is just that no one wants to pay up.'

And then she started a litany of accusations about Chakki who listened quietly. 'You don't want to pay him either,' Karuthamma concluded.

Chakki denied it vehemently. Karuthamma made another decision. 'I am going to speak up.'

'Oh my dear child, please don't!'

'Do I have a choice?'

After a little while, she continued, 'After this grand wedding, on our way to my new home what if he accosts me and tells me, "Pay up the money you owe me and then leave", what will we do?'

Chakki hadn't considered that until then. A horrifying picture rose before her eyes. Chakki asked her anxiously, 'Why would he ask you for the money?'

'He gave the money because I asked for it.'

'But that was merely a joke!'

'Says who?'

The vision of him accosting Karuthamma refused to leave Chakki's eyes.

Pareekutty was dejected. And he was facing total ruin. In that precarious state of mind, he would do anything.

Karuthamma continued, 'I have decided to tell Achan everything. I will do it today. Why can't I?'

'My daughter, you mustn't!'

'I will.'

In the end, Chakki promised to pay the debt off one way or the other before the wedding.

That day the wife had a fresh piece of news for her husband: their daughter had no objections to that marriage. However, there was the weight of an unspoken 'but' that lingered in the air. Could that 'but' be voiced though?

Chembankunju didn't particularly care whether Karuthamma was agreeable to the wedding or not.

Chakki could think of no means to get her husband to agree to pay Pareekutty's debt off.

The price of fish had fallen. It wasn't just Chembankunju, but no one on the shore knew any peace. A few days later, things picked up again. All the dried shrimp at Kochi and Alapuzha had been loaded onto ships. But there was a fall in price at Rangoon. Everything was selling at half price, the traders claimed. And a ship was lost at sea. So all settlements were made at half price.

Pareekutty lost a thousand rupees.

Karuthamma felt a great change enter her. She was perhaps changing to adapt to changing circumstances. She had grown up. She had acquired a certain courage, a will of her own. She sought a chance to talk to Pareekutty. She had so much to tell him.

They met. She stood on one side of the fence and he on the other. That day she was the one who began the conversation. A conversation that neither had a structure nor was peppered with giggles.

She asked, 'Bossman, your business is at a loss, isn't it?'

That wasn't the opening Pareekutty had expected the conversation to start with. He didn't speak.

She continued, 'We will return your money, my Bossman.'

Pareekutty replied, 'But Karuthamma, you didn't take any money from me.'

'Nevertheless, I should be the one to pay it back.'

'How can that be?'

'But that's how it should be, my Bossman. For only after your loan has been paid off…'

Karuthamma couldn't finish the sentence. A lump clogged her throat. She felt faint. Her eyes brimmed.

Pareekutty completed the sentence for her. 'You want to pay the loan off and get married, isn't that it?'

Pareekutty would not allow himself tears. But he asked, 'So you want to sever our ties, I suppose?'

A question that pierced her like a sharp weapon. How could he be so heartless to ask that? Pareekutty knew she was helpless. And yet he expected an answer of her.

She said, 'No, no, my Bossman, I want you to do well…'

Pareekutty wasn't that simple-minded swain any more. He smiled. A mirthless smile. 'I do well, Karuthamma?'

She understood the irony. He would never do well. Karuthamma couldn't bear it any more. She walked away. Pareekutty stood there for a little more time and then left.

That night Chembankunju had an announcement to make. He was in high spirits. He whispered to Chakki, 'Palani doesn't want a dowry!'

Chakki couldn't believe it. She said, 'As if.'

'Yes, of course! He says he'll marry her without a dowry!'

Chakki looked at Chembankunju carefully. Chembankunju proclaimed, 'I swear it is the truth. I swear it by the mother of the sea!'

Chakki demanded with a gleam in her eye, 'Just because he says he doesn't want a dowry, shouldn't we give it to him?'

She challenged him to refute it.

If someone said he didn't want any money, was there any obligation to pay it? Hence he was astounded at what Chakki was asking of him.

Chakki asked harshly, 'You must have convinced that simpleton of a boy. Didn't you?'

Chembankunju hastened to reply, 'I didn't say anything to him.'

Chakki had a serious question, 'Why do people need money or wealth?'

'Do I have any money of my own?'

'This dowry is something we give our child.'

'But what if he doesn't want it?'

'So whom are you making all this for? That's what I want to know.'

Chakki spoke a great deal. To enjoy in one's old age; to make a mattress and pillows; to bring a good-looking woman home – all this may suffice for him but there was so much more to be accomplished in life. Without bowing to Chembankunju's dictatorial stance, Chakki said, 'You wouldn't have made all of this without me!'

Chembankunju tried to soothe her with a smile. 'But I want the two of us to enjoy it all! The mattress is for you as well…'

Chakki hopped in rage. Her voice rose. Chembankunju began to worry that if this turned into a quarrel, all the secrets would be spilt for the neighbours to hear. He got up and left so that the argument would come to a natural stop.

Karuthamma arrived on the scene then.

'I don't want a dowry, Ammachi!'

'How is that possible? It is not seemly for a girl to be married without a dowry. Don't you need some money of your own?'

A moment later Karuthamma said, 'But I don't have a sister-in-law or a mother-in-law waiting there for me! Isn't that the kind of set-up you are sending me to?'

Chakki felt those words stab at her throat. They were sending her to a home without a family!

'But daughter, won't people talk?'

'Big deal!'

Karuthamma continued, 'You can send me off any which way. But please pay off the Little Boss's money.'

A little later, in a voice choked with emotion, Karuthamma said, 'He is ruined. I can't leave here seeing him ruined as he is. And if I go, he will die...'

Karuthamma spoke all that was in her heart. There was nothing left to say. But Chakki didn't understand. If she had understood any of it, as a mother she would have had so much to ask of her daughter. Or perhaps Chakki had understood all of it! A woman, even if she is a mother, would understand her daughter's love story. And then keep quiet about it.

'Daughter, I will pay that loan off.'

'But Achan won't pay it!'

What should she do? Chakki asked her. Karuthamma suggested that Chakki steal from Chembankunju. There would be murder, if he discovered it. And Chakki didn't have the gumption to get away with it.

Karuthamma asked, 'Amma, are you afraid?'

She was. That was why she hadn't done it before even though she had wanted to.

In the early days of the big catch season, there had been plenty of cash. In those days, if she had filched some, it would have been undiscovered. Karuthamma tried to bolster Chakki's courage. Besides, Chakki fully understood how important it was to sort this out. And so when Chembankunju went out to sea at dawn, the mother and daughter opened his box and took some money out. They spent that day petrified. Chembankunju locked the day's earnings away in his box. Unusually for her, Chakki wanted to know his share of the takings of the day. He said, 'No one wants shrimp.'

'But what did you get?'

'Why do you want to know?'

Every day the mother and daughter secreted away a little cash.

One day, Chembankunju counted his money carefully. That day Chakki and Karuthamma held a searing coal in the pits of their stomachs – eating into their flesh, hurting, threatening to consume them any moment. When he locked his box up, they sighed in relief. Their crime was undiscovered.

The daughter asked the mother, 'How much do we have?'

In all these days, they had been able to put aside only seventy rupees. And there was a large stock of dried fish as well. That would fetch about twenty rupees. Even if the amount was small, they decided to give it to Pareekutty.

Nine

The wedding was fixed. It didn't require much planning or organizing. Palani didn't have anyone to speak on his behalf. Or to vouch opinions. He mentioned it to the owner of the boat he worked for. Chembankunju went with Palani to make an offering of betel nut and leaves to the Shore Master of Palani's shore. Chembankunju also made an offering to his Shore Master.

Now no one could find fault with him for not having got his daughter married off. He stood up straight and demanded of his wife, 'Do you see this? Chembankunju got everything sorted out!'

Chakki retorted tartly, 'But look at the boy! He has neither home nor family or anything to speak of. Wonderful!'

'Shut up, you old broom! What do you know? He is a good worker. Look at his brawny body! There isn't a young man like him anywhere around.'

Chakki couldn't dismiss that. Instead, she laughed and said, 'In which case, we can now go ahead and have a good time.'

'I am going to have a good time. Enjoy myself like Pallikunnath Kandankoran.'

Chakki responded, 'Shouldn't you have paid that Muslim boy's money first?'

As if it was an irritating thought, Chembankunju said, 'Why

is it that you always bring this up when we refer to Karuthamma's marriage?'

Chakki was shaken. He had hit on the truth unknowingly.

Each time Karuthamma's wedding was discussed, this thought hinged itself to the conversation. But Chakki had never expected Chembankunju to bring it up.

Chakki came up with an explanation, 'Aren't we going to frolic around like young lovers? I thought it would be best if we sorted that matter as well!'

There would be a way. Chembankunju hadn't forgotten. One by one, he would fulfil his obligation depending on time and circumstances. He told his wife in all seriousness, 'Listen, we don't have boys of our own. What if we bring him into our home as ours?'

Chakki beamed. 'But he is our eldest son!'

As if Chakki hadn't really understood it, Chembankunju explained that Palani was all alone, so why shouldn't they ask him to stay with them? They had two boats now. If Palani came in, it would be a fine thing. Chembankunju explained this at length to Chakki and asked her what she thought.

Chakki thought about it a bit. It was a good idea. It would fill the vacuum of not having a boy of their own. But Chakki had her doubts.

'But would he agree?'

Chembankunju said, 'Why won't he?'

Chakki said, 'Do you think any able fisherman will choose to leech on to his fisherwoman's family?'

Chembankunju thought a while and replied, 'I am sure he will be happy to do this. He is a gullible chap, a rather simple boy!'

'That's true!' And then Chakki continued, 'But when you married me, you wouldn't even agree to spend two days in my home!'

'I had my father and mother!'

Chakki wasn't convinced that Palani would want to live there.

Karuthamma discovered her father's plans. Chakki was perplexed by Karuthamma's opposition. She turned to her daughter, 'What a creature you are! The moment your wedding has been fixed, you have no need for your parents, is it? So what was the point in enduring all this hardship in bringing you up? Just a mere hint of this fisherman coming into your life, and suddenly you don't want your mother and father any more! You are quite a girl!'

Chakki's words pierced Karuthamma's heart. She hadn't expected such a response from her mother: Did they think that her opposition to their scheme was because she didn't love her parents? She hadn't even thought that there was any loss of face in her staying on in her parents' home after her wedding. She would always be her mother's daughter. Her mother was prepared to do anything for her. How could she bear to be separated from Panchami? The day she left this house – how was she to bear that moment?

And yet all Karuthamma wanted was to flee that shore, that land. Karuthamma was choked with emotion as she said, 'Ammachi, I didn't mean it like that! My Ammachi, please don't speak like this. Whom do I have other than the two of you, my mother and father?' She fell onto Chakki's shoulders, weeping loudly. Her mother gathered her in her arms.

Chakki hadn't really meant any of what she said. Neither had she thought Karuthamma would be so hurt. Karuthamma wept as if her heart would break. Chakki too wept.

Karuthamma said, 'I ... my ... I don't want to live on this shore any more. Or, shall we all leave together?'

Chakki asked in a voice full of love for this child of hers, 'What are you saying, my child?'

Unable to bear the pain in her heart, Karuthamma said, 'I …
if I were to live on this shore…'

'What is it, daughter?'

Karuthamma had something to say. Chakki thought her
harsh words had wounded Karuthamma. But there was a bigger
grief hidden in Karuthamma's heart. But she hadn't thought that
it would be so intense.

Even as she wept Karuthamma spoke through clenched teeth,
'If I continue to live here, this shore will be doomed! Doomed!
Do you hear me?'

Chakki's eyes filled up. 'My daughter, you mustn't speak like
this!'

'No, Ammachi, all I want is to go away from here! Only
then is there hope for me. Whom else can I say this to but you,
Ammachi?'

Karuthamma had no one else to bare her soul to. But even
then how much could she reveal? Was it possible?

Even then Chakki persisted, 'That Muslim boy has bewitched
my child!'

Karuthamma denied it. It wasn't bewitchment; no one had
cast a spell on her. Karuthamma asked, 'Has this shore ever seen
a woman like this?'

'What kind of woman, my child?'

'Don't you know, Ammachi?'

'Oh my mother of the sea. My child is talking nonsense!'

'I am not mad, Ammachi. I was asking you, have there been
other women, another woman – like this?'

Karuthamma didn't know how to explain what was in her heart.
But she wanted to know about that woman. A fisherwoman who
fell in love with a man from another community; a woman who,
despite all her efforts, felt her love only grow rather than lessen;
had there been such a woman on this shore? A woman whose

every breathing moment was overwhelmed by that fiery love. Had that shore ever known such a love? What hope was there for a love between a fisherwoman and a man of another religion? Had the grains of sand of that shore heard such a lover's song and sprung alive? What happened to that lover?

Could she ask her mother any of these?

Perhaps there once was a pair of heartbroken lovers who walked this shore. Unable to do anything but hide her inextinguishable love in her heart, had the woman allowed herself to become another man's wife? Or perhaps, had she killed herself? Or perhaps, was there another way?

Karuthamma decided that only she must be as unfortunate. Only she must love a man like this. Even if there had been other love stories on this shore, only she could know such pain.

Chakki asked bewildered, 'Did something happen, daughter?'

Karuthamma didn't understand her mother's query.

Chakki continued, 'Girls of a certain age...'

Karuthamma dismissed Chakki's hint with a matter-of-fact, 'Ammachi, no, I am all right!'

There was courage in that claim.

Karuthamma had only one plea. That she be allowed to flee. An unknown dread had filled her. A monster with gaping jaws. She had to flee its dark shadow. And her mother agreed to help her escape. She would be sent away on the day of her wedding itself.

Karuthamma became the focus of attention amidst the women of the neighbourhood. They performed a ritual that went as far back as time. Once a wedding had been fixed, it was the duty of the neighbourhood women to instruct the bride on the religion of wifehood. If she were to make a mistake, the society would blame these good women, in fact.

Nallapennu told Karuthamma, 'Daughter, we are entrusting a

man to you. It isn't as simple as what you think. We are not giving a girl to a man. On the contrary it is the other way round.'

Kalikunju had something else to say, 'Our men live in a sea where the waves rise and fall, daughter!'

Kunjipennu warned her, 'Daughter, women have hearts that are easily turned. So you have to be careful!'

And so all of them advised her. They had all in turn accepted such advice. And now they were only passing it on. That was their duty. None of them had ever been blamed for the misconduct of a woman who had been married from that shore. It was all advice that was untainted by envy.

Karuthamma listened to each word carefully. She was overwhelmed. But she still had a query of her own. The one she had meant to ask her mother. 'Has it ever happened that a woman loved a man on this shore? And the man returned her love. But she married another man? Has anything like this ever happened on this shore?'

It was a question that resounded within her. Yet she didn't dare ask: What was the story of that unfortunate woman?

Karuthamma thought that she saw the soul of that cursed woman with her unfulfilled longings wandering through the winds of the shore. Sometimes in solitary moments, she heard an incomprehensible story being narrated to her in an alien language. Once, the shore had known women like her. Women who turned into grieving creatures, living a life of sorrow. Those were the tales of loss the wind too told her. The sea's heaving voiced the same. The grains of sand knew it too. There was more. The bones of these crones had crumbled to dust and were now part of the sands of the shore. They too must be trembling.

One day Karuthamma asked Nallapennu, 'Auntie, has this shore ever had any woman who went astray?'

Yes, there had been so. Most unusual tales. One or two back

in time. They didn't go astray of their own choice. One of the old sea ditties told the story of one such woman. Her fall from grace caused the waves to rise as high as a mountain and climb onto the shore. Dangerous serpents foamed and frothed as they slithered on the sands. Sea monsters with cavernous mouths chased the boats to swallow them whole. It was an old story. Nallapennu sang a few stanzas of that ditty.

That was also a story of love. Perhaps in many years' time, Karuthamma's story too would be the subject of songs sung.

Nallapennu said, 'This is the way of the shore.'

Karuthamma asked with great curiosity, 'Even to this day?'

'These days there is none of that strict code of purity. These days the men too have changed.'

People and customs change. But a daughter of the sea has to safeguard her virtue.

Little girls asked her, 'Karuthamma chechi, are you going away?'

Karuthamma had important matters to tell those little girls. They mustn't flit around these shores like dried leaves in the wind.

Karuthamma said her goodbyes. She was born there; grew up there; and now she bid farewell to that place. But could she really forget that seashore?

What would the new shore be like? She had thought a great deal about it. Would the sun set there in a burst of golden light like it did here? Even when the sea was tossing and turning in a storm, it had a beauty of its own. She had never feared this sea. Even as it sang the song of that cursed woman, the winds of this shore knew only how to caress. Would that shore be the same? Would it?

What about the people there? Even if they were loving, this

shore that had reared her had a certain tenderness. And it was this she was going away from.

She said her goodbyes one by one to everything familiar.

It was a moonlit night. The sea lay calm. There was a particular beauty to the moon. A song wafted in the air meshing with the moonlight.

Was that Pareekutty singing?

But it didn't resound as his song in Karuthamma's ears. Pareekutty the man didn't exist any more. She was beckoned into a world of joy. This was the call of a seashore drenched in moonlight. It was the youthful call of her own longings. The music of the shore she was going away from. She had so many poignant memories of that shore!

The strains of that song entered her. Karuthamma sat up. An image of Pareekutty appeared before her. Was he, in fact, calling out to her? What else did he have as a consolation, as a reprieve, but that song? Not just that night but he would sing every night. He would continue to sing even after she left. He didn't care if anyone listened to him or not.

Her mother was asleep. Her father was away. She knew the shore would be deserted. She felt something stir in her that made her want to open the door and step out. The singer's heart hadn't broken yet. But he sang as if he wanted it to shatter. For it was a song that evoked the past of that fallen woman who lived on this shore once!

These were the lines Nallapennu had sung to Karuthamma. She didn't remember the words. But the very essence of that song, the pain and depth of the emotion moved her heart.

Had the woman too walked to the shore in a trance lured by a song? She too must have heard the call of the radiant moon that night ... And, so one more woman followed her path.

The waves would rise high as hills. Sea monsters would rise above the waters with cavern-like gaping jaws. Venomous serpents would crawl on the shores.

Karuthamma drifted into another stream of thought. A deep stream. She was leaving. She had said her goodbyes to everyone and everything she knew. She was prepared to leave. But she hadn't said her farewell to the moon on that shore; to the sea washed in moonlight; to the sweet song of the moon. She hadn't bid adieu to that messenger of the moon god.

It could happen that the song might not be sung again tomorrow or the night after or till the day she left this shore. And that night the singer's throat might finally crack. What if he stopped singing? And thus the moon on that shore would be muted in sorrow.

Yet another impulse overwhelmed her. Never again would she be able to merge with the moonlight or the song. Perhaps this was her last chance. Karuthamma couldn't let it pass. Once more she sought the shadows of the beached boat on the sands. Once more she sought a joy that was to be denied to her forever.

She ran on the shore as a child. It was on that shore she became a maiden and fell in love. And now she was to be the chaste wife of a fisherman who braved winds, squalls and treacherous waves when he went out to sea to fish. It was an important phase of life she was stepping into. The life that lay ahead would be weighed with gravity, substance and meaning. All she had left were these last few days of fecklessness.

But Karuthamma also knew fear. She didn't trust herself. She would succumb. Be tainted. Until then she had never feared this of herself.

She would beseech him to never sing again. That he shouldn't move the moon on that shore so. She had so much to say to Pareekutty. Many words of regret to utter.

Karuthamma stood up. She opened the door softly. Outside, the world was bathed in moonlight. She stepped out!

She walked through the long shadows of the coconut palms to the shore.

Suddenly the song paused. He had propitiated his goddess to appear before him with his relentless singing. For a moment he couldn't believe his eyes. He asked, 'Karuthamma, are you leaving?'

What else could he ask of her?

'Once Karuthamma leaves … will Karuthamma ever think of me?' It was a sincere query.

'Even if you don't think of me, I will sit on this shore and sing. Even when I am an old man with no teeth, I will continue to sing.'

Karuthamma had something to tell him. 'My Bossman, you must marry a good girl, have many children, become a big trader and live happily.'

Pareekutty didn't speak.

Karuthamma continued, 'My Bossman, you must forget our childhood days. Of the times we played on this shore.'

Pareekutty wouldn't still speak. And Karuthamma went on, 'That would be best for my Bossman and me.'

Karuthamma wouldn't pause. 'We'll pay back the money we took from you before I leave. My Bossman, I want you to do well…' She couldn't speak thereafter. She wished to tell him she would pray for him. But she wasn't sure if she could. A fisherwoman was allowed to pray for only one man's welfare. The man she was entrusted to. Her tradition wouldn't allow her to pray for another man. So how could she say that to him? But of its own volition, words tripped off her tongue.

'I will think of you every day, my Bossman.'

'Oh, but why? You mustn't.'

There was silence for a while. However, it was a silence filled with unspoken words.

A night bird rose off a coconut palm and flew across the moon as if to suggest that it had witnessed the scene. A little farther on the sands, a dog stood watching them. And thus there were two witnesses.

Pareekutty asked, 'All of it is over, isn't it? The games we played, the shells we picked on this shore.' He sighed heavily and continued, 'And so a period in our lives comes to an end!'

Karuthamma agreed. Pareekutty said, 'I will be alone on this shore.'

Those words pierced through Karuthamma. He continued to speak, 'I thought Karuthamma wouldn't say goodbye to me.'

He finished abruptly, 'But I don't have any complaints. If Karuthamma went away without telling me, I would be sad. But I won't ever complain. How can I ever criticize my Karuthamma?'

Karuthamma hid her face with her palm and wept into it. Pareekutty sensed it.

'Why are you crying, Karuthamma? Palani is a good man, a capable man.'

In a choking voice he continued, 'All will be well, Karuthamma. You will be blessed.'

She couldn't bear it any longer. She said, 'My Bossman, you mustn't stab a corpse so.'

Pareekutty didn't fathom what she meant. He was astounded at the fact that he had said something to hurt her. But what had he said?

With a deep sorrow she said, 'But, my Bossman, you never liked me.'

'How can you say that, Karuthamma?'

He swore that his greatest desire was to see her well. He said, 'I will sit here and sing. Sing loudly.'

She replied, 'I will listen to your song even if I am far away on the shores of Trikunnapuzha.'

'I will continue to sing till my throat cracks and I die.'

'And I too will die of a broken heart.'

'And then there will be two souls flittering in the moonlight on this shore.'

'Yes,' Pareekutty said.

Then they didn't speak.

In silence, she walked towards the east. That was how she took leave of him. He continued to watch her. And that was how he bid her farewell.

So they parted.

Ten

Chakki wanted to make something of the ceremony. All the neighbours presumed it would be a wedding with pomp and splendour. Chembankunju had money and Karuthamma was the oldest girl. So the wedding would have to be a big affair.

However, Chembankunju didn't want any of that. He had had to spend money on buying Karuthamma some gold jewellery. He said he didn't have any money left to splurge on a lavish wedding. Yet there was no way he could curb the expenses.

Chakki and Chembankunju quarrelled about this. And it was Karuthamma who had to intervene and make peace between the two. It hurt her no end that she was the cause of their everyday squabbles.

All she wanted was to get past that day. She was a nuisance to so many people! Everyone associated with her seemed to be hurting. Who else was she going to bring trouble to? Who else would she end up hurting? she asked herself.

They had to invite the Shore Master. Only then could the rituals begin. Chembankunju made an offering of betel leaves, tobacco and some cash to the Shore Master and sought his permission. The Shore Master was delighted and promised to arrive early for the wedding.

The wedding day. It wasn't such a big event. Nevertheless,

it had somehow exceeded Chembankunju's planning and expectations.

The Shore Master reached there early. There were about fifteen people from Trikunnapuzha. There were no women in that group. Palani had no female relations to take Karuthamma home. The women gathered there began to speculate about this. Everyone knew Palani was an orphan. But it hadn't truly struck them what that meant until now when Palani arrived with a group of men and not a single woman. It was indeed a serious shortcoming. Chakki saw it as a failing too.

Nallapennu spoke up impulsively, 'Couldn't these fellows have at least asked a woman from the neighbourhood to have come along with them?'

Kalikunju agreed adding her two bit.

Kunjipennu asked, 'How do you send a girl away with a group of men?'

Lakshmi said, 'What else are we to do?'

Nallapennu was acerbic in her observation. 'This is a new tradition indeed! There ought to be many women with the groom's party to accompany the bride. That's how it is done!'

Chakki heard titbits of the women's gossip. Chakki too had thought on the same lines.

It was time to pay the bride price. The amount was to be fixed by the Shore Master. Only after that would the marriage ceremony begin. The Shore Master called Palani and his people. All of them stood in rapt attention. He said, 'The sum is fixed for seventy-five rupees.'

The groom's party was astounded. They hadn't expected such a large amount. Besides, they thought it was way too much. Only a netsman would usually be asked to pay as much.

For a while no one spoke. The head of the groom's party spoke up courageously but in the most deferential of tones. 'Father, you

mustn't think me rude but we too have come from a place with
a Shore Master of our own. You could decide on the bride price
and we are obliged to pay without any objection, but this…'

The Shore Master demanded, 'Tell me … go on, tell me, what
is it?'

Achuthan, that was the man's name, said, 'It is your right
to tell us to pay the bride price, Father. But you should have
consulted with the groom's people first.'

The Shore Master had made a mistake in his calculations. But
when it was pointed out to him, it drew forth his ire. He asked,
'What is there to consult or discuss?'

Achuthan wouldn't back off either. He wasn't seeing a Shore
Master for the first time. There was an illustrious Shore Master
on his shore as well. Achuthan said, 'Of course, it has to be
discussed!'

'So tell me, what is it?'

Achuthan retorted firmly, 'Is it that you don't want this
wedding to take place?'

Achuthan had exceeded himself. The Shore Master snarled
at the accusation.

Achuthan defended his point of view. How could the bride
price be fixed unless someone had ascertained how much money
the bridegroom had? How could the wedding take place under
such circumstances? That was why he had said as much.

The Shore Master was contemptuous. 'Are you such vagrant
riff-raff?'

Even if he wasn't their Shore Master, he was the Protector of
this shore. So they quietly stomached his calling them riff-raff.
They were obliged to do so. In fact, they would put up with more
abuse if it came their way.

Nevertheless, Achuthan had something to say about that as
well.

The Shore Master asked Chembankunju, 'Chembankunju, are you marrying your daughter to a vagrant who doesn't have seventy-five rupees of his own?'

The women gathered there approved of this. Each one of them had thought as much. They were all perturbed by the fact that a comely young girl from their shore was being married off to a man with neither a home nor a family. Chembankunju was to blame for this. And now when the Shore Master asked him this to his face, they were all pleased. Nobody else would have dared to do so.

Chembankunju stood silent.

Achuthan said, 'That's true. He's a rootless vagabond. None of us is his kin. We are just from the same shore. That's why we said you ought to have discussed the bride price.'

Achuthan began talking about Palani. The women felt sorry for Karuthamma. It was better to have drowned her at sea, the women whispered.

But the Shore Master was still adamant. He said, 'All that's fine. But is the bride price based on the boy's financial status?'

Achuthan accepted that it wasn't so. The Shore Master continued, 'She is a good girl. If you want her, you have to pay the price worthy of her.'

One of the groom's men muttered something. He didn't like either what the Shore Master was saying or the way he said it. Unable to contain himself, he had found himself kvetching.

The Shore Master snapped at that impertinent man, 'What are you whinging about?'

He didn't say anything. The Shore Master demanded, 'Say it, you...'

The man decided to speak his mind. Perhaps he had always meant to bring it up. Perhaps he had wanted the wedding to be stopped.

In a ringing voice, he challenged, 'Please don't tell us how good a girl she is!'

'How dare you?'

'Isn't this wedding just meant to get rid of her from this shore? Just so this shore isn't ruined. Let our shore be wiped out, that's it, right? And despite all this, you want the boy to pay a bride price that is beyond what is paid usually. Wonderful, indeed!'

All of them were shaken. What was he insinuating?

Chakki fell down in a deep faint. Karuthamma gathered her mother in her arms. Her cries of 'Oh my Ammachi' sent everyone rushing in. Chakki lay unconscious.

Chembankunju ran around like a mad man. Was his wife about to die? The marriage party was breaking up.

Some of the people gathered asked that brazen man what he had meant. They accused him of slander. He shouldn't have spoken as he did. But the man didn't show any remorse. In fact, it made him even more belligerent.

'Listen, I come to this shore. I know everything that goes on here.'

It was inevitable that everyone would assume that the girl had some sordid secret. But no one wished to know more about it then. All they wanted to do was shut him up. After all, they were away from home and on an unfamiliar shore.

Achuthan gritted his teeth and mumbled, 'Will you shut up?'

Nallapennu and Kalikunju tended to Chakki. She opened her eyes. She coiled an arm around her daughter's neck and moaned, 'Oh my daughter!' And slipped into a faint again.

The women consoled Karuthamma and attended to Chakki. When Chakki was a little better, Chembankunju called Palani and Achuthan over. He was prepared to give the seventy-five rupees. They should accept it from him and pay the bride price. Palani consented and so did Achuthan.

Thus, with the bride price Palani entered the wedding pandal. Everything quietened down a bit. No one thought any more of Pappu's allegations.

The money was paid. As per custom the Shore Master took his share. The rest was given to Chembankunju. Despite all the kerfuffle, they had kept the appointed auspicious time. And so the first part of the wedding was complete.

Even though Chakki was propped up, she still felt dizzy. Suddenly she felt her vision cloud and her ears buzz.

The bride was brought to the pandal. One of the elders explained what was to be done. The thali was tied and new clothes were given. Palani's palm was thrust into Karuthamma's. Chembankunju thought he saw her stiffen. Then she pulled her hand back. It seemed that she hadn't held Palani's hand. All that had transpired was that his palm rested in hers briefly.

What was Karuthamma thinking of? What was she remembering? Who knows. She did everything she was asked to almost mechanically.

The women supported Chakki and brought her to the pandal. At the muhurtham, Chakki fainted again.

It was a bad omen, a few women said. Could anyone fault them for thinking so? Chakki surfaced again. She will be fine once she has rested enough, some people said.

It was time for the feast. Again there was a problem. Some women went away without eating. They were unsure of Palani's caste and hence were reluctant to eat at the feast. Many of the groom's party including the troublemaker Pappu left.

None of this bothered Chembankunju. But he fell at the Shore Master's feet and pleaded for his intervention. Chakki was totally incapacitated. Karuthamma had never left home until then. And now she was to go all by herself to a strange place. And there were no women in the groom's group. Given all this, was there some way they could prevent the girl from leaving home that day? Let Palani also not go. He could stay the night here as well. If Karuthamma left, Chembankunju's home would fall apart. There wasn't anyone to even wet the invalid's lips.

Chembankunju was in a frenzy. The Shore Master sympathized with his plight and said, 'What you say is right, Chembankunju, but how can we prevent them from taking the girl if they want to?'

Chembankunju said, 'If Father himself insists, they will agree.'

The Shore Master smiled mirthlessly. 'They are from Trikunnapuzha. An arrogant lot. Haven't you seen it for yourself, Chembankunju?'

Chembankunju had no one else to turn to but the Shore Master. If she left, what was he to do? If the Shore Master was adamant, they would succumb.

The food was eaten and the betel leaves passed around. Achuthan said it was time to leave. Karuthamma continued to sit at her mother's side. She wept ceaselessly. Chembankunju pretended to be busy as he hustled and bustled around. It was time to leave. Achuthan spoke up again. When he said it for the third time, Chembankunju had to pay attention. He asked Achuthan, 'Is it really necessary to take the girl back today itself?'

No one had expected such a query. Achuthan didn't know what to say. The Shore Master waited for an answer though.

Achuthan asked, 'What do you mean?'

'What do I mean?'

'After the wedding, how can the bride be left behind?'

The Shore Master knew he really didn't have an argument. But he could use his authority to full effect. So he did, describing the state of that home. But they already knew that.

The Shore Master said, 'All I am asking is for you to consider if you can let the girl be here till her mother can at least sit up.'

'It is up to the boy to decide that,' Achuthan said.

To add weight to his argument, the Shore Master brought up yet another matter. 'You really can't insist on taking the girl with you now.'

Achuthan demanded, 'Why is that?'

'Isn't it customary that a woman be there to accompany the bride to her new home?'

Achuthan retorted brusquely, 'Why marry your girl to a fellow who doesn't even have a single female relative then?'

The Shore Master feigned anger. 'Are you arguing with me?'

Achuthan retreated into silence. Now it was left to the groom to decide. Let him, Achuthan told himself.

The Shore Master hoped that Palani would be willing to make a concession.

Time sped. No one was willing to commit to anything. 'It's getting late,' Achuthan said. 'Let Palani stay on here,' the Shore Master instructed. But no one responded to that either. Palani was the one who would have to decide now.

Achuthan told Palani, 'Look here boy, what have you decided? We have to leave.'

Palani squirmed. He didn't know what to say. He had heard all of what had been said. But he hadn't been able to make up his mind. Was it because it was beyond him? Whatever it was, Palani didn't seem to see it as an important problem. He was unmoved.

Achuthan spoke in disgust, 'Say something, will you? Why are you putting us through this?'

Then he accused Palani, 'Look, we came here on your behalf and now seem to have got everyone's back up.'

Chembankunju waited eagerly to see what would trip off Palani's tongue. Palani was a simple man. He wouldn't be so heartless. Besides, it was only a matter of taking her there. He thought the whole world as his home. Chembankunju thought that Palani would send the others off and stay behind.

Achuthan spoke again, 'Say something, will you?'

Palani looked at Achuthan's face. Then at everyone else's face. He could find nothing to help him decide. Nevertheless, a phrase fell off his tongue, 'I want to take the girl with me. Now.'

Chembankunju was startled. It was unexpected. He hadn't expected Palani to be so blunt. Chembankunju beat his chest and cried, 'Son, look at the plight of that woman and then make up your mind.'

He should have added, 'Weren't you also born of a woman!' But Chembankunju didn't say it.

Was Palani moved by the plea? It was hard to know. All he did was look at Achuthan's face again. But there was no advice on offer. But Palani sensed that Achuthan thought the girl must go with them.

Palani reiterated, 'I want to take the girl with me.'

A little later his mind began functioning. He put forward a few reasons for wanting to do as he had said. He was a man with neither a home nor a family. But it was to have a home of his own that he had wed. He wanted to start his life. So he couldn't accept this business of getting married and leaving his bride behind. He had many things to accomplish. And none of it could wait.

'So I need my bride to go with me.'

That Palani was able to say as much was amazing in itself. And it seemed a firm decision. Palani felt that his friends were pleased with his decision. But no one noticed how it affected Chembankunju. Chembankunju wept and pleaded in a manner that would have touched anyone's heart. 'Son, this is a father speaking. A father who brought up a child. One day you too will be a father.'

Palani was unmoved. Perhaps if Achuthan and the others had agreed, he would have accepted Chembankunju's plea.

The Shore Master's heart melted. Anyone would have felt the same. Achuthan's too, perhaps. But he wouldn't reveal it. The Shore Master was annoyed. He said, 'This was bound to happen! He didn't grow up in a family. He doesn't know what it means to have a father or mother. You learn about love and tenderness from your home. How will an orphan from the seashore know any of this?'

A little later, the Shore Master told Chembankunju, 'You are to blame for choosing such a vagrant as your daughter's husband.'

Chembankunju didn't agree with him. But in his mind he was already beginning to doubt his decision. Chembankunju hadn't realized that Palani could be so heartless. Chembankunju too felt that the Shore Master was right in his reading – Palani was such a brute because he hadn't been reared in a family. What would he be like in the future? Perhaps Chembankunju was already – on the very day of the wedding – beginning to regret his choice. Palani had no love in him. It was obvious even this early.

Achuthan who seemed to have comprehended the situation thought of a solution, 'Palani, why do you have to be cursed and slandered? It's the girl who must go with you. Ask her what she thinks. Let her decide!'

Chembankunju was relieved. Palani too must have felt the same. The Shore Master too approved of that suggestion. He said, 'That's right. Let her decide. Call her...'

Chembankunju called out for Karuthamma. She was seated at her mother's side. With a face wet with tears, she came to the doorway. The Shore Master himself asked her, 'Girl, do you want to leave your mother in this state and go? Or, are you staying behind? There isn't anyone here to even light the hearth for your father.'

He paused and then continued, 'After the wedding, it is customary to go with the groom. But you have to decide…'

What could Karuthamma say? She didn't have the strength to make up her mind. She had already bid farewell to this land. She thought of the future with trepidation. She had been waiting to flee this place. The day had arrived. But her mother had fallen ill and there was no one to tend to her father's needs either. All of it demanded she stay back but … She burst into tears. She couldn't speak.

Everyone waited to hear her response. The Shore Master said, 'The poor child! What can she say? But she still has to speak. It is up to her now!'

She went to her mother, laid her face against her mother's and sobbed. Chakki too must have wept. She muttered to her mother.

'What did you ask, daughter?'

She couldn't speak then. A little later, she sobbed, 'I … I … am not going, Ammachi!'

Chakki spoke up suddenly, 'My daughter, you mustn't say that. My daughter must go. If you don't…'

The woman couldn't complete the thought. Chakki knew what would happen if Karuthamma didn't leave. Karuthamma too feared the same. The mother could see that horrific scene play before her eyes.

Chakki didn't mind being left like this. With not a soul around to offer her a drop of water. But she couldn't have her daughter ruined. Chakki too wanted her to leave at the very earliest. She must go. She must go. 'My daughter, go tell them that you want to go.'

Chakki prised Karuthamma away from her body. She insisted, then admonished her with clenched teeth, 'You can't leave that Muslim boy, isn't that it?'

Karuthamma summoned courage from deep within. She went to the door and said, 'I would like to go.'

Once again the mother and daughter locked in an embrace. Their hearts were breaking.

Karuthamma fell prostrate at Chembankunju's feet and clutched at it. He shook her off and turned away. She lay there for a long while and then rose. Her mother blessed her. 'Heed my words,' her mother advised.

Palani went to take his leave of Chembankunju. But the latter wouldn't speak. This wasn't a grief-stricken Chembankunju. He wasn't weeping any more. He had transformed. His face was red and swollen. He had turned into a deity of fury.

The group of men walked in front. She followed behind. Chakki propped herself up on her elbow to see her daughter leave. Suddenly she collapsed. Nallapennu, with tears in her eyes, held Chakki's head up.

Grinding his teeth, Chembankunju roared, 'She isn't my daughter!'

A sobbing Panchami called out, 'Chechi!'

Nallapennu and Kalikunju stayed with Chakki.

Karuthamma walked into her future. Who knew what it would be like? Had she really escaped danger and temptation?

No one prayed for her. Neither did she. Perhaps Pareekutty had said a prayer for her.

And so Karuthamma left her familiar shores.

Would that song echo on that shore again? Who knows? But there wouldn't be anyone to hear it.

Part Two

Eleven

Even the sea here seemed strange. The water a different hue. It wasn't a quiet sea here. Beneath the waves lay a capricious undercurrent that would churn the sea up into a swirl causing treacherous whirlpools. The sands too were coloured differently.

Several people came to see the new bride. Karuthamma didn't know how to introduce herself or how she was to be with them. Everyone scrutinized her carefully. Karuthamma flinched.

But she knew that she had to leave a good impression on them. How was she to do that?

At the crack of dawn Palani went to sea. It was the sardine season. Karuthamma was the mistress of a house. She had many things to do.

All there was in that house was a pot, an open-mouthed pan and a ladle. That was all! There were so many things necessary to turn it into a home. Some rice, chillies and salt had been procured and kept in a basket. Palani hadn't ever lived in a home of his own before marriage. And there wasn't anyone in his life to tell him what was needed in a home. She would have to do all of it on her own.

Karuthamma boiled the rice and strained the water away. She made a theeyal with shallots. She borrowed the pots and pans for it from the next-door neighbour. She went across to use their grinding stone as well.

The old woman in the northern house said, 'We have entrusted a young man to you. You are responsible now!'

All that she had heard at Neerkunnath shore was echoed here as well. Everywhere any new bride would hear the same. Or, was it being told only to her? She felt that everyone looked at her suspiciously. Did they know her secret?

The women there huddled around and speculated about the new bride. They had enough material for that. She was the daughter of a netsman with two boats of his own. So why would someone like that marry her off to a man with no kith or kin?

One woman said, 'Maybe the father doesn't have boats and nets of his own!'

Kochakki didn't think so. Her children's father had gone to Neerkunnath during the big catch. He knew all about him. 'He has boats and nets; money, lots of money!'

Vavakunju asked, 'So why then did they give her to this fellow?'

Kochakki demanded, 'What's wrong with him?'

Kotha had a suspicion. 'I think there's something wrong with the girl!'

It seemed as if Kotha knew something. Everyone was curious. What did she mean? they demanded.

Kotha ventured, 'The girl must be a slut ... they must have got rid of her from that shore!'

The old woman put her hand on her bosom and trembled in fright. 'So is she going to ruin our shore?'

Everyone began asking probing questions of Kotha. But she didn't reveal anything more.

Once Karuthamma had cooked rice and curry, her job was

done. Nevertheless, the women were still hovering around. She felt everyone treated her as if she were a strange creature.

All of them had heard of Chakki's pathetic state too. Would any daughter leave when her mother was as ill? Wasn't a mother more important than a husband? This made them wonder even more about Karuthamma.

By noon, Karuthamma had turned into a choice piece of gossip. In each home, she was the topic of discussion: she was a slut. A vile creature they had got rid of by any means. In which case ... wasn't that a problem?

Karuthamma thought of her mother. She wondered how her mother was. Had she done right in leaving her mother in that state? Her father had cast her off for good. Her father's words echoed in her ears: 'She isn't my daughter.'

Karuthamma knew Chembankunju well enough. He would never ever accept her as his daughter again. Karuthamma felt that hers had been an act of bravado and little else. Would any daughter have behaved like her? No, it wasn't possible. They must all be blaming her at her home shore, cursing her too. But her mother had blessed her. It was with her consent that she left home.

Her mother had to put up with so much. That was what it meant to be a mother. Her father would blame her mother for not having anyone around to even boil him a cup of water. All of that her mother would tolerate. And she would endure even more for her sake. But her father would never ever forgive her.

Karuthamma considered her future. She once had a father and mother. Her father was a hard-working man who made his money. There was a certain security to her life. Her desires and needs, even if they were limited, were all fulfilled. She had never known want. And she had disdained all of that security to come here. Into a new life; into a new world. What would it be like?

Would she be fed? Would there be enough to clothe her? She had never known hunger. Who knew what lay ahead? Who could be sure? Would she be able to open her heart and laugh? Would she be able to breathe right? All of it was uncertain, precarious...

She used to be loved.

The man she had come away with: Would he love her? That was a big question indeed. She knew nothing about him.

Despite her mother's pathetic condition, he had been almost inhumanly adamant about leaving. What kind of a man would he be? If he hadn't insisted on taking his bride away, there would have been none of this trouble. Two days would have sufficed. So how was she to earn his love and affection? And how was she to make those feelings endure? It was quite possible that he would be as heartless again. How could she keep this love without any impediments?

She had no one but him. He was all she had. His likes and dislikes would be the basis of her life. And she knew nothing about his likes and dislikes.

Karuthamma could endure any hardship. All she wanted to be was one of those countless fisherwomen who lived their lives out willing to put up with anything and everything. She didn't want anything significant happening in her life. All she wanted was to be an ordinary fisherwoman to the end. But would that be possible? That was what Karuthamma feared. A voice in her head told her that she would never be that. A thought that had begun a long time ago. Events that didn't happen in other people's lives happened in hers. And there might be many more such occurrences. They would twist her life into unforeseen tangles. She had always been haunted by that thought. A thought that had now taken concrete shape.

If only Palani would love her. She desired that. But could she expect it of him? That was her fear.

All women desired their husband's love. But do even one of them have an inkling of what love is? Karuthamma had known love. The pangs of love. Which was why she feared whether she would know love again.

She felt that Palani was incapable of love. So what was the point in her leaving her home? Hadn't it been a dangerous act? But if she had continued to live there, it would have been an even more hazardous proposition.

When it turned noon, Palani came home from the sea. She carefully served him his rice and curry. It was the first time she was doing so. Would he like her curry, she wondered. Would he be content with the meal? She wasn't certain. Palani began eating. He ate with relish which was a relief. She stood by the kitchen door. She spoke standing there. But she didn't say: 'Please love me. I will love you back.'

'There wasn't a pan to make another curry.'

'There may be grit in the rice.'

She didn't have a vessel to clean the rice. There was just one ladle. The theeyal she had made wasn't all that good. She had borrowed a skillet from a neighbouring house. She had done her grinding there as well. She stopped with that. Then again, 'We must buy pots and pans and many things.'

'Yes, we will. But not all of it at the same time.'

'No, that's not necessary. Just a few things at a time.'

He had finished eating what she had served him first. She served him more rice. Even though Palani said he had enough, she served him one more ladle of rice. That was how it should be. She knew that.

He said, 'There's too much rice here.'

'So what? You can leave behind what you don't want.'

A little later, she summoned courage to ask, 'The theeyal isn't good, right? I don't think you were satisfied with the meal.'

'The theeyal was delicious. Didn't you see how much rice I ate?'

'Is this a lot? Oh my goodness…'

'I don't usually eat as much.'

The coy smile of a new wife. Karuthamma said, 'You must eat much more and more. Or I will have to feed you myself.'

Palani too smiled. It was an eager smile. She felt something akin to solace settle on her much bruised heart. He was a gentle man, willing enough to listen to her. More than anything else, there was a certain glint in his gaze. Wasn't that enough to start with?

She served herself some rice in the same plate and began eating. He washed his hands. Palani lit a beedi, entered the kitchen and went to sit by her.

'Let me serve you.'

She didn't speak. She felt her heart bloom as rays of love caressed that bud.

'Look at this. You have hardly eaten.'

'I am full.'

He peered into the pot. 'Isn't there any rice left?'

'There is enough. But I am full.'

'That's not enough.' Palani served a ladle of rice into her plate. Enough. Enough. Karuthamma gestured. But she did eat what had been served to her.

Karuthamma was beginning life as a married woman. Not as a lover but as a housewife.

And Palani had become the master of a house as well. After lunch, when she had washed the dishes, he asked, 'What are the things you would like me to buy? Tell me!'

'Do you have the money to buy everything?'

He opened a pouch at his waist and counted the money. He had only four rupees. He gave her an account of money earned and spent that day. The catch was poor. He paid off quite a bit of the money he had borrowed for the wedding. This was all that was left.

Karuthamma asked, 'So what's your share?'

'Fifty!'

'It's sixty on our shore.'

Karuthamma continued, 'You must ask for your share based on how it is in neighbouring shores…'

Palani tossed back a careless 'That's how it is here!'

She narrated to him how Chembankunju rallied the men together on their shore and increased the share to sixty.

Palani said, 'Nothing like that has ever happened here.'

He asked her again about the things needed for their home.

Karuthamma asked, 'Are you going now to buy it?'

'Yes.'

Karuthamma said, 'Why don't you rest a bit? You don't have to go out now. You've just come back from the sea. Everyone will accuse me of having chased you out to buy pots and pans. Rest a bit and then go!'

Palani seemed to accept her advice. He rolled out a mat and lay on it. Then he called, 'Karuthamma!'

Perhaps she too had been waiting for that call. She went to him. Palani said, 'Come here.'

She went to his side shyly. It was possible that she was beginning to feel secure. She would do her best to be a good wife. He gathered her into a tight embrace with his muscular arms. Her eyelids drooped, her breath stuck in her throat, she sank against him almost faint.

She had loved a man once. And once she too had been loved by a man. But she had never been touched by a man. Perhaps she had craved for it. But Karuthamma wouldn't break the rules. She was a married woman now. With the right due to him, a man held her close to his body. She submitted obediently. Even if she had loved one man, a man's touch, the submission to a man, the rapture of that breathlessness, all of it came from another man. She was his now. Her body was just for him. She had kept it unsullied until then for him. And she would keep it chaste for him.

She didn't know how long she lay in that languorous submission. Young blood coursed hotly in those veins. The hungers were rapacious; dams had been burst through and a deluge followed, unrestrained.

When she came to consciousness of the world around her, Karuthamma was bashful. It wasn't just shyness but a fear too. A fear that sat upon her. She had revealed far too much, she feared. She didn't have a clear picture. It was like a trance. An uninhibited blatant greed. How could any girl be so? What would her husband think of her?

Karuthamma feared all of it had been wrong. All her secrets were out. He knew. Palani was a stranger. That he had made her his was true. But how could she have abandoned herself so in such a wanton fashion with a strange man even if he was her husband? What must he think of her? How could she have been so uncontrolled? She was a very demure woman. She worried every minute that there would be a life-destroying query soon. The question would be, 'So have you played the field?'

She could truthfully answer, 'No.' But would she be believed?

How could she trust him? If she didn't, it would be a crippling blow to life itself.

Even before the question was asked, she wanted to ask for forgiveness. But what was she to say? That she didn't know.

Were all girls like this? Even if he was a stranger, would you become a reckless wild creature with your husband? She didn't know.

She thought uncertainly of this hunger that had come to her. She couldn't accept that she was an ordinary girl. Once long long ago there had been a few such extraordinary women on her shore.

A voice in Karuthamma spoke: You loved a man once. That is, when you thought about that man you knew a stirring of the soul, a great delight. Which meant you felt desire for him. And so when you found a man, you became this intemperate woman. You went mad. Other women are not like this.

Was that love that had stirred her so?

The question that Karuthamma feared wasn't asked.

Palani was going out. 'What should I buy?' Palani asked.

She said, 'You must buy what you can for the money you have.' Then she detailed what was urgently required. That itself was a long list.

When Karuthamma was alone at home, her thoughts reverted to Pareekutty. How would he be? He must be bereft. They hadn't paid his money back either. Her mother was laid up. They might never pay it back. He was ruined on that front as well.

She wasn't able to erase thoughts about Pareekutty. Wasn't that a sin? How could she, a wife, think of another man? Nevertheless, someone inside her said she wouldn't be able to forget Pareekutty ... ever. It was a nightmare that would haunt her for life!

His song perhaps still resounded on that shore. Karuthamma felt restless. When and how would she find some peace? Perhaps she was destined to never know serenity.

Palani came home with pots, pans and ladles. On the way, his friends had teased him. When he reached home Karuthamma found fault. The pot wasn't good enough. It had hairline cracks. And that wasn't the kind of pan required. The wife was declaring her competence. Her superior housewifely abilities. And Palani acknowledged that. He said, 'How do I know what pots and pans to buy?'

She laughed. It was all in jest.

They didn't sleep at all that night. They had so much to say to each other! So much was said and they still couldn't stop. Their expectations from life was what they talked about. And during the course of it, she asked, 'When my mother was laid up, why did you insist on bringing me away?'

Karuthamma felt comfortable enough with him to ask him that. It was a question that troubled him. Nevertheless, Palani replied, 'Is it befitting a man to leave his wife behind in her house after the wedding? It isn't right!'

She realized that he thought it an act of impropriety to leave her back in her home. Then Palani explained. The people who had gone with him were not happy for him to come away without her. No one liked that. So he had to say as much.

With a trace of shyness Palani asked, 'Were you willing to come with me?'

She retorted instantly, 'Yes, I was.'

The reason behind that 'yes' stayed hidden.

Then, Karuthamma remembered something important she had to discuss. About her father. 'My father will not be there for us any more. That's his nature! He won't recognize me as his daughter any more.'

Unruffled, he said, 'Fine. If he thinks he doesn't have a daughter, you must think you don't have a father.'

She couldn't have received a greater oath of troth from him. He meant that even if she didn't have her father, he was there for her.

Palani continued, 'Your father is an avaricious and peculiar man! And so also your Shore Master. He insulted us!'

Palani's self-esteem grew and found a voice. 'Even if I have no one or nothing, I too am a son of the sea. All of this is my wealth too. What do I lack? I am like all other fishermen. But I have something else. I know my job. I can sail through any tide. And avoid the suck of any whirlpool. So there was no need to insult me as he did!'

Karuthamma didn't speak. She began to wish that she hadn't brought up the matter. Palani was getting angry. He had no regard for her father at all. Not just her Shore Master, he would defy his Shore Master as well if needed.

He asked, 'Why would I humble myself? No need for that.'

But Karuthamma still had a point to make. 'My mother is a timid soul!'

He didn't respond to that. But his thoughts veered in another direction. 'Let me tell you something. I am not going to your home till that man, your father, comes here first.'

Like her father, her husband too had made a firm decision. Nothing would shake that either.

Karuthamma voiced her thoughts: She had neither a father nor a mother now. She only had her husband. He must love her. She would be a responsible and dutiful wife.

He listened.

She had no one but him. She would endure anything and obey everything. All she wanted was to be loved.

He didn't ask of her that she love him back. Perhaps he had no need for that love. She too probably didn't feel the need to make that declaration.

That was a failing. On the one hand one person wanted to be loved. But the other person didn't ask for the same. She had promised to be a good wife as was expected of her. But even if Palani hadn't asked to be loved, shouldn't she have said as much? But she didn't. Did that mean that she wouldn't love him? If Palani had asked that of her, perhaps she would have unconditionally offered him her love.

And so that first night was spent with minor splintering and no major rifts. But they had arrived at a common consensus. To set up a home together.

With a laugh, Karuthamma said, 'I don't have relatives or friends. I have neither a house nor family.'

At the crack of light, the shore rang with calls and cries. It was time for Palani to go.

Karuthamma had learnt a few norms of daily living. She had been taught as much before her marriage by the women of her neighbourhood. One of those lessons came to her mind.

When he stepped out, she asked anxiously, 'Are you going straight to the boat?'

He didn't understand what she meant.

'Hmm ... why?'

Karuthamma didn't know how to say it. She said, 'People shouldn't leave their homes like this...'

'So how else are they to leave?'

'People going to the sea must be clean and pure.'

He stood there unable to comprehend. He asked, 'What are you getting at?'

Shamefaced, she said, 'Why don't you have a bath before you go?'

She helped him bathe and then bathed herself.

When Palani reached the boats, the Shore Master asked, 'Did you have a bath, boy?'

Twelve

Karuthamma had been taught many lessons at her home. She knew how to bring prosperity into a house. She had seen her father and mother toil for it. In fact, her father was a shining example. She had seen how with much discipline and by curbing excessive expenditure he had kept aside money to buy a boat and nets.

When Karuthamma was by herself, she pondered about her home. She had a role model to lead her on.

She had sent Palani to work after ensuring that he had a bath and was clean enough. Nevertheless, until the boats returned, she was filled with an anxiety. That day, she didn't stop with one and instead made two curries. She felt closer to him than she had the day before. And so she waited.

There was a huge catch of sardines that day. They hadn't seen anything like it in recent times. He got thirty rupees. As they were washing up after they had shaken the nets out and cleaned it up, Ayappan asked the group, 'Shall we go to eat at Haripad?'

None of them protested. They all had enough money. The sea mother had blessed them. So what was wrong in having a good time once in a while! Palani alone didn't say a word.

Veluthakunju asked, 'Hey Palani, why are you so silent?'

Aandikunju teased, 'What are you saying? When he has a

bride waiting for him with rice and curries, he would prefer to be at her side and eat there.'

'What's wrong with that?' Kochayyappan demanded. It was natural for young people to feel that way. All of them in that group were married and had children.

Velayudhan generalized about the state of marriage, 'All of it is wonderful for the first four days! Then you won't find any food at home and even if you do, it would be tasteless!'

When all of them had washed up, Veluthakunju asked, 'Palani, are you coming?'

Palani said, 'I am!'

But he said it without really wanting to go.

The group went to the road and took a bus to Haripad.

Karuthamma waited for a long while. When Palani didn't turn up, she went to the beach looking for him. All the boats were hauled onto the shore. Not even one boat was at sea. There wasn't a single soul on the beach either.

At that moment, Aandi's fisherwoman Paru arrived there. She began to make small talk, 'What is it, new bride? Why are you standing here staring at the sea?'

Karuthamma flushed coyly. 'Nothing. I was just looking at the sea.'

Paru understood. 'You are looking for your fisherman, aren't you? All of them went away together to Haripad. They have money in their hands, child!'

Pretty much the same would happen on Karuthamma's shore as well. There they would all go to Alapuzha. That was the only difference. But Karuthamma hadn't expected Palani to go that day.

Karuthamma and Paru chatted for a while. Karuthamma was disturbed. She felt all of this ought to be changed. So much could have been accomplished at home if they had the money he would spend at Haripad. The thought rattled within Karuthamma.

Paru said, 'Anyway, when your fisherman returns from Haripad, you can be sure he'll bring the new bride a beautiful length of cloth.'

Karuthamma responded, 'But chechi, we don't even have a vessel to drink out of. We have just two pots!'

Paru, who was older, said, 'Who has more than two? You can think about all that when the big catch season comes. And later when the sea is barren, we'll sell those and live off that!'

A dog followed Karuthamma. It was looking for a chance to sneak in. Karuthamma went into her shack.

She waited. When it was almost twilight Palani came home. He had a little packet in his hand.

Karuthamma wondered if she should sulk. It wouldn't be a pretence. She really was furious. But she worried if Palani would like it. She wore the beginning of a smile on her face. She asked, 'Did the boats get in only just now?'

Palani didn't understand the sarcasm. Instead, he replied, 'No, but look…'

He gave her the packet. As she tore it open, she asked, 'When you go to sea here, do your nets fill up with cloth?'

He laughed. And she laughed.

It was a beautiful kasavu neriyathu, a fine cloth to drape herself with, and it had an ornate zari border. Karuthamma opened it out. It was wide and of fine quality! Palani told her its price. They had bought five such pieces. Veluthakunju, Velayudhan, Kochuraman, Ayappan and he, and they had taken one each.

Velayudhan's child was ill; his wife had gone to Paru's house to borrow some money for the medicine, Paru had just told her. That day there was trouble in Ayappan's home as well. All those homes that had new pieces of cloth.

With a hearty laugh Karuthamma asked, 'What's the use of a beautiful new neriyathu when we don't even have a vessel or a glass to drink out of?'

Perhaps overwhelmed by the heartiness of that laugh, he failed to understand the underlying irony yet again and instead laughed out aloud. And then he said, 'Do you know why I bought this for you?'

She asked, 'Why?'

'To go for the Mannarshala Ayilyam. Drape it around you and let me have a look.'

Palani's feelings reflected in his eyes as he looked at her. A glance at her high-raised breasts. She turned. Now that glance fell on her buttocks that were covered by just a sheer mundu.

Palani took a few steps forward. Then she said, 'I am covered in sweat and grime!'

Even if there wasn't a drinking vessel, was it wrong to have bought that beautiful neriyathu? It was what he desired. To see his wife dressed and decked up. Was life just about purpose and making things happen? Was life just about buying things for the house and making money? Wasn't there an emotional dimension to life? Yes. There is. There certainly is.

Karuthamma hadn't seen anything like this ever in her life. Which is why perhaps it would seem unnecessary to her. Nevertheless, the thought that her husband wanted to see her well turned-out made her happy.

She put aside any further thoughts of scolding him for having bought the neriyathu.

Their bodies were locked in a tight embrace. Lips met. They were one. Eyes drooped languorously as they sank into a trance-like state. Hands wouldn't unclasp. Separation was so hard.

Karuthamma began to think that a kasavu neriyathu was vital

fish being caught with their eyes open and breath floundering, it ceased to affect him. But money made out of such mindless violence to life couldn't be set aside; it just wasn't possible.

Why else would the people of the sea starve as they did? This wasn't just Palani's way of looking at life; this was the philosophy of the shore passed on from generation to generation through centuries. Karuthamma too had heard as much. But there was one man who had protested against it. Her father. Those days she hadn't been convinced by her father's arguments. However, she wasn't merely convinced now but she also understood the gravity and importance of his reasoning. Nevertheless, she didn't voice them. She didn't have the courage to enter into a debate.

Palani said once again, 'Why does a fisherman have to save money? What lies spread before him is his wealth. What is that we don't have? Even if he doesn't set aside anything, the sea mother will bless him with enough. That's how it is!'

She retorted, 'So why then does everyone starve when there isn't a catch?'

'That's to be endured.'

Karuthamma thought of her mother and father. Of how they managed to own a boat and nets. Suddenly, as if a burning ember had touched her heart, she felt a searing pain. A pain that coursed through her veins. How did they come to own a boat and nets? That guileless Pareekutty was ruined.

Palani asked, 'Is it because of your father and mother?'

It seemed that his expression had hardened. He continued, 'That must be where your avarice came from! Everyone wants to know when we are going to visit your parents!'

All the women there had asked her the same. She too didn't have an answer. After the wedding, it was unseemly not to be invited to the bride's home. But she was doubtful whether it would ever happen. She said, 'We left home when my mother was on her deathbed. Who is there to come over here and invite us?'

A little later, she spoke up with a laugh, 'After the wedding, has anyone from the groom's side invited us for a visit? Isn't that too a tradition?'

Karuthamma had only meant to tease. Nevertheless, it contained a tiny sting. Palani felt as if he had been slapped. He was hurt. He didn't think it was funny. Nor did he take it that way. His expression changed.

'Didn't you know that there wasn't anyone to invite us for a visit? So why then did they send you with me?'

Karuthamma's face paled. Palani was angry. She hadn't expected that. He didn't pause.

'But that wasn't it, right? Here was an orphan, who has no one to weep for him or celebrate with him. And here is a girl unfit for the shore. So let's burden him with her. If he died at sea, there won't be anyone to grieve for him. That's what happened.'

It was an unjust accusation. A girl unfit for the shore! How could she bear that? Nevertheless, wasn't it true? The niggling feeling of guilt that lay hidden within her seemed to have taken shape. In these first days after marriage, her husband was already saying that.

Karuthamma covered her face with her hands and sobbed furiously. Her body quivered and shook with the force of that sobbing. Palani sat there looking at her. For some time, all that was heard was the sobbing. Did he feel sorry for her? A voice from somewhere spoke in her ear: 'This isn't me saying so. Everyone else is saying it!'

It seemed Palani's heart had softened a little. He said, 'I didn't say this.'

A little later he said, 'It is that Pappu who is saying all this!'

And so, after the wedding, for the first time tears were shed in that family; and attempts at reconciliation were made.

A grey pall enveloped the surroundings. An unease that stretched through the night. Through her sobbing came a plaintive cry, 'I ... I ... I am unfit for the shore!'

She pleaded with him to believe in her. She wouldn't behave in a manner that would cause her husband to be lost at sea. She wouldn't be the reason why giant waves would break over their roof. Venomous snakes wouldn't slither and crawl on the shore; unnamed sea monsters wouldn't rise from the waters with gaping jaws and cause whirling winds; she would live as a fisherwoman. She asked him a thousand times if he didn't trust her. He wouldn't respond. All she could do was lay her head on his wide chest and try and melt its hardness with her tears.

Palani asked, 'Why do you keep on asking me, "If I believe in you, if I believe in you..." as if you don't trust yourself?'

Once again a burning coal seared through her. He did have some suspicions about her dark secret. Some quisling had filled his head with gossip.

She didn't speak thereafter that night. Whether he knew her secret or not, wasn't it better to have revealed the truth to him? But if she told him the truth, would he forgive her? So how could she tell him? Instead of someone making up false stories around what really happened, it was best to tell the truth.

It was a dilemma. A decision had to be made. Several times she began to tell him, but what was she to say? Should she say, 'I had loved a man once'? Would any husband have the fortitude to hear that? Or should she begin with: 'In my childhood, I had a companion'? That too wasn't possible. If she began recounting that, in the sweetness of that memory she would say way too much and even end up praising Pareekutty. And he would think that her affection still lay with Pareekutty. That wasn't right.

Should she say, 'A Muslim on the shore bewitched me'? No, no, she couldn't say that! For she would have to describe Pareekutty as a bad man. As a despicable man. Karuthamma couldn't do that either. Pareekutty wasn't a despicable man; he hadn't bewitched her or deceived her. She saw before her an image of him broken, teary-eyed. She could see that even in the dark. She felt as if she had stamped and walked all over his feelings to reach here. She had ruined him in every way. He wanted nothing more of life. Even when he was seventy-five, he would sit on the shore, singing his song. And so he would sing to his death … she could see all of this. Her lips moved to speak. She forgot where she was. She failed to recognize that her husband lay next to her. The core of her being spoke up, 'I love you!'

She said that to Pareekutty. The sound of her words shook her.

Palani asked, 'What are you saying? You love whom?'

Karuthamma woke up. Had she given herself away? She said, 'Yes.'

He asked, 'Whom?'

She spoke a bare-faced lie, 'My fisherman!'

The cock crowed. A sound rang through the shore. It was time to go out in the boats. She insisted that Palani leave only after a bath. Again she helped him bathe.

It was later than usual when Palani reached the boats. It had never happened before. That day the other boatmen had to wait for him. Velayudhan joked, 'That's how it is! Once you are married, getting up becomes very difficult!'

A harmless joke! And the truth, in fact. But Palani didn't like it.

'Oh be quiet, Velayudha cheta!'

Velayudhan snapped back, 'Hey boy! Why are you snarling at me?'

Palani had worried that Velayudhan would bring up other matters. What if he mentioned Karuthamma? A thought that niggled at him.

The boat set out into the sea and sailed towards the west. Palani was on the stern. There was no sign of fish anywhere. Boats were scampering this way and that without casting their nets. But Palani continued to furiously steer the boat to the west. It was as if he had no definite purpose. His iron-like muscles rippled. It wasn't enough, the sea wasn't big enough. The oar was light. When he leapt, the stern buckled and leapt with him. As if to tear through the horizon and go beyond it. All his vigour had roused itself.

The boat was deep in the ocean. Land was nowhere in sight. Aandi demanded, 'Where are you taking the boat?'

All of them took in their oars. But the boat continued to leap and course forward. Palani had turned into a demon. The horizon his goal.

Kumaru quaked with fear. 'You son of a bitch! Just because you have no one…' Kumaru shouted at Palani. 'Go kill yourself! You have a slut for a wife! You'll drown in the sea. That's your destiny. But we have children and a family!'

Velayudhan grabbed Palani's oar from him. He dragged Palani towards Aandi, seated him there and turned the boat back.

Palani was silent, as if exhausted from that long ordeal. Much later he began rowing. They cast their nets in the waters where the other boats were.

They didn't catch anything. No one had managed to get anything. Palani's boat netted some small fry. Each one of them received a rupee and a half.

As they were bathing, Velayudhan asked, 'What happened to you, Palani?'

All of them were curious to know the same. He had lost his sanity. Palani used to steer the boat with vigour and courage. But he would never be driven by a rage such as this.

Palani said, 'I don't know. Something happened to me!'

Aandi said, 'Son, we all have wives and children!'

Kumaru opined, 'I don't think Palani should man the stern any more. He will drown us all in the middle of the sea.'

All of them had to agree. Some demon had possessed him. That was it!

Thirteen

O n the fourth day after the wedding it was customary for the bride and her groom to be received at her home. But there was no one here to go and invite them.

Chakki was laid up on the wedding day. She hadn't got out of bed since then. That good neighbour Nallapennu dropped in every once in a while to tend to her. Panchami was in charge of the house. Chembankunju didn't seem very concerned about Chakki's rapidly worsening condition. Nallapennu kept saying that a doctor had to be called in. But he wouldn't even reply.

In the days after the wedding, he was busy with everything. He would go to the door of the room Chakki lay in and peer. And so once when he went to stand there, Chakki said that someone ought to go to Trikunnapuzha and invite Karuthamma and Palani home.

Chembankunju forgot himself in his rage and bellowed, 'I am not going! And I don't want her in my house either!'

A distressed Chakki sank into a faint. That day Chembankunju brought a doctor home.

The girl hadn't been invited to her home after the wedding. Everyone wanted to know why. He snapped at them in response. But they wouldn't budge either. And so Chembankunju fell out with everyone.

Chembankunju seldom went far away from home. The two boats did go out to sea every day. But the catch was poor. It seemed that he was on bad terms with the workers in the boat as well.

Everyone at Trikunnapuzha also speculated and gossiped about Karuthamma not being invited to her home. Someone ought to have come along and taken them as per the norms. Everyone knew that she was a girl with a family. Which meant she had been kicked out from there. Even the poorest of people would invite their daughter home after the wedding. Karuthamma too waited for the invitation to arrive at any moment. She hadn't expected her father to abandon her so. She was anxious about her mother too. But she was too scared to speak to her husband about this. How would he take it? Nevertheless, she made up her mind to bring it up.

One day after lunch she thought that she had found an ideal time. She said aloud as if to herself, 'I wonder if my mother is alive or what?'

He didn't respond. She looked at his face carefully. She continued to look at him and said hesitantly, 'Shall we go across?'

'Don't even think about it!' A retort that stung like a slap in the face.

She hadn't expected him to be so stern. The truth was the change in his expression frightened her. It was like biting down on grit in freshly harvested rice.

Karuthamma put on a smile. 'How can you say that?'

He asked her in a forbidding voice, 'Hmm ... say what?'

'We will have daughters of our own. And when they have their fishermen husbands, we'll have to pay for all of this!'

Palani had a stinging retort for that as well. 'I'll bear that when that happens!'

What more could be said? So she left it well alone. When an opportunity arose next, she asked, 'Could I just go see my mother?'

He didn't object to that. But he had one thing to say, 'If you want to, you can go, but don't bother coming back!'

A little shard of anger shook itself free in Karuthamma's heart. It displayed itself as, 'Good heavens, what kind of a heart do men have?'

And then she put on a smile.

So the days passed with no consideration for the feelings of either Chakki in her Neerkunnath home or Karuthamma in her Trikunnapuzha home. Those souls wept. When Karuthamma was all by herself, she cried. Chakki's heart seared and burnt. But no one knew about it.

Hearing that Chakki's health was failing, Pareekutty went across one day. Chembankunju wasn't there. He was not on the shore but elsewhere. When Chakki saw Pareekutty, she burst into tears. Pareekutty was disturbed to see her sob so.

Pareekutty was a much changed man. He wasn't the eager-to-please, full-of-life Pareekutty he used to be. In between her weeping, Chakki said, 'I … I … I am dying, Boss.'

Pareekutty could see Chakki was very debilitated. Nevertheless, he said, 'What are you saying, Chakki? You are not all that ill!'

She gestured to him to seat himself by the cot. He sat down. Chakki continued to sob glancing at him. Pareekutty didn't know what to tell her. And then as they sat there Chakki said, 'I have so much to tell you, Little Boss!'

Pareekutty asked her to speak her heart.

It was the money she wanted to speak about first. Pareekutty asked her not to worry about that any more. Chakki cursed her husband. She said he was a greedy and wicked man.

'What can a helpless person like me do? He won't give the money back to you!'

'Don't worry thinking about that!'

'That's not it, Little Boss!'

It was difficult for her to go on.

A little later Chakki continued, 'I didn't send my child off to a good home. There isn't a moment when she is not in anguish!'

Since it had to do with Karuthamma, Pareekutty didn't have an opinion to offer.

Chakki continued to speak, 'I am lying here on my deathbed and my child hasn't even been brought here.'

A mother's anxiety reared its head. And didn't she have many things to worry about? Her daughter had had a love story. But she was married off to another man. How was she to know that the love story wouldn't cast a shadow on her new life? A new chapter was beginning. But how could she be certain that the past would have no influence? Above all this, she had been sent away with a man who had nothing or no one to call his own. How could she be sure that Palani would love her?

Chakki said, 'I have thrown my daughter out to sea on a mere coconut frond.'

Pareekutty comforted Chakki. 'Don't think like that. Palani is a good worker. He will look after her.'

She nodded in agreement. Chakki continued to voice her emotions, 'The two of you played and frolicked on this shore.'

A soft chord struck in Pareekutty's heart. Old memories awakened. Chakki saw that. After all, she too knew of that love. Perhaps she even knew how strong it had been, how it had touched the two lives to the core.

Ill as she was, it was Chakki the mother who said, 'My belly didn't ever spawn a boy.' With a deep sorrow, Chakki continued, 'I have a son.'

Pareekutty looked at her face wanting to know; and Chakki stared back at him as if to ask, 'Don't you want to know?' Chakki clasped Pareekutty's hand tightly and said, 'This is my son Pareekutty, you Pareekutty!'

Relief coursed through Pareekutty's much bruised heart. The one he had loved was taken away from him. But she still was his in a fashion. He was a part of her life.

Chakki had no hopes about Karuthamma's marriage. She remembered the times Pareekutty and Karuthamma played and grew up on this shore. Now she had acknowledged him as her son. And fresh shoots sprang up from the ashes of Pareekutty's hopes. Would Karuthamma be Pareekutty's ever? Even if not, would her mother want it? In a moment, Pareekutty arrived at a conclusion which was neither real nor possible.

That troubled mother told Pareekutty, 'My son, you must find yourself a bride, do your trade well and prosper!'

Words that resonated indelibly in Pareekutty's ears. That last night Karuthamma had said the same to him. But Pareekutty couldn't reply to Chakki like he had responded to Karuthamma.

'My son, you mustn't upset Karuthamma any more. She has a fisherman. You must not trouble her.'

Pareekutty was shaken. The words rang through his ears like a voice from above. You mustn't interfere in her life, destiny commanded. Or, was it just a thought? No, Pareekutty did hear it. 'Pareekutty is Karuthamma's brother. She doesn't have a brother of her own. My son must be her brother.'

Chakki had uttered those words. He had no doubts about that. Chakki spoke much thereafter. Chembankunju had abandoned Karuthamma; Chakki was dying; Karuthamma had been sent away with a man who had neither a home nor a family; whom did she have except Pareekutty? And so Chakki defined their relationship. Siblings!

Chakki asked, 'My son, will you always be a brother to Karuthamma? Only a brother!'

Pareekutty's eyes welled up. Chakki saw the tears roll down drop by drop. Chakki knew what that meant. She also understood what had caused the teardrops to flow.

Chakki elaborated the essence of that love story. 'My son, you were in love with Karuthamma. But you must now be her brother. That is the measure of your love for her, don't you think so?'

Pareekutty didn't have an answer. His throat was choked with tears. If he loved her, he should be her brother now – that was how it should be, he was being told.

Silent moments passed. Chakki asked, 'Isn't that so, son?'

Pareekutty replied mechanically, 'Yes.'

'Then my children, you must be brother and sister henceforth!'

A second later, Chakki continued, 'If she was here, as I lie here dying, I would tell her the same...'

Chakki became even more distraught and pleaded with him to be Karuthamma's brother. Just her brother! And if she had no one, he would look after her! And if she didn't arrive before Chakki died, he would send someone to fetch her! Pareekutty agreed. But Chakki felt that it wasn't the right manner in which to proclaim his acceptance. So she pleaded again.

That night Chakki heard Pareekutty sing from the shore.

Times were hard for Chembankunju. He was unable to go out to sea. And that was why the catch was poor, he told himself. And there had been yet another loss. He had to get a great deal of money from Khadar Boss for the fish he had sold him. One night Khadar took all the stock in his shack and fled. That loss was a great blow to Chembankunju. He decided to go back to sea once again. How long could he wait it out on the shore?

That day and for a few more days, Chembankunju was seen on the stern of his boat. But he was sitting there and not standing. The boat didn't have the same speed any more. It no longer raced. The oarsmen rowed. But Chembankunju was unable to stand on the speeding stern any more. His legs trembled. He no longer had the courage to stand on that narrow plank anchored by only the grip of his big toe. So how would they be able to go forward?

It just might happen that Chembankunju and his boat would never again be able to race the other boats; or come back to shore with the greatest catch. This boat floated like the other boats. The sight of that leaping, racing boat might never again be seen by the people of that shore.

They turned the boat back even before it was time. The oarsmen wanted to know why.

'Let us go back; this is enough for the day!'

Chembankunju had never ever been able to think 'enough'! On the way back to the shore, Chembankunju stumbled on an oar and fell into the water. The oarsmen pulled him back into the boat. Thereafter, Chembankunju didn't sit on the stern any more.

That day Chembankunju didn't even haggle. He gave his catch away at a throwaway price. He went back home fatigued. It was the gait of a defeated man.

Had Chembankunju's plans gone awry? Panchami was waiting for her father. She had cooked rice and made the curries he liked. From within, a weak voice fluttered, 'Daughter, serve the food; it's time for your father to come home.'

Panchami brought out the rice and curries. He stuffed his mouth, but with neither taste nor relish. He was just performing a deed called 'eating lunch'. When he rose, a perplexed Panchami said, 'Ammachi, father didn't eat at all!'

Chembankunju washed his hands and went to Chakki. She looked at him carefully. Both their eyes became tearful. It was the first time in Chembankunju's life that his eyes had teared up. Chakki said, 'What is to be done? It's fate!'

Chembankunju swallowed those tears. He didn't allow even a drop to be shed. He still had that much of his will left. He asked, 'Can't you get up?'

'I tried. What can I do?'

He stood there silent for a while and then asked, 'What am I to do now?'

Had he already started considering a life without her? A life where she was no longer of any use? That sort of a life would be incomplete and had no future. What could Chakki say?

He sat on the cot beside Chakki. She felt as if her husband's vigour and strength had drained away. Chembankunju described the accident at the sea. 'My legs gave way!'

Chakki couldn't think of her husband having an accident at sea. She hadn't even imagined it ever. That too had happened now. And might happen again.

'What am I to do, Chakki?' A helpless Chembankunju asked. Who else could he ask this of? Who else had the right to answer this? She was the factor most responsible for a life of discipline. But she was laid up now. And with that the systems and discipline fell apart. Not just that, the light itself disappeared! The man huddled on the bed was a defeated one.

Chakki took his hand in hers, pressed it against her bosom and asked, 'When I am gone, what will you do?'

Chembankunju started weeping. 'Don't say that. What will I do?'

The grip on his hand tightened. As her chest heaved, his hand was thrust off. And even as her eyes focused on him, a voice spoke, 'You must marry again!'

She had said that! Chakki's body quivered. The beat of her heart slowed.

Chakki continued to lie there looking at him. Chembankunju asked, 'What did you say? Marry another woman?'

There was no answer.

She knew that it was essential to have a life partner. She was showing him the way. Chembankunju had never considered something like that.

'Say something, Chakki.'

A film clouded Chakki's eyes. Chembankunju was frightened. He shook her awake. 'Chakki!'

All was still.

'Have you gone?'

Chembankunju fell onto Chakki's bosom. Her clasp on his hand was still fervent and tight.

Fourteen

Nallapennu consoled Panchami who wailed, 'But I have no one now!' Chakki had entrusted Panchami to Nallapennu. Instead of four, she had five children now, Nallapennu told her. But was that enough to comfort the bereaved?

Achakunju and the others prised Chembankunju away from Chakki's body. There was so much to be done. The Shore Master was informed of the death. He arrived. That Karuthamma ought to be informed came up for discussion. Someone asked, 'Shouldn't someone go for the girl?'

The question rang through the grieving Chembankunju's ears.

'No!' A roar.

Chembankunju claimed that it was Karuthamma who killed Chakki.

Everyone gathered there fell silent for a while. They were all perhaps thinking whether that decision was right or wrong. Or, perhaps they were waiting for the Shore Master to come to a resolution.

The Shore Master voiced his opinion.

'She went away even though she saw her mother lie like a fallen tree. Well, she went away not wanting any part of this. Let her stay there!'

Everyone there thought of what had happened on the wedding day. What she had done had been heartless.

Only Panchami called for her chechi. Who else did she have but her sister? But who paid any attention to her?

The preparation for the funeral was complete.

Pareekutty, as befitting a man of another faith, skulked in the periphery. He was probably grieving for Karuthamma without whom the funeral was happening. But how could he intervene in what was their business?

She would be heartbroken! If they were to meet again, she would ask, 'How could you have not let me know, my Bossman!'

Besides, would the woman who lay dead there ever forgive him?

Pareekutty felt as if he had much to do in this matter. But he wasn't sure what it ought to be. He was Karuthamma's brother; he had made her his sister. Now he had to do his brotherly duty.

That night he couldn't sleep. At the dead of night, he sat up. Much later, he stepped out and locked up the shack. He walked. The sea breeze seemed to hum a strange tale. The waves too had something to say... Where are you going? To Trikunnapuzha? Why? To inform Karuthamma of Chakki's death? But what right did he have to do that? And if someone were to question him about it, what answer did he have?

And when he found Karuthamma, what would he say to her? Questions that ought to have held back Pareekutty. But he continued to walk. He had a certain intrepidity. He was her brother. Her mother had made him her brother. But would she be his sister?

When Pareekutty had found Karuthamma, what would come of that rendezvous? Had Pareekutty considered that?

When dawn broke, Pareekutty reached Trikunnapuzha seashore. He saw a fisherman about to leave in his boat. Pareekutty asked him where Palani's house was. During the big catch, this fisherman had been at Neerkunnath. He recognized Pareekutty.

'Why are you looking for Palani, Little Boss?'

The question threw Pareekutty off kilter. Pareekutty replied, 'Palani's wife's mother is dead.'

A piece of news for Kochunathan. He knew Chembankunju and Chakki. Kochunathan praised Chakki. Then he posed a dangerous question. 'But why did the Little Boss have to come with the news of the death. Aren't there any fisherfolk there?'

It was a question that Pareekutty had expected. And he had found an answer to placate himself. But he hadn't expected a stranger to ask him this, or that he would have to answer it. Nevertheless, he replied, 'They decided that they were not going to inform Palani and his wife.'

Pareekutty narrated to him what had transpired after the death. But Kochunathan's questions wouldn't cease. 'What was the need for you to come in the middle of the night, Little Boss?'

The only answer he had for that was to tell him how he had been anointed a brother. But if he were to tell that, he would have to rake up what lay beneath that. How could a Muslim man be the brother of a fisher girl? Why had the mother ordained him as a brother? Pareekutty fumbled for an answer. In the end he claimed that he had come moved by the utter heartlessness of what had happened. Who knows if Kochunathan believed it? He told him where Palani's house was.

How was he to start talking to Karuthamma? Should he give her the news straight away? How would she understand?

All the boats were out at sea. Pareekutty stood in front of Palani's house. That little house was silent.

Pareekutty's tongue dried up. His throat was parched. For a while he stood like that. Without his knowing, a sound escaped his throat – Karuthamma. No one answered his call. He called again.

'Who is that?' A voice came from inside the house.

Pareekutty recognized Karuthamma's voice.

'It's me, Karuthamma!'

'Me? Who's me?'

'Can't you make out who I am?'

'Who?'

'I ... I ... Pareekutty.'

Silence! It stretched. Dense.

'I have something very important to tell you, Karuthamma!'

The voice from within the house cracked as it cried out, 'Won't you let me be in peace even when I have come away?'

A second later, she continued, 'No, no, I am not going to open the door. I don't want to see you.'

She was crying.

Words that pierced Pareekutty's heart. It was true. She had gone away seeking refuge. But she had no peace even here. He wondered if he should return without saying a word. No, he wouldn't do that. He would tell her the news even though she was inside the house. But how could he say something like this so abruptly? Pareekutty beseeched her again to open the door.

'Don't you know me, Karuthamma?'

She clenched her teeth in a fierce anger as she said, 'I do!'

'Why won't you step out then?'

There was no reply to that. He said, 'I am the same old Pareekutty. And I know that Karuthamma has a fisherman in her life now.'

Helplessly she said, 'I can't see you.'

He didn't know how but Pareekutty felt courage grow in him.

'You mustn't say that. We will have to see each other again! We have to talk face to face!'

'No, oh no, no … he's gone out to sea! To a wind-tossed, stormy sea!'

More silence!

'Karuthamma!'

As if fated to despair, she answered, 'What?'

'I am your brother!'

'Brother?'

That deep bond of theirs had not been frittered away. Instead, it had now evolved into something else with a name. She knew the relief of the dying man who found something to clutch at. Pareekutty said, 'Yes sister, your brother, you have a brother now!'

'No.'

'It's your brother calling! Your mother said I ought to care for you like a sister.'

'My mother?'

'Yes. Open the door. Let me tell you…'

Karuthamma lit the lamp, opened the door and stepped out.

How was he to tell her that momentous news? But it emerged in its harshest form. 'Karuthamma, Chakki is dead!'

Karuthamma wept loudly. By the time the neighbours arrived, Pareekutty had left. The neighbouring women tried to console her. They were disbelieving of the news. Even in that moment of deepest sorrow, she wouldn't reveal to any of them how she had come to hear of the news. They said that she had dreamt it.

As it became light and much tears had been shed, she began to question herself about the logic of it all. She began to disbelieve the news herself. Couldn't it be the treachery of a lovelorn lover? If her mother was dead, wouldn't someone have come to inform her?

Her husband had gone out to sea. When he returned, food would have to be served. A sense of wifely duty pushed her into doing her household chores. As usual, she managed to cook some rice and curry. And waited for someone to come with the news any minute now.

Palani reached the shore earlier than usual. Karuthamma wailed, 'My mother is dead!'

It didn't seem as if he had heard. She saw a graveness on his face which she had never seen before. She wept. 'I killed my mother.'

Without any trace of sympathy, he asked, 'Who came here to tell you this?'

She faltered, unable to find an answer. He looked at her carefully. 'That Little Boss.'

'And where is he now?'

'He said what he had to and left. I haven't seen him since.'

Why was he so grim? Was it because Pareekutty had come? Or, was it because the announcement of the death hadn't been made in the proper way?

Palani asked, 'Did your father send that Muslim man?'

Karuthamma didn't have an answer. Palani asked, 'Don't they have any fisher boys to send across?'

What could she say? Not just that. Was this the time to talk of norms and strictures? Palani had something on his mind. But she doesn't know what. She had only one thing to say, 'Let us go.'

'Where?'

'To Neerkunnath.'

He twisted his mouth into a smirk. It meant that he had no intention of going.

'It's my mother who's dead.'

That didn't seem to move Palani either. 'She loved you like you were her son,' Karuthamma said. Her mother was faultless. She was the one to blame. And it was because her mother insisted that she had come away with him. She said, 'By the mother of the sea, when I hesitated, it was my Ammachi who said I should go. Let us go!'

She hugged his feet and cried. He stood there like a statue. It was Chakki who showed Palani what a mother could be. It was she who had died. Could that death have not touched Palani? Perhaps it might have. From deep within him, he said, 'They pushed me back ashore.'

Karuthamma asked, 'So that we could go to Neerkunnath?'

'That's what they said. But it isn't that.'

'Then?'

A second later Palani said, 'Kochunathan chettan saw him come here. That Pappu's been spreading vicious gossip all over the seashore. So ... so ...'

His voice choked. He swallowed and continued, 'They have children. That's why they sent me back.'

Karuthamma understood. So this too had come to pass. She had only one thing to ask of him. She asked him, 'Do you doubt me?'

He didn't know what to say.

'After he came here with the news, where did that Muslim go hang himself?'

'I didn't see him.'

'Why did he come here?'

It was the moment to reveal everything, just about everything. Could she tell him all without hiding a thing? She could. But she couldn't find the words. Palani asked, 'What did he say?'

'That my mother's dead.'

This was the moment that would determine this little family's future.

At that point a story was spreading across the sea. That the old woman was dead was probably true. Everyone knew she was laid up. And that she might never rise from her bed was also known. But why did that Muslim man have to come bearing the news?

Kochunathan said, 'He was anxious. I could see that.'

Pappu had much more to say. 'That Muslim man and she would run around night and day on that Neerkunnath shore, I hear! In the night he would sing and she would step out and go to him. That's why I raised such a ruckus at the wedding.'

Pappu was triumphant. But all of them were sad about one thing. Palani was a nice man. Such a pity that his wife turned out to be like this!

Someone asked, 'So how do you take him on the boat with you?'

Everyone understood the implication of that query. Palani's house was defiled! So if he was in the boat, an accident could take place.

Velayudhan bristled, 'Who said his house is defiled?'

Aandi took sides with Velayudhan. He asked Kumaru, 'Can you be completely sure? Who can actually claim that their house is totally pure?'

No one was willing to go that far. They had to believe their homes were untainted. For none of them had any accidents yet.

But there was a general suspicion: Hadn't Palani dragged the boat to deep sea because something was on his mind?

Pappu's stories were yet another irritant. Anyway they also opined that the girl was good.

Apart from Kumaru, everyone else made an effort to believe Palani's home was untainted. Kumaru had a question; but who could answer it with clarity? 'Do fisherfolk send Muslims to carry tidings of death? And why did he come at the crack of dawn?'

Suspicion all around. All of them sympathized with Palani.

Uncertainty continued at Palani's home. Karuthamma

beseeched that they go to see her mother's dead body; to make that last plea of penitence. She spoke not with the right of a wife; but with the numb grief of a bereaved woman.

He wouldn't speak.

She asked, 'Do you trust me?'

He said, 'I do, girl!'

But he wanted to know many things. That was clear from his assurance of faith in her. She was prepared to tell him whatever had to be said. She wouldn't hide anything. But she had neither the strength nor the skill to speak the words. It was a big moment for Karuthamma. But Palani wouldn't understand how important it was. It wasn't just her mother's death, Palani wouldn't be able to fathom the significance of any mother's death.

Karuthamma cried helplessly. She voiced a thought. That she be allowed to go by herself; she would return the same day. He didn't give her a clear answer to that either. What if she defied her husband and went? But it would mean that she would never be able to return.

No, she wasn't prepared for that. She was born a fisherwoman and would die one. That was her deceased mother's desire.

She would cling to his feet and die there. There was no reason to even think that her father, who didn't have the compassion to even send someone to inform her of her mother's death, would take her in. Neither did she have the right to claim it. She had defied her father and left her home for good to go with a man. She would have to live her life out in this little hut.

Karuthamma thought about Panchami. She could almost hear her plaintive cry of 'echechi echechi'. When they dug a hole in the salt-soaked sands and laid her mother there, Panchami would be crying bereft and alone. She would have to live alone in that home now.

There would be other Pareekutties on that shore. Palani who

sat silently looking at the far distance too seemed to have lost his peace of mind. He was someone who had never ever had to live with chaos. Any place on earth had been heaven to him until then.

Karuthamma went to his side and asked, 'Don't you want to eat?'

'I am not hungry.'

'Why is that?'

He asked, 'Why did that Muslim come?'

Karuthamma revealed the truth. 'If you ask me, it is to ruin me, why else?'

She was willing to take her troubles head-on. Karuthamma had the fortitude for that. Palani too was strong-minded. He asked, 'Who is he to you, Karuthamma?'

She understood exactly what he meant and she decided to tell him everything. All she was in doubt about was how she should tell him that story. She didn't care how she began. When she had decided to reveal everything, how did it matter how she began.

'From our childhood, we played on the seashore...' and then she began telling the story.

Palani listened, showing neither anger nor any emotion. Wasn't he affected by the graveness of her story? She was petrified by his demeanour.

When she had spoken for long, she asked, 'Do you believe in what I have said?'

Palani said that he did. A woman was telling her love story to her husband. There was no need to disbelieve her. Wasn't she smearing filth on herself?

But she couldn't continue telling her story in that vein. The narrative didn't have the flow.

In her tale Karuthamma is now eighteen. But she didn't talk about the money. She didn't tell him about the song. And she didn't tell him about that final farewell either. She spoke of all else. Did Palani suspect that she had kept quiet about many things? Who knows?

She said, 'I don't have a brother. He is my brother.'

She didn't think it worked.

When Palani had heard everything, he asked, 'So it is true what everyone says – you were sent away from Neerkunnath – isn't that so?'

The wife had only one answer to that: She would always be a proper fisher-wife befitting this shore.

Fifteen

Everything that Karuthamma had told him was the truth as she knew it. Even though he believed her, it had lessened his fervour for her. Palani was lost in thought. His enthusiasm flagged. How could he confront Pappu face to face?

She was chaste; and he believed in her. But what if Pappu said she was unfit for the shore – how could he defy that? He had dragged her by force from her father's. His sense of duty, his beliefs shaped by being a fisherman wouldn't allow him to abandon her. If he were to forsake her, where would she go?

She had opened her heart to him. She placed her faith in the confession. That she had been at fault, she accepted with tears day after day. The past had to be forgotten. It was certain that henceforth she would be virtuous. Palani had no doubt about that.

He could no longer give in to the temptation to kiss her. His embrace no longer tightened around her. With tears in her eyes, and with twice as much fervour, she would mumble this and that. She kept trying to gather him back to her. Knowing that he had escaped her and not knowing how to bring him back to her, she clutched at him. But each time she felt him slipping away. All she could ask him was if he trusted her. She dared not ask him if he loved her. She felt she had lost the right to ask him that.

Palani who never ever quarrelled now got into fights. One day Pappu looked into his eyes with a mocking expression and said a few things. Palani had heard all of this from Karuthamma. But how could he bear it when another man flung it in his face?

They pushed and jostled each other. Palani hit Pappu.

But the quarrel didn't end there. Pappu belonged to a big family on that shore. He had numerous family members. It wasn't seen as a mere slight. Instead, it was seen as an act of arrogance – was Palani man enough to beat up the fisherman from the Thengumkoottathil family?

Thus, Karuthamma's plan to make a home frittered away. Those days the sea too lay fallow. Palani showed no enthusiasm to go to work. Neither did Karuthamma have the courage to ask him what had been his share of takings for the day.

Didn't he want to deck her up and take her to Mannarshala? Shouldn't that hovel become a house with a room and kitchen? There was a grinding stone. But there were so many other things to be acquired! Forget about the boat and nets; that was a long-term plan. It may or may not happen. Managing everyday affairs itself was getting to be difficult. Everything was falling apart. She needed a cloth and blouse. Palani had only one lungi.

One day Karuthamma asked, 'Shall I start going to the east to sell fish from tomorrow?'

Palani didn't answer at once. Did he have to think about it? Nevertheless, he didn't speak. She told him of its benefits. And that she would go only if he permitted it.

He said, 'In which case, go!'

In two days' time she bought a basket. The next few days, when the boats drew closer to the shore, Karuthamma reached there in preparation to go sell fish in the east.

She was still a new bride and she was already on the shore. Kochupennu asked, 'Why are you doing this?'

'I too am a fisherwoman of this shore.'

That day it became the topic of discussion. Opinion was divided about that as well.

It wasn't a job that Karuthamma was familiar with. Had she ever considered that she might have to do this? Who knows? Her mother had done it. Had Chakki ever thought that her daughter would have to lug a leaky heavy basket of fish? Had Karuthamma too hoped to put aside some money?

When the boats drew in, she too went with the other women. One merchant took the entire catch of a boat. Karuthamma and a few women bought all of it from him.

All the other women ran ahead of her. It was what they were used to on a daily basis. She was unable to lug that heavy load and run. She was the last one. It was possible that they might have to go at least four miles to the east. Neither was she familiar with people or the places. The other women had already been through the various settlements. She didn't know how to find a new beat. She stood at every door and called. In some homes, they had already bought fish for the day. So they didn't need fish.

At some homes, they wanted to know what fish it was. No one was interested in small fish. At other homes, the price wasn't right. Despite walking a great distance, she didn't sell at all. All she wanted then was to get rid of it even at a loss. How could she take it back? And so having sold at a loss, she returned home bone-tired. But she did accomplish one thing. She was ensured of the custom of several homes on a regular basis.

Palani sat smoking a beedi. She was exhausted and her face was drawn and tired. She could barely walk. She thought that the sight of her exhaustion would prompt him to ask her a few questions. Wasn't it her right to expect such a query? Well, if it didn't happen, so be it. She had just started a new venture.

Shouldn't he at least ask her how much she had made that day? Wasn't she doing this for him as well? Palani didn't ask anything. He sat as if she had been there all day. Did she have the right to confront him on such apathy? Or, could she at least lose her temper? No, what right did she have? No, she had no right at all.

Nevertheless, she was his wife. Even if she had no rights, she had her responsibilities. She asked, 'Have you eaten?'

He said, 'Yes.'

When she finished her bath, she didn't have fresh clothes to change into. She continued to wear the sodden clothes.

Even though he didn't ask her, she described her day's trade to him. She had made a loss that day but she had set up everything for the next day. She wanted his permission on one another matter. She wanted to try her hand in helping make a 'Kambavala'. She wanted him to introduce her to someone who dealt in it.

He said, 'Forget it. I can't.'

The next day the catch was mackerel. Karuthamma bought as much as she could with the money she had. Like the previous day, she lagged behind all the other women. Many of the people she had arranged with waited for her. The other women had sold two for an anna. Karuthamma sold five for two annas. Even though the profit was small, she was again assured of regular custom in many homes. They asked her to come again the next day. That new fisherwoman is a good sort.

A few days later a huge quarrel erupted on the shore. All the fisherwomen who sold their fish in the east ganged up against Karuthamma and abused her. Karuthamma's tongue wasn't long enough to confront even one among them. So how could she take on five or six women? She stood there weeping. One woman bristling with rage said, 'A slut who lay with a Muslim somewhere. She's come here to ruin us all!'

Then the others said, 'She'll get enough business. The men in those houses want only her … she's a shameless flirt, that's what she is!'

All of this was said to Karuthamma to her face. Her ears hurt with their venom. She went home crying. There wasn't a creature in this world to stand up for her. No one knew her truth. So she didn't have the right, it seemed, to earn a living like other fisherwomen.

Palani who had come home from the sea didn't ask why she hadn't gone to sell fish that day. He just looked at her carefully. It wasn't the first time he had seen her tear-stained face. That's how he had seen her most of the time anyway. But that day she was even more woebegone. He asked her the reason. Nothing, she replied. For that was all she could tell him. How could she tell him of what had happened?

Had none of the women at Trikunnapuzha ever committed a fault? When people quarrelled in Neerkunnath, they slandered each other with tales of the past. Each one had a story of their own. That was how it was. But she knew nothing about anyone here. If she did, she would have brought up stories about them. Why shouldn't she? What grievous wrong did Karuthamma do?

Don't boys and girls play together on this shore here? Hadn't she seen them pick mussels, make sand tunnels and fish for minnows?

These women were girls on this shore once. For a moment Karuthamma thought about how she could collect tales about them. Did the breeze on this shore contain an old love story? Had the sinful soul of a fisherwoman flitted on this shore on moonlit nights? No one had ever heard a song sung like that.

Karuthamma stopped going to the east to sell fish. But she began another line of work. She would buy fish from the shore, salt and dry it and build a stock. When there was no fresh fish, she would be able to get a good price for it. Or, she could sell it to the shack owners.

Thus Karuthamma set herself up anew. But in truth, hadn't it always been so? An inner life of which she could talk to none. She lived there by herself. She didn't make a friend there as well. There were days when she didn't speak to another person.

And so it was for Palani. Each day he would go to work. He had lost his vitality and enthusiasm. He used to have friends once. It seemed as if he had forsaken them all.

Karuthamma and Palani's life entered a realm of flatness. The ardour of those first days was gone. It was natural for things to settle a bit. If their lives had naturally plateaued, the ardour too would have settled into a plane. But this wasn't like that. A leaping flame had been snuffed out in a moment. Dreams and plans for the rest of their lives had collapsed all of a sudden. And if you were to still ask how was it they lived as husband and wife with no passion, didn't such cold marriages exist in this world?

Was Karuthamma content? Perhaps. Palani? Perhaps he too was content. When Karuthamma became a topic of discussion on the shore, Palani too became one. When he walked by, people whispered about him behind his back. And even if it didn't happen he suspected it did.

Some months ago when he lived on this shore and his ties with the community was still a tenuous one, anyone who met him greeted him with a bright smile and some chit-chat. He was regarded as a good man. But now as he went by, they whispered about him stealthily. What a change! Palani hadn't committed a sin against anyone. Ever since the day when he steered the boat like a mad man to the deep sea, that expert boatsman had never been given the helm oar. Everyone was scared. Not just the men in his boat but everyone. Perhaps they believed that he was possessed by an evil spirit; or that as Karuthamma was a fallen woman, being with her man in the same boat invited a disaster – a threat the fisherwomen frightened their menfolk with. After all, it was an age-old belief.

There was not a single creature in that place to speak up for hapless Karuthamma. And so it was for the destitute Palani. Anyone could slander them. There wasn't anyone to oppose it.

Palani's boat was owned by Kunjan Valakkaran. He was from a family that had always owned boats and nets. However, these days his sole wealth was that one boat and net. He had mortgaged even the land and the house they lived in. If he didn't have that one boat and net, he would starve. Nor would his status allow him to go to work in another man's boat. Not just that, he was also an elderly man.

The gossip about Karuthamma trickled into his ears. What a disaster! A fallen woman's husband going to sea in his boat. He didn't have a moment's peace until the boat returned to the shore each day. Since Palani was in the boat, it was quite possible that it would capsize and smash to bits. The boat could be caught in an undertow and dragged deep into the sea. Any kind of accident could happen! He could lose everything.

Kunjan Valakkaran called for a secret meeting with all the boatmen except Palani. All of them had the same fear. And day after day their women fanned that fear. Each day the women called to the mother of the sea. So when Kunjan Valakkaran called for a discussion, they were relieved.

Kumaru said, 'Valakkaran's fear is about losing his boat. For us it is our lives at stake. God in heaven, twelve families will be destitute.'

That was an opinion that not even Velayudhan opposed. He too was scared within.

Kunjan Valakkaran said, 'Yes, yes, you are right. You don't mess with the sea.'

None of them had any doubts about that. Even if times changed, the laws of the sea didn't. Neither did the rules that governed the fishermen on the shore. Overcome with fear Kumaru said, 'When we are at sea, what if that Muslim comes here ... can you imagine the plight?'

Kunjan Valakkaran quivered in fright. 'Yes, yes, what would become of us?'

Aandikunju said hopelessly, 'Everyone says that the Muslim still visits this shore...'

Kunjan Valakkaran asked, 'Really? What if we finish him off?'

Velayudhan, 'That will be an even greater mess than this...'

The women in their homes were disturbed. From the moment the boats went out to sea, they were in tears. It was only when the boats drew close to shore that they knew some peace.

Aandikunju continued, 'If the women are right, would the mother of the sea have looked after us? If the old laws worked, none of us would have been around. All of us would have been deep under the sea.'

Veluthakunju said that Pappu claimed he had seen Pareekutty on that shore quite recently on a moonlit night. He was seen walking on the sands singing a song! It seems he did that every night!

Despite all this, they felt a great pity for Palani. He was a good lad. Such a shame that his fate was this! What could anyone do?

Perplexed, Kunjan Valakkaran asked, 'So what is the way out now?'

Kumaru said there was only one thing to be done. Palani had to be left behind on the land. That was the right thing to do! It was the only solution. For the hundredth time, Kumaru narrated how Palani had taken the boat to the deep sea as if he had been possessed.

'What if he gets into one of those states again? I sit facing him in the boat each day so that I can watch his expression change.'

All of them accepted the veracity of that. Even if the steering oar wasn't in his hands, one false move of the oar would do.

Kumaru's suggestion was accepted by all of them. But it was a matter that caused heartache in each of them. Palani had worked for Kunjan Valakkaran ever since he was a boy. First he was thrown into the water to help spread the nets. No one worried too much about tossing an orphan into the sea. Then he became an oarsman. When he took the steering oar and stood on the stern, he helped them fetch at least two rupees more than anyone else. Kunjan Valakkaran asked all of them, 'Hey Kumaru, ever since he put the steering oar down, hasn't our earnings come down?'

Kumaru agreed. But what else could they do to escape this great danger? Nothing! But who was going to tell him this and how? Kunjan Valakkaran said he couldn't. He didn't have the strength of mind for that. Neither could it not be mentioned. He spoke to Kumaru, 'One of you must tell him!'

None of them would. So how then could they put the plan into action? Karutha had an idea. 'We must go out to sea before he gets there. Isn't that how you lay off workers at the shore?'

Kunjan Valakkaran knew that. But he also knew that the laid-off worker would demand to know why. When he saw Palani, how would he face him? That was what troubled Kunjan Valakkaran.

But that was the only way out. The boatmen decided on that and left. Kunjan Valakkaran arranged for another man to take Palani's place.

Palani woke up as usual at the crack of dawn and went to the shore. But the boat had already left by then. Palani hollered loudly. It changed into a roar. The shore had never resounded with a sound like that. The realization that he had been grounded aroused the man in that child of the sea. In the lull that followed, muscles cramped. The child of the sea was being cast out of his element. It was a body hewn to battle with the wind and storms. For years it had wrestled with the forces of nature. But as of this day, it was being denied that. In that denial, his might was awakened. The west wind carried that roar into the alleys between the houses. If the boatmen had heard it, would they have come back to the shore? But perhaps they didn't.

The boat he so loved fled deep into the west – as if to proclaim it had no use for him.

The forces that had been awakened wouldn't be contained. He understood the purport of what had happened. Palani leapt into the sea. To catch up with the boat; to once again establish his right. Like an otter, like a dolphin, he raced to the west. It was his need to live his life as a fisherman, as the son of the sea. A giant wave, a wave that until that day had never risen as high, rolled over his head. The next second, draining him of all his strength, the sea flung him into a heap back on the shore.

Palani lost; he was defeated. He got up and ran to Kunjan Valakkaran's home. He had a question to ask, 'Am I unfit to go to sea?'

Kunjan Valakkaran shifted uneasily, unable to find an answer. 'That…'

'That's a lie! Bare-faced lies. She is not a fallen woman. I know that!'

'But that's what everyone's saying.'

Bristling with anger, Palani said, 'Yes, that's what they are saying!'

He turned and walked back.

Sixteen

When Palani returned home Karuthamma was surprised. She couldn't understand the reason. She asked him what had happened. He said, 'You are a fallen woman. So they have declared I am unfit to go to sea.'

Karuthamma was astounded. So many people had branded her a slut but her husband had never accused her, ever. This was the first time. In fact, he wasn't accusing her as much as repeating hearsay. And so, because of her, a good fisherman was cast away from the sea.

Palani asked her, 'Didn't you know you are a fisher girl? So why then in your childhood did you frolic and play with that Muslim boy?'

That was true. No one had ever asked her such a question. Even when her mother had scolded her in the past, she had never had to answer such a severe or obvious query. Karuthamma was perplexed. She understood all the implications of that question. She was obliged to answer it. But what could she say? And so Karuthamma accepted it as her fault. With tears she said, 'It happened. Please forgive me!'

His ire wasn't directed towards her. He said, 'Why should I blame you? It's not your fault.'

Karuthamma felt relieved. He had forgiven her. He believed

all of what she had told him. He was blaming her indifferent upbringing. It was a great relief.

Palani continued, 'They let their daughter gambol with that Muslim boy, and now it is their daughter who has to suffer its consequences. Shouldn't the father and mother be the ones to look after their children?'

But Palani's anger didn't stop there. He stared into her face and asked, 'I suppose your father acquired his boat and nets by using you as bait to lure and cheat that Muslim boy. Wonderful indeed!'

Palani was justified in his suspicion. That was a secret she hadn't revealed to him. She should have, Karuthamma thought. One day she would tell him about that as well.

Palani instructed his wife, 'Look, just as your parents did, you must bring up that creature in your belly. If it is a girl, you must make sure that she brings harm to some fisher boy on the shore. Do you hear me?'

'No,' Karuthamma said. She understood his sarcasm. She would never allow the child growing in her to experience what she had; she had endured so much, learnt so many lessons. Even if it was the most difficult phase in her life, Karuthamma knew a respite. It was the first time he had referred to the child growing in her. And the first time he had openly spoken about her misdemeanour. Palani didn't believe in any of the rumours that had spread everywhere. Whew, that itself was a relief!

Though they had stayed together for a while in the same house, she didn't dare take advantage of that. Instead, like a helpless creature seeking solace, she went to sit by him. He didn't kick her away. That was a big thing. It truly was a remarkable thing.

She asked, 'How will we live?'

Palani hadn't considered that.

She cursed everyone, 'Bloody back-stabbers! They won't even let me go sell fish in any of the settlements! And won't let you go to the sea either!'

Palani straightened up. He said firmly, 'I am a fisherman, girl. Will live as a fisherman and die as a fisherman!'

She saw a man filled with masculine vigour. Muscles that had toughened with work rippled. She was under the protection of a fisherman with fortitude. Palani clenched his teeth and said, 'Who has the right to declare that I am unfit to go to sea? I am born to work the sea. Everything in the sea is mine. Who has the right to deny me that?'

Palani's being quivered with righteous indignation. He was the owner of a cornucopia of riches!

'A fisherman won't go out to till the soil or dig the ground. Palani will not do that either. That's for sure.' And then Palani assuaged his wife. 'You don't worry. Palani will live off what comes from the sea.'

It was the time when the nets were being hauled in. He had lived on the sea since he was five. It was the first time he was sitting at home without any work.

When he looked to the west, Palani could see the boats in the mid sea. It was a day when the catch was mackerel and kuruchi! Palani became restless. What could he do? Bristling with rage, he sat there grumbling, feeling his repressed masculinity protesting.

Karuthamma felt something stir in her. If he was a fisherman, she was a fisherwoman. She too must live off the wealth of the sea. No fisherwoman lived by husking coconuts or spinning rope. It wasn't meant for her. She asked, 'Shall I go east to sell fish?'

Palani refused, 'No, you stay at home. There is no need for you to haul a heavy basket around dragging that belly with you.'

'I am all right, I am not yet weak or tired.'

Palani said forcefully, 'I brought you here knowing I could look after you. I have the strength for that. You don't have to do a thing.'

Karuthamma didn't accept that suggestion wholeheartedly. But she took strength from it. As a woman at fault, she had worried about what was to be of her. But in declaring that she needn't work, he was saying he would take care of her.

It was a memorable day in her life. For wasn't this the day when she truly became a wife? What else could she want for? Was there such an able husband as hers on this shore? Every aspect of the bond between a husband and wife was explored on that day. There was just one thing left. Just one aspect.

Palani said, 'Karuthamma, there is one thing to remember … you must be careful to never stray … no one can deny you a place on this shore as a fisherwoman then.'

Palani spoke his mind. Until then she had always clung to his feet or laid her face to his chest crying her innocence. He had never asked for such an avowal. In reality, it was the right of each husband to ask such a troth of his wife. Without that her sense of belonging would never be complete. Such an avowal was contained in the ritual of marriage: You mustn't ever stray. And it was a primary factor in a husband's love for his wife.

It was a grateful wife who sank onto his wide chest in complete fulfilment. The dams in her eyes burst open. She spoke as if to his very heart, 'Why do you say that? I know I am at fault. Will I ever stray?'

Palani continued to caress her back. He consoled her, 'Don't cry. You mustn't cry.'

The died-out fervour blazed again. His strong muscular arms almost suffocated her with the strength of his embrace. Sensual rapture was found again. Orphan Palani had someone to consider now. And she, hapless woman shorn of kith and kin, had him to depend upon – Palani. He for she. And she for him. They would hold hands and fight their way forward.

The boats drew close to the shore. Palani could see the hustle and bustle of trade. Palani said his friends would be asking themselves how he would survive now. But they wouldn't be able to put him down. They needn't even try. Palani wasn't one to give up.

Karuthamma had a query of her own. 'Didn't any of their wives ever make a mistake?'

'Of course! Liars, they are all just silent about it, keeping it to themselves…'

She wanted to know all about it. She wanted to know about the past of each one of them so she could fling it back onto each one of their faces. Her tongue was sharp enough for that.

She said, 'If not now, but later I will ask each one of them.'

All decisions had been resolved. And they were one. But what were they to do now? How would they survive?

'What do we do? Why don't you speak about that?'

He couldn't but think about it. It was a serious issue.

Karuthamma continued, 'I have twelve rupees with me.'

It wasn't enough to accomplish anything. A net would cost about thirty rupees.

Karuthamma had a brainwave. 'Why don't we buy a fishing rod?'

'But don't we need a canoe if we buy a fishing rod?'

'And one more person to go in the canoe. But who would come?'

Palani dismissed it airily. 'Don't worry about that. If there was a canoe, I would go on my own and make enough for us for each day.'

There were a few canoes on that shore that were ideal for fishing. Karuthamma wondered if they could rent out one of those.

'No one will give it to us. If there is an accident, the boat will be lost.'

'So what is the way out?'

Palani thought for a while and said, 'Give me the money. I'll buy a fishing rod.'

Karuthamma counted out the money and gave it to him. Palani left to buy the rod.

The wife of a man who had decided to take life on was fortunate. Once again the house, things for the house, a boat, nets and suchlike appeared on the horizon. An uncelebrated Mannarshala Ayilyam, had gone by. But there would be more.

She prayed that the child in her wouldn't be a girl. She had endured the trials of having been born a girl. And if it was a girl, what if history repeated? No, she wouldn't allow that. She wouldn't let that girl child play or grow up alongside a boy child. She wouldn't let her get entangled in a love affair.

And if it was a boy? She wouldn't allow him to be the cause of trouble for any girl.

She cooked rice and curry in the kitchen. She thought that once again they would eat off the same dish. She would roll a ball of rice and place it in his mouth. Not a small ball of rice but a big one. Karuthamma dreamt of many such things.

Even if they were starving, she would put up with it and everything else. Her husband loved her. He had forgiven her for her trespasses. What more could she need? Her god had protected her.

Palani came home after dusk with the fishing rods. Big and small ones! He turned them around and began fixing the lines on them. And so everything was prepared.

When the shore fell asleep, Palani stepped out with the rods. She would let him go only after he had disclosed his agenda. He would borrow a canoe from someone without his permission and sneak out to sea. Before the shore awakened, he would fish and return. 'I too have to live off the sea.'

Karuthamma was frightened. To go by himself at night into the sea? Anything could happen.

She said, 'But. But…'

'Why not?'

'But alone!'

'I am a son of the sea!'

As he walked she said, 'You mustn't chase after fish into the deep seas!'

He didn't say he wouldn't.

Karuthamma couldn't sleep. She sat beneath a coconut tree to the west of their hovel. Further to the south, she saw a canoe go into the sea.

Karuthamma's heartfelt prayers must have worked as a talisman for him.

Before anyone woke up, Palani returned. He had got some fish. Early in the day Palani reached the market at Karthikapalli. He had fish for eight rupees.

A canoe was needed. If they were going to save for it, it would take a long time. If they had one hundred and fifty rupees, they could buy an old canoe. There was a way. She had her gold. But Palani didn't want to sell that gold to buy a canoe.

'That came from your money-grubbing father.'

She retorted, 'No, it's mine! My mother made it for me.'

'Nevertheless, I can't … I can't use a girl's wealth.'

'So am I not yours?'

He didn't reply. Buying a boat with money from selling his fisherwomen's jewellery wasn't part of his scheme of things.

And yet he took the gold from her and sold it. He then bought a small boat. Even if it wasn't what he wanted, it was the best he could get for that amount.

The neighbourhood was agog with the news of Palani having bought a boat. Perhaps there was much speculation about that as well. Why wouldn't they say the money for the boat too came from that Muslim?

Palani's new enterprise began well enough. Some days he got five or ten rupees. And some days there was nothing. His vigour and well-developed muscles were not satiated. The boat was much too small. He didn't feel as if he had done any work; his vigour had no outlet; he didn't tire enough. Moreover, the boat and oars were not big enough for him. He needed a big boat for himself. And at the helm of it, he wished to stand with a giant oar. And to pursue the big catch with a whorl of nets.

Karuthamma asked him, 'Would you go on your own if you had a big boat? No one will go with you!'

'If I have a boat, they'll come sniffing like street curs!'

Meanwhile though, Palani made up his mind about one thing. 'I won't go to sea in another man's boat!'

Karuthamma's pregnancy made her tired. Her belly too was swelling up. When he went out into the sea, his thoughts lingered at home. He couldn't spend too much time at sea.

One day when he came home from sea, there were a few women gathered there. They beamed at him and said, 'It's a girl!'

A newborn baby was being bathed in a trough made from the outer bark of an areca palm. It was bawling its head off. The midwife handed over the bathed baby to Palani. He didn't know how to take it in his hands. He had never held a baby before.

When the husband and wife were alone, he asked her, 'Why are you so dull?'

She was listless.

'Is it because the baby is a girl?'

She said, 'If it were a boy...'

She continued, 'Doesn't the father feel the same?'

'Oh, I don't think so.'

'You are just saying that!'

'No, how does it matter if it is a boy or a girl?'

She revealed her decision to him in one sentence. 'I won't bring this girl to be another Karuthamma!'

Palani smiled. 'And neither will Palani be a Chembankunju!'

The arrival of that baby brought into their lives a new meaning, a new density. The two of them were living for another being as well. Another life depended on them. For Palani, the child was only a source of joy. While he waited for fish to snare on his rod, it was that angel's tiny clear eyes he thought of. And then he would yearn to come home. Karuthamma taught Palani how to hold the baby. She would scold him, 'If you keep cuddling the child, she will be spoilt!' Frightened, Palani would put her down.

As far as Karuthamma was concerned, the child had birthed with it a few reasons for anguish. Her mother wasn't there to see that child. When she gazed at the baby's face, she would think of Panchami. Panchami, who had flailed and kicked her arms and legs in such joy as a baby, had once been her life. Panchami had done no wrong. But the relationship with her too had been severed. How was she coping? Karuthamma wondered. That worry blazed in her.

One day Palani came with a piece of news. Chembankunju had brought home a woman from Cherthala or so. Someone from Neerkunnath had mentioned it and that was how it had reached Palani's ears. And so in that house where Karuthamma was born and reared, a home that her mother had ruled, a strange woman had taken over as queen and keeper. Her mother had built that home; everything had been her mother's. How would that strange woman treat Panchami? When Palani walked around holding the baby close to him, she would think of how once her father too must have held her so. Her father had loved her once.

Soon as she began to feel she could take liberties with Palani even to the extent of finding fault with him, she chose a moment to bring up the matters of her home. 'My father had hoped that you would have stayed on in my home after the wedding.'

He asked, 'Do you think any able fisherman would stay on in that manner in his wife's home?'

Another time when he was dandling the baby she said, 'I am reminded of my Panchami's baby face when I see her face. I would never put her down.'

With tears in the corner of her eyes, Karuthamma continued, 'Poor child! She will have to put up with whatever the stepmother does.'

Palani asked, 'Why is that?'

'That's how stepmothers are!'

'What can be done?'

She ventured cautiously, 'I would like to see her.'

Palani didn't respond.

Yet another time in a moment of play and laughter, Karuthamma asked, 'Shall I go to Neerkunnath just once? To see my Panchami.'

He didn't like that. With an enchanting smile, she said, 'Listen, we have a daughter. She won't come to see her father!'

He demanded brusquely, 'What do you want? To see that Muslim? Are you using Panchami as an excuse to go there?'

Karuthamma was stunned. Nothing had changed. The nature of the beast was the same. Hadn't that black shadow called 'that Muslim' not disappeared yet? Wouldn't it ever be erased?

Karuthamma felt she had put the wrong foot forward. She said, 'No, I'll never go to Neerkunnath. Nor will I ever ask to go there.'

But there was no consolation. Wondering if her life would turn murky again, she asked with tears in her eyes, 'Don't you trust me?'

A black shadow stretching as far as life itself. How could she escape it?

Nothing, there was nothing she could do. Once again she would have to make amends for life to return to what it had been.

Seventeen

When a wife dies, it is said that her soul comes to her husband's bedside at night. She becomes one with the air around him. That's the afterlife of a deceased wife.

'Marry another woman!' Why had Chakki said this? Perhaps she must have thought it the wisest counsel given the circumstances. Or perhaps he needed the comfort of another woman. And she must have whispered this to him knowing her husband's need for sensual fulfilment.

As Chakki's eyelids had closed, Chembankunju had muttered several times in her ear, 'What should I do?' He had prised open her closed eyelids and demanded, 'Don't you want us to be together, Chakki? To enjoy ourselves?'

Everyone said Chembankunju had lost his right hand. It was indeed the truth. All the prosperity and grace in his life had come from Chakki. There wasn't another fisherwoman as capable as she was. What would Chembankunju do now? Could a young girl run a house? Karuthamma wouldn't come. Nor would he send for her. What was it that he said? A twig that refused to blaze had to be cast out!

'Marry another woman!' Those last words kept booming in Chembankunju's ears. He sought Achakunju's advice. 'What do you think about my bringing in a new woman?'

Achakunju said, 'You will need to do that! The girl needs a mother, doesn't she?'

'But I won't find another Chakki!'

'That's never going to happen, no matter whom you find!'

They left Panchami with Nallapennu and went out seeking a bride for Chembankunju.

Achakunju advised Chembankunju on many things in the pretext of talking about the marriage. Chembankunju should remember that he wasn't the Chembankunju he used to be. He was now a man of means, a man with some prestige. So he ought to seek a woman who was his equal in wealth and status.

Chembankunju liked that line of thought. Not just that, he was also worn out, body and soul. He was unable to work as he used to once. Now was the time for him to rest and relax. That wish to enjoy life to its fullest reared its head again. Pity! For Chakki too had slaved alongside him. But she had never known a moment of pleasure.

And so, in Chembankunju and Achakunju's search for a bride, they heard about a likely candidate. Pallikunnath Kandankoran Valakkaran's wife. Kandankoran Valakkaran had passed away. Papikunju wasn't all that well placed any more.

Without any further thought, Chembankunju agreed. His notion of comfort and pleasure had been born in Papikunju's home.

She too was agreeable. She said there was no need to inform the Shore Master. Chembankunju went across and fetched her home. And with her was her almost grown-up son.

Even though Papikunju had been in some distress after Kandankoran's death, she was still an attractive woman; a radiant woman. But Panchami didn't like the woman stepping into her house. She ran to Nallapennu and muttered angrily to her.

Nallapennu advised her, 'My child, you mustn't say anything.'

'Why not?'

'Your father will be angry!'

Panchami began crying. Why was she crying?

For the first time Chembankunju felt ashamed of his home. A mean-looking hovel. And it was here he had brought Papikunju. With an abashed smile he said, 'This was put up when I had neither boat nor nets. My Chakki didn't care too much about these things. So we never built another house.'

He had been to Papikunju's big house. Even if it was someone else's now, she used to live there once. Chembankunju decided he would buy a plot of land and build a house there. And he told her this.

His beloved Chakki had advised him to marry another woman. Would she be pleased with his choice? He looked around him. Surely his Chakki was somewhere around!

Chembankunju summoned the weeping Panchami. Didn't she want to meet her new mother?

Nallapennu told Panchami, 'Go child!'

With tears in her eyes, Panchami said, 'No, I am not going!' 'I'll come with you!'

Nallapennu wiped Panchami's face with the end of her sari. She wasn't to cry, she was told. Leading her by her hand Nallapennu took her across.

Papikunju looked at her carefully and asked, 'Why are you crying, girl?'

Chembankunju said, 'She is a child; must be crying for her mother!'

Holding his daughter close, Chembankunju said, 'She is a good stepmother; don't cry, my darling!'

There was much he could have said to console her. That it was at her mother's behest he had brought home a stepmother;

that it was for her as well, etc. Shouldn't he have also told her to consider her stepmother as her real mother now?

Papikunju's son Gangaduttan lived in that house like burr on a dog. He was unable to come to terms with either his stepfather or Panchami. Gangaduttan was a young man. He was a burden to Papikunju. Just as Panchami wondered about his presence there, it seemed he too asked himself what he was doing there. As if he felt that it had been wrong on his mother's part to have accepted the protection of another man. Perhaps she had done this to leach him off her. She hadn't done it just to ensure a life for herself.

The taste of the food at Pallikunnath when Chembankunju had gone there to buy his boat still lingered on his tongue. His concept of pleasure in life was born of that meal. He had thought that he would eat food like that three times a day now. But the curries didn't taste like what he had eaten at Pallikunnath; it just didn't seem to be the same. His meals didn't give him a sense of relish or satiation.

Chakki had been unable to lie on the bed she had bought. Neither had the mattress been ready. As far as she was concerned, there hadn't been time for that. Many things had to be accomplished before the time was right. She had neither been able to rid the tan off her skin nor plump herself up.

Chembankunju had a mattress made. It was covered in the same cloth as was used in the mattress at Pallikunnath. But he felt as if Papikunju was losing her looks. Would even fair ones lose their complexion in the stiff breeze from this sea? It seemed as if Papikunju had lost her radiance.

He played in his mind the scene he had recounted to Chakki with some embarrassment. It had been that which had always rounded and coloured his concept of pleasure. When Papikunju entered the room, he too followed her in.

But there was no heat to that kiss. No heights or depths could be reached. Their hands wouldn't clasp tightly enough. Neither did it last long. 'My Chak...' was what emerged from his mouth in that moment of release. And she too muttered another name. Perhaps the name she had used to call Kandankoran Valakkaran by.

It just didn't seem possible for them to be one. There were two people between them. Chakki and Kandankoran Valakkaran. Chakki's and Kandankoran's manner had been different. Perhaps if Chembankunju and Papikunju had been together in their youth, things would have been different.

There was an effort to introduce laughter and frolic into the house. There were smiles, a parody of a smile with no real mirth. And play-acting of merrymaking.

This new life had a form. But with it Chembankunju also sensed a smouldering within. An unknown undefined anxiety raged in him. He couldn't stay idle. He wasn't used to that.

Dressed in a mulmul mundu and draping a fine cloth with a narrow lined border on his shoulder, he would go to the shore as the boats returned. He would trade the catch. That was how Kandankoran Valakkaran had been. But was this the old Chembankunju?

With Chakki gone, his desire to move up in life too had disappeared. Now he was turning into Pallikunnath Kandankoran.

Even though he didn't have much to do, Chembankunju's looks didn't improve. He lost some of his tan. But it was a faint change in pallor.

One day Chembankunju told Papikunju, 'These days the takings are meagre.'

Papikunju had nothing to say about that. Perhaps she had never spoken on such matters. She wasn't used to it. He continued, 'This is not the kind of earnings I used to bring back. My takings are based on the boat, nets and the helm oar … and was always twice as much as any other boat!'

Despite stating a fact, Chembankunju's face wore a glimmer of embarrassment. He went on, 'And when I entrusted it to my Chakki, she would stretch and make it grow and grow...'

He described all the various things Chakki had done to make money for them. Going to the east to sell fish, helping build Kambavalas, and drying fish – he told her about all of this. As he spoke, he glanced at Papikunju. He saw sorrow on her face.

Suddenly he said, 'I don't mean that you should do any of that! Chakki was used to it ever since she was a girl. But you are not like that.'

But Chembankunju realized that Papikunju was unhappy as she couldn't do any of what Chakki had managed. Everything there, including the bed they slept on, was a result of Chakki's efforts.

And then there was Gangaduttan who pestered his mother all day. She had promised to help him make a life. But nothing had happened as of yet. It was necessary to send him away at the very earliest. He said, 'I am frightened of that girl's glare. She will say something nasty very soon. I have to leave before that!'

How could she find some money to send Gangaduttan away? Papikunju knew there was no money. And she didn't want to ask Chembankunju either.

Panchami had a new plan. She stayed by her father all the time. She, it seemed, wouldn't allow Papikunju a chance to get close to Chembankunju. Nor did Papikunju make an attempt to push her away.

She had lived well. All of it was ruined now. When there was nothing else left, Chembankunju had become her means to her future. And that was how Papikunju had got there.

It hadn't been a need for sensual pleasure that had made her accept a new husband. If there had been another way she wouldn't have chosen to put on this guise as wife. She was only pretending to be a wife. Play-acting. Yet Papikunju was loyal to her protector. She neither tried to establish her rights nor did she demand them. She listened to his bidding.

Chakki had helped make money for Chembankunju. And perhaps Papikunju was ashamed that she couldn't be of such assistance to her husband. Chembankunju may not have expected that of her, but shouldn't she have nurtured such an aspiration? Had Chakki given Chembankunju permission to marry a woman like her? Surely not! Chakki would have wished for a wife who could have been the wife she was. A woman who knew how to lay a foundation to build a great big family upon. And a woman who took care of her husband's each and every creature comfort.

As for Panchami, she was a headstrong girl. She cared little for her stepmother. She would make faces at Gangaduttan. Everything she did indicated what she thought: they had no business being there.

One day as Papikunju walked, Panchami trailed her mocking Papikunju's gait. When Papikunju turned suddenly, she saw Panchami ridiculing her. Nallapennu was standing by her house laughing. Papikunju began crying.

When Chembankunju came home, Papikunju said, 'You need to bring this girl up properly.'

Chembankunju wanted to know what the matter was. She was evasive. 'She will have to live in another home one day. The love we have for her should be contained in our hearts. She's turning into a monster!'

Chembankunju persisted in knowing what the matter was. Papikunju was scared that he wouldn't like her finding fault with his daughter. So it was with much hesitation that she spoke. Chembankunju was worried about his motherless child. So Papikunju said with great care, 'She treats me with disdain. It is all the neighbour's doing!'

Chembankunju called Panchami. She was standing towards the northern part of the house. She was frightened by his summons. She came after he had hollered a few times. Papikunju pleaded that Chembankunju mustn't punish her. Nevertheless, in a flash of anger, he slapped Panchami twice. Not because he was angry with her but to show his disgust for the neighbours.

Panchami wailed, calling out for her mother. It broke everyone's heart. Nallapennu came running and held her. She asked Papikunju, 'What is it, woman? Are you planning to do away with this motherless child?'

Papikunju retorted, 'I don't want her spoilt!'

In it was suppressed her resentment for the neighbours. Nallapennu demanded, 'What do you mean she is spoilt?'

Nallapennu turned to Chembankunju and continued, 'You mustn't listen to her and hurt your daughter!'

Papikunju asked Nallapennu, 'What business of yours is it?'

'It's to me that Chakki, the woman who made all this, entrusted this child as she lay dying!'

Papikunju might have been a timid creature but she too was a fisherwoman. The fisher wife in her was aroused. She said, 'Hold your tongue! This is Papikunju, the woman who once lived with Pallikunnath Kandankoran!'

Nallapennu's retort was a slap on her face. 'Now you are Chembankunju's wife; and what you are eating is what Chakki made. So back off, will you?'

Chembankunju stood helplessly. Papikunju forgot herself in her anger. 'What is it to you? Who is Chembankunju to you?'

'You … bloody woman … you,' Nallapennu was speechless with rage. Then she claimed her right. Not as Chembankunju's other woman but as the wife of her husband's friend. The men went to sea together when they started their lives and it was because of Chembankunju that her children had food to eat. She loved her fisherman. That was her claim on Chembankunju.

Ever since the day Chakki came to this house they were friends; they were one. They might have quarrelled but they loved each other. That was her claim. Nallapennu reiterated how Chakki in her deathbed had asked her to be responsible for Panchami. Then she went on to speak of her bond of love with Karuthamma and Panchami from the moment they were born. 'I didn't have a place for them in my belly but they grew up as my children. That's my right!'

Nallapennu looked at Chembankunju and asked, 'Chembankunju accha, you must get rid of this double-faced woman … I'll bring up Panchami!'

She continued, 'You deserve this! You killed that nice woman, with your ambitions. You are a greedy man. You sent your older child away on a nowhere road. And now there's this child. In the end there will be … I am not going to say anything more!'

Nallapennu's anger wouldn't quell. Her ire turned to Papikunju. 'On this shore, when our fishermen die, we don't go off with another man. That's how we are!'

Papikunju couldn't restrain Nallapennu's vicious tongue. Neither could Chembankunju. After a while, the rage subsided but she still wasn't ready to relinquish her right over Panchami. She asked, 'Are you coming with me, girl?'

Chembankunju stood stupefied. Nallapennu was calling for his daughter. Panchami followed her.

Papikunju had never been so insulted in her life. She had had to listen to such abuse; what was left to be said? Unable to bear her sorrow and anger, she asked, 'I was living a quiet dignified life. Did you bring me here for this?'

Chembankunju stood there helplessly, unable to speak. Papikunju continued, 'Fisherwomen have never talked in this manner to me, who was born into the family of the Shore Master of Ponnani.'

To console her, Chembankunju said, 'These creatures are like this!'

'But you still remained silent!'

'What could I have done?'

Gritting her teeth, Papikunju mumbled, 'What do you want me to do now?'

She continued, 'I lived with a good man once ... now it's my fate...'

Chembankunju had to pay for the abuse she had to endure from Nallapennu. Her anger was directed towards Panchami. 'Your precious daughter went with Nallapennu when she asked her to.'

Chembankunju said, 'The two girls were brought up by her.'

'So!' Unable to suppress her rage, Papikunju cursed, 'That one's also going to be a slut like her older sister.'

Chembankunju was shaken up. It was a fierce curse. His older daughter was no longer his child. All he had left was Panchami. Would she also not be his?

Papikunju wouldn't stop. It didn't matter if her life was shattered but she wouldn't stop till she had spoken her mind. 'This one will also turn out to be the same. Like her elder sister, she too will entice some Muslim boy and frolic on these shores!'

Lightning flashed in Chembankunju's head. There was nothing more to be asked or said.

Enticed a Muslim boy?

The story became clear now. The enthusiasm to return

Pareekutty's money. In an instant everything made sense now. She, she ... Had Chakki too been party to this? That was all he needed to know.

Chembankunju felt his senses leave him. He ran to Nallapennu's home. He dragged Panchami off Nallapennu's lap, took a stick and flailed her with blows. He kept asking her if she too would entice a Muslim boy. Nallapennu stood with her mouth open. Panchami kept crying out for her mother. Between blows, he screamed, 'Tell me you won't lead on a Muslim boy, tell me...!'

When it seemed he wouldn't stop, she said, 'I won't lead on a Muslim boy, Accha.'

Poor girl! She didn't even know what she was saying. Or perhaps she did. Hadn't she too seen all of it?

He chased her back into his house.

That day Chembankunju was seen digging up Chakki's grave. Who knew what he was thinking of? Perhaps he wished to question her himself.

Eighteen

Chembankunju's fit of madness disappeared in a few days. But he seemed to have fallen apart. He became silent. He seemed defeated, devoid of all hope. Look at it from his point of view. How else would he be? Money began dwindling. Now that could be endured. All the material goods accumulated until then too disappeared. If his senses hadn't taken leave of him, imagine his plight? How could he have looked the world in the eye?

Chembankunju's two boats needed repairs. They were unfit to be put out to sea. The nets too had several holes; they hadn't been mended on time. A mackerel net was torn to tatters by a pig. He needed a big sum of money urgently. The family had many expenses to meet. And he didn't go to the shore as he once used to.

Papikunju was the one responsible about many things now. She talked to Chembankunju about repairing the boats and mending the nets. There was nothing to be done but borrow the money. Chembankunju agreed to take a loan.

But whom was he to borrow the money from? There was no one on that shore but Ousep. When her mother was alive, Panchami had made some money selling white bait. She brought out the twenty rupees she had put aside and gave it to her father. Chembankunju took it in his hands and burst into tears. Panchami said, 'If I had been able to pick the fry every day, I would have had more…' She continued, 'Or even if Ammachi had been alive…'

Chembankunju didn't speak. Strong emotions didn't stir his heart any more.

Gangaduttan began insisting that he wanted to be sent away. But Papikunju hadn't been able to present his case yet to Chembankunju. She was having to put up with so much merely to survive, to be able to look after Gangaduttan. Panchami hadn't ceased in her run of cruelty. Papikunju even felt that Gangaduttan didn't have the right to eat in that house. Above all else was Chembankunju's diminished faculties. She had never ever thought things would turn out to be like this.

Papikunju hadn't thought Chembankunju would be so destroyed. She hadn't meant to devastate him. He was her protector, after all.

Perhaps she was unhappy that she wasn't able to make money like Chakki had. If she could have gone east to sell fish or knew how to build a Kambavala, things might have been better. It was only natural that she began thinking on those lines.

Papikunju had nursed a husband. That she knew how to. She loved Chembankunju too. It was impossible to not love him. But Chembankunju had to make his place in a slot that had once been occupied by another man. Just as she had to find her place in a home that had been filled by another woman. Like Chembankunju thought of Chakki in his moments of crisis, it was Kandankoran Valakkaran she thought of when she needed counsel. Perhaps she was begging for his forgiveness.

Papikunju knew no peace. Everything was falling apart. And at times she was plagued by a guilt that she had been the cause of it all. Chembankunju had prospered when Chakki was around.

And was ruined when Papikunju took her place. Chakki was the wife of a fisherman. And Papikunju that of a netsman.

The boats were beached on the shore. Papikunju feared the outcome. She decided to send for Ousep. After dinner, when Chembankunju sat lost in thought, Papikunju went to him and asked, 'How can you sit around like this? Don't we need to repair the boats?'

He looked up and into her face. He didn't speak. She asked again. 'Yes,' he replied and retreated into a silence. Ideally a discussion should have followed.

She asked, 'Shall I send for Ousep?'

'Call him.' The answer came quickly. Did he even realize what he was saying? Chembankunju knew more than anyone else on that shore what it meant to borrow money from a shark like Ousep. So didn't that mean that he had spoken without contemplating it seriously? Would he have said that if he had deliberated about it? He didn't seem too concerned about his boats lying idle on the shore.

In that house, such after-dinner scenes had been played out before. Discussions regarding the laying of a firm foundation for a future. In those days the witness to those discussions had been a wick in a broken kerosene lamp. In those days Chembankunju used to be sharp and vigorously bright, and with him was his Chakki who had come to him as a child bride. They would think deep into the future. Within the hut their two children lay asleep lost in pleasant dreams. Now Panchami squirmed in the coils of a nightmare.

Papikunju asked, 'What should I do?'

He didn't speak. She continued, 'I am a burden. I am unable to manage things. What do you want me to do? I am used to being fed by what the man brings home!'

Chembankunju listened to her silently. Papikunju began to

weep. 'How many people have I ruined? The moment I stepped in here, everything was ruined.'

Chembankunju's mouth opened. 'So what about that now?'

'What do you want me to do?'

'Do something!'

Gangaduttan began insisting for five hundred rupees. Papikunju had dragged him into this life. So she had to give him what he demanded. How she did it was none of his business. Chembankunju was obliged to pay up. He had bought Papikunju's affections. Gangaduttan's mother had sold herself to another man. In Gangaduttan was Kandankoran Valakkaran. Sometimes Papikunju felt it was Kandankoran standing there and demanding money and more from her.

Papikunju sent a man to fetch Ousep. She told him about what had to be done. Ousep agreed to lend them the money. But the two boats and nets would have to be pledged. If the principal and interest were not paid back in time, the boats and nets would be his.

Chembankunju didn't speak. Ousep asked, 'Chembankunju, why don't you say something?'

Chembankunju said, 'What am I to say? I need the money anyway.'

The next day Ousep brought a letter of agreement. Chembankunju didn't even bother reading it. He signed it. Ousep counted out seven hundred ninety-five rupees. He said there were certain expenses that were paid out from the balance five rupees. Chembankunju locked up the money in a box.

It seemed that the silence in him had begun to abate. He began talking a bit: About having the boats repaired. And that the money had to be paid back within the stipulated time. Or, it would be big trouble. Ousep was a heartless man. Papikunju promised to do her best.

Perhaps Gangaduttan sensed the presence of money. Or perhaps not. But he began pestering Papikunju like never before. He had to be sent away. He couldn't bear to stay there, not even for half an hour. Papikunju pleaded with him. Let the boats be repaired and put out to sea. She would find him the money he needed.

He was adamant. 'I can't wait that long!'

Papikunju grew angry. 'If you can't, that's up to you. What more do you expect of me?'

'In which case you can forget you have me as a son.'

Papikunju could find nothing to respond to that. She was his mother; the woman who had given birth to him. She had trampled upon the memories of his father and come to Chembankunju.

Helplessly she asked, 'How can I ask that man?'

'Amma, you have to find a way to send me off.'

He wouldn't listen, no matter what she said. His implication was that only if she were to send him away would she be Chembankunju's alone.

'It's also for your sake, son, that I came here!'

'That may be so. But you have to let me go.'

Papikunju didn't have the courage to broach this uneasy subject to Chembankunju. But it was growing to a point where it couldn't be contained in secrecy any more.

Papikunju was agitated. Chembankunju behaved as if everything he owned was no longer his. And on the other hand was Gangaduttan's insistence. She shouldn't have taken up with another man. But then how was she to live? How could she have known that there would be such troubles ... she wished she hadn't ventured into this at all. Neither would she have had to put up with Gangaduttan's demands nor with Chembankunju's unhappiness. She had begun her life on a fault line. If she had been an ordinary fisherwoman, she could have put a basket on her head and gone east to sell fish. She could have eked out a living in that manner. Everything had gone wrong. She had thought that she was attaching herself to a prosperous boat owner. What was the future going to be like?

In that fierce tussle within her, it was the mother who triumphed. It was only the mother who could be victorious. At the worst, she would have to starve, beg … and Papikunju had the courage to endure that. What was her tie with this house? If she were to think about it, nothing at all. If Chembankunju was ruined, well, she would starve. But if Gangaduttan could be sent off with some money and he flourished, she would too. And if she did, surely Chembankunju would too. And so the mother in her won that battle.

One day when Chembankunju was not there, Papikunju opened his box. Panchami wasn't there either. She took two hundred-rupee notes from the bundle Ousep had given them. She locked the box and secured it once again.

That night Panchami saw the mother and son huddled to the west of the hut whispering. She tried to hide behind a coconut palm and eavesdropped. Panchami made some sense of what was being said. Papikunju was asking him to be content with two hundred rupees for now. The rest would be found later.

The son went away with his mother's blessings. The mother watched her son. Her eyes filled. She wiped her face and came back in.

Panchami had a new weapon. She decided to make use of it. Stepmother had given her son some money. She didn't realize that it was from the money that Chembankunju had kept aside. But she had no doubts where that money had come from. It was from their home. She would whisper that secret to her father. While her father had to pledge his boats and nets because he had no money, stepmother had money of her own. And it was that she had given her son.

The next morning when Chembankunju went out to the shore, Panchami too went along.

A little later he rushed in like a mad man. Chembankunju opened the box and peered inside. There was only five hundred rupees there. The next instant there was a bellow. 'Did you take the money from here?'

Papikunju confessed; she confessed everything. Unable to contain his anger, he shook. His decree emerged as yet another roar, 'Get out of my house!'

Papikunju stepped out silently. Panchami was pleased with it. 'Go to the shore!'

Papikunju walked to the shore. He shut the door. 'Don't dare enter this house again!'

Papikunju didn't answer that either.

On that long, long shore, a hapless destitute woman wandered. Once Kandankoran's wife, now Chembankunju's wife.

Once again from somewhere aggression and vitality shot through Chembankunju. The vim and vigour that had dulled and diminished for sometime now surfaced.

That Chembankunju had thrown out Papikunju from his home spread like wildfire through the shore. Papikunju was seated under a coconut palm on the seashore. Where could she go? There was no place on this earth. Neither did it seem that Chembankunju's heart would eventually melt. But the matter couldn't be left alone to resolve itself, everyone there said. A destitute woman wandering on that shore!

The elders of the community got together and went to the Shore Master. Right from the beginning the Shore Master had not been happy about her choosing to make a life with Chembankunju. This woman belonged to the Ponnani Shore

Master's family and had been Pallikunnath Kandankoran's wife. It had seemed a slight to Shore Masters everywhere. Which is why he didn't want to hear a thing about a woman who had no respect for tradition, he said adamantly. The Shore Master was furious. But the elders wouldn't budge either. This was a serious issue. A woman with no place to sleep during the night was on the shore. Was that right?

The Shore Master said, 'Do what you want! Beat him or her to death and fling them in the sea!'

Ayankunju asked humbly, 'How is that possible, sir?'

'What else do you want me to say?'

'You must call for Chembankunju and talk to him.'

'I can't. What can I tell him?'

'What are we to do then? Who else is to resolve such matters?'

Faced by that question from the elders of the community, the master and protector of the shore had to bow down. Something had to be done.

A woman from a Shore Master's family was wandering like a vagrant on this shore. The Shore Master said, 'This is the result of forgetting traditions and values. Would something like this have happened to her if she was in a Shore Master's family?'

All of them agreed with what he said.

The stepmother who had usurped her mother's place was cast out. Everything was clean again. Panchami clung to her father. She had something to accomplish. She was looking for an opportunity to broach the subject.

The subject was trivial. There was no one at home. Why don't they fetch her elder sister back? If that happened, the house would be the home it once was.

That Ammachi was not there would be its only shortcoming.

But if Karuthamma was there, Panchami could bear even that. But she couldn't find the right moment to bring it up.

Chembankunju wasn't idle even for a moment. He was serious all the time. With that reawakened vitality and strength, he seemed a different man. He had decided to revert back to being the Chembankunju he once was. He kept finding fault with everyone all the time. Papikunju was an omen of destruction; from the moment her shadow fell on this house, ruin set in. He was cursed the moment he decided to marry her.

'I think my brains must have been addled then! I was smitten by her skin, her hair and her curves!' That was what he claimed. He spoke about Karuthamma as well. She enticed a Muslim and then when a fisherman appeared, she went after him. She wasn't his daughter. She had ceased to exist for him.

Occasionally, he would ask Panchami, 'What will you turn out to be?'

He didn't trust her either.

He was going to start a new life. So what if in the middle there had been a run of foolishness.

Nallapennu took Papikunju to her home. Panchami was upset to see that comet of destruction stationed close by rather than sent to some distant part of the universe. She could have borne it if anyone else had done it. When her mother was dying, it was to Nallapennu that Panchami had been entrusted. So why was her foster-mother now turning traitor?

Chembankunju too was rubbed raw by this. But he found an explanation for that as well. Achakunju had always been envious of him.

Panchami felt a compromise would take place one of these days. But before that chechi had to be brought home. And finally after biding her time for a long while she said, 'Accha, why don't you ask chechi to come home? She is a simple girl. Everything said about her is all lies!'

Chembankunju shook in anger. 'Whom do you want brought here, you brat?'

Panchami grew frightened.

'That Muslim's shack may be in pieces, but he still lives on this shore. I am not going to let a slut like her enter my home.'

Panchami didn't speak. Chembankunju asked, 'Do you also want to do the same as she did? In which case, you can get out right now!'

Chembankunju's anger grew by the moment. He lost control, forgetting the place and himself, and shouted, 'Get out! Get out!' It seemed as if he was going to kick her too out of his home.

Chembankunju began ranting about Karuthamma. And then about Panchami. She too was going to take after Karuthamma! He left Papikunju alone. He had stopped talking about her. Karuthamma and Panchami now became the objects of his ire.

Meanwhile, the Shore Master arrived there to examine the situation. The elders of the community, Chembankunju and Papikunju were sent for. It was a momentous event. A great many people gathered there. There was only one person praying fervently that no compromise be arrived at: Panchami.

'My mother of the sea, my departed ammachi, let that not happen!' That was her silent prayer.

The Shore Master called Chembankunju and asked, 'What is all this, Chembankunju? Why are you behaving as if you have no regard for norms and rules?'

The Shore Master had many serious accusations. He had married again without asking for his permission. What was his explanation for that?

It was a very serious crime. Chembankunju should have

offered betel leaves and tobacco to the Shore Master and sought his blessings before he brought Papikunju home.

Everyone waited to see how Chembankunju would respond. Along with others, Achakunju too was one among the involved. They too were obliged to respond to that accusation. Some of them began moving away slowly.

The Shore Master demanded with the authority vested in him, 'Tell me, Chembankunju, why?'

Chembankunju stood straight. It seemed he had grown taller and wider. He didn't give a toss, his face set into a grave expression. No one had ever seen a Chembankunju like the one standing there!

The Shore Master repeated his query. An answer shot out like a bullet. 'I didn't marry her.'

It wasn't what she expected to hear. All of them were shaken up. The Shore Master sat down gulping. When he recovered, he said, 'How do you explain the presence of this woman then?'

'I brought a woman to work for me. What's wrong in that?'

The Shore Master was defeated. His first accusation had crumbled to dust.

All the other accusations too fell apart.

Papikunju was summoned. The Shore Master examined from head to toe the woman who had flung custom and norms to the wind. He asked her, 'Is that the truth, woman?'

Everyone expected her to deny what Chembankunju had claimed. Chembankunju didn't seem too concerned even then. He didn't seem to care if she replied that all he had said were lies. It seemed as if he had decided to disregard and disrespect everything. He wasn't going to give in to anything.

The Shore Master repeated his question to Papikunju. A little word that astounded everyone slipped out. 'Yes.'

'So Chembankunju didn't marry you?'

'No.'

'So were you a maid here?'

'Yes.'

The honourable Shore Master was unable to speak for a while. Chembankunju himself hadn't expected to hear such a response. The Shore Master looked at Papikunju, who had just buried her honour, with the disgust meted out to one who has brought dishonour to her family and said, 'You deserve all of this! You who once lived with a decent man...'

He didn't finish his sentence. But neither was he going to let Chembankunju who stood there completely unconcerned go scot-free. He asked Chembankunju, 'Even if she is a maid, you can't throw a woman out.'

There was an immediate answer to that. 'She is a thief!'

Again the Shore Master was dumbstruck.

Even if it all sounded right, that wasn't the truth. Everyone knew that. Papikunju had been offered a podava by Chembankunju and brought home.

The Shore Master thought of a new trick. He decided to frighten Chembankunju. 'Your arrogance is a little too much. Not just now. But always. Do you know what the outcome of that is?'

With a mocking curl of his lip, Chembankunju asked, 'What's to know? What new thing will you tell me now? Chembankunju gives a toss for Chembankunju knows he has the sea in front of him and the sky above him!'

He continued, 'I have nothing to lose. Everything is over. I am not going to listen to anyone, so please don't get me wrong. I have no intention of obeying anyone. Tell me ... Why should I? Only the man burdened by money need fear his every step!'

The Shore Master threatened him, 'Don't mess with us!'

Even before the Shore Master finished speaking,

Chembankunju spoke up, his body trembling in indignation, 'Quiet! If you want to keep your dignity, stay silent…'

No one had ever spoken to the Shore Master in that manner. And that too in the presence of the whole fishing community. He wasn't just insulting a man; he was insulting the entire community.

What was Chembankunju thinking of? Was he mad? Wasn't he thinking of what was to come? No one understood a thing.

Chembankunju walked away without saying another word.

The Shore Master was insulted. The rest of the people stood there looking at each other's faces. Papikunju followed Chembankunju.

All that Panchami had hoped for was ruined. She stood watching Papikunju follow Chembankunju.

Chembankunju didn't ask Papikunju to go away.

Nineteen

The next day Panchami went missing. Where was she? The poor child had run away to escape her lot, the women said. She had been chased away, they added.

All the women there had a certain respect for Papikunju now. She didn't betray Chembankunju. Would any other woman have done that? Papikunju was a decent sort. There was nothing to be surprised about that. She had once been a noble and valorous man's woman. So that was how she would be.

Everyone waited to see what would happen to Chembankunju who had insulted the Shore Master. How was he going to bear the Shore Master's wrath? Who was to know what form that displeasure would take? Not just that. The two boats would end up being Ousep's. How would he live then? There was no way he could go to work in the sea.

Meanwhile, away from all this commotion and gossip, another life was falling apart on that shore. A life with no purpose and yet there wouldn't be a Neerkunnath without its presence.

Pareekutty! Neerkunnath had many boats, shacks, fishermen, fisherwomen, and then there was Pareekutty. He too was part of that shore. Once in a while he would sit on a boat hauled up on the sands and sing. After its many renderings the song had acquired a particular tune. A style and tune that were his. No one else sang that song as he did. Had he, that son of the sea, ever thought his verses would take this form? Pareekutty had made it his. With him that style and tune would cease to be. No one else could sing it as he did.

Pareekutty's shack fell apart. It crumbled into dust. On that shore there had been other shacks; and some that had been ruined. The ruined shack owners were never seen again. But he continued to live on this shore. Didn't he have another place to go to? Perhaps not.

In the twilight, he would be seen walking on that shore with a downcast face. As if he was searching for something lost among the grains of sand. Wasn't that the truth? A life was lost in the sand. It had to be sought for and found.

Once or twice he had been the subject of discussion. Each time there had been rumours about his having enticed and seduced Karuthamma! But it would also die quickly. So many shack owners had seduced so many women; and then left these shores, until even the gossip came to nothing. No one took it very seriously. No one really knew the gravitas of that relationship. Could a Muslim shack owner be in love with a fisher girl? No one said love couldn't happen. But it had never happened before. That's the fact.

Hence no one had heard about the shattering of that love.

Even today when the boats drew to the shore, Pareekutty would go there. He would watch the trade. He would eke a living out of brokering some deals. That was how he lived.

He would go and stand by Chembankunju's hauled-up boats and gaze at it. Perhaps he did that when memories kindled within him. Perhaps he was reminiscing about the history of those boats. Once, as he was standing there, Chembankunju came there unexpectedly. He didn't see Chembankunju approaching.

Pareekutty hadn't met Chembankunju in a long time.

Whenever he saw Chembankunju in the distance, he would take a detour. What was the nature of his crime? Yes, Pareekutty had actually perpetuated a crime against Chembankunju!

When Chembankunju suddenly drew close to him, Pareekutty was dismayed. The man who stood before him was neither the Chembankunju of yesteryear nor was he Chembankunju's ghost. In one glance he could make out that something was amiss with Chembankunju. And did Chembankunju too see the Pareekutty that he once knew?

A moment was spent sizing up each other.

Chembankunju flung a question at Pareekutty, 'How much money do I owe you?'

Pareekutty had never bothered to keep track of accounts. He didn't know. He had no idea.

Chembankunju asked, 'How much?'

Pareekutty didn't know what to answer back. He had nothing to receive; neither did Chembankunju owe him anything. There was so much to be said. But he was afraid of saying it. He was as tongue-tied as a borrower. The creditor in him was strangled to silence.

What was the real nature of that give and take? Pareekutty was in love with Karuthamma and Karuthamma had loved him in turn. That was the truth. And that love was without a blemish. The deal with Chembankunju and Chakki had been brokered in the days when that love was blossoming. Even then, as he lent the money, he had said he didn't want it back! So had he meant to have her parents obliged to him to facilitate the smooth progress of that love? To blind them with cash? Bribing them to get the girl! But that couldn't be. Pareekutty had never sought to entice or seduce Karuthamma; he hadn't even tried to. So shouldn't he have asked for the money back when another man made her his and took her away? When a job couldn't be done, doesn't one take back the bribe? Did he give the money because she asked him to? In which case, it wasn't given in secret.

For lack of that money, he had been ruined. Not just ruined, but completely penurious for he only had the clothes on his back. His house and land were no longer his. Nothing was left in Pareekutty's life. There was neither a purpose nor a goal. Couldn't he start a shack in a small manner? Make something of his life again? If for nothing else but to keep him going till death. Karuthamma would never be his. He should forget that episode in his life. Faced with harsh experiences and impediments in life, men changed, became different. But even today he was that hapless lover.

Chembankunju undid a pouch from his waist. He asked again, 'How much is it, boy?'

There was no answer. Pareekutty stood there guilt-ridden. Chembankunju continued, 'I thought you were a good sort. But you, you … are not.'

But what sin had Pareekutty committed? Had he deceived Karuthamma? Had he created impediments to stop her wedding? Had he trespassed into her marital life and made trouble there? What had he done?

He had fallen in love. He hadn't chosen to. Not to bring trouble to her family or her. He was born a man and so fell in love with a woman. And even then he had walked away from her life. But he still stood there as if he had transgressed. Chembankunju said, 'You gave me the money then only because of my daughter, isn't that right?'

'No,' the reply rolled up his throat. But it wasn't spoken. Shouldn't Pareekutty have refuted Chembankunju's accusation with a 'no'? He didn't do that. Chembankunju said, 'The moment I asked for it, you swept up everything and gave it to me. Without any hesitation. I thought you did that because you were naïve. But that wasn't so. You had an ulterior motive.'

Chembankunju undid the pouch and began counting out the money. Suddenly he asked, 'Do you know the implication of your crime?'

Pareekutty was still as a statue. Sans any emotion, sans any thought. Chembankunju's eyes were moist. 'You don't know; you really don't know ... but how would you? You are a demon.'

Pareekutty didn't speak.

'You wrecked a family. Ruined it. Turned my life into nothing. Do you know how many lives you have destroyed?'

It's time to take a look at that family's history. From the time when in their quest to acquire a boat and nets Chakki took a basketful of fish to the east to as it was now. If one were to look at that history as a whole, doesn't that accusation carry some bearing?

Chembankunju's voice quivered as he spoke, 'My Karuthamma who like Chakki had played and frolicked on this shore ... you ruined her. It began since then ... isn't that what this is all about?'

That was true indeed. If Pareekutty wasn't in love with Karuthamma, none of this would have transpired. In normal course, a fisher family with a purpose would have made some progress on that shore. But a destiny as Chembankunju had hoped for would have remained a mere illusion. For Chembankunju was a brawny fisherman who tussled with natural forces constantly and was a man whose life was dictated by the norms of that community. What did Chembankunju have now? Neither a wife nor children; and the boats he had worked for relentlessly were gone. No nets, nothing was left ... even his special relationship had fallen apart. When all of it was counted, there were five hundred ninety-five rupees left. That was all he had after a lifetime of Chakki's and his efforts. And an old debt remained.

Like an evil worm, Pareekutty had bored and wriggled into

the annals of that family's history. A flame had been lit to make it shrivel in its path. So wasn't it right for Chembankunju to question him? If Pareekutty was a man with some humanity, he ought to curse that day when he first came to this shore as a little boy clinging to his father's hand. That day Chembankunju's family too came under the evil influence of Saturn ... but on that day the girl who came to pick the small fry fallen off the boats had looked at him without blinking. He had asked her for a small pink shell she had picked. 'Will you give it to me?'

She gave him the shell. But didn't she give her heart too with the shell?

But he was not responsible for all this. Pareekutty hadn't insinuated himself into the family wanting to do so. He had stepped into the inner rhythm of that family unknowingly. He could be accused of many things. And Pareekutty might stand as befitting one accused. But who was to know his truth? And how could he let anyone know? Only one person knew it – Karuthamma. But did even she accept it? When she saw him, thought of him, wasn't she struck by anxiety? He had turned into an object of fear for her. Pareekutty. That was he.

Chembankunju said, 'I only have one liability left. Your debt. The money you gave me to seduce my daughter and ruin me ... Here!'

He stretched out the money.

Pareekutty stood frozen. Chembankunju said again, 'Here ... here take it!'

'Hmm,' a grunt.

It was a grave command. Pareekutty stretched out his hand mechanically. Chembankunju put the money into his hand.

'This is all there is. I don't know what I owe you. That only my Chakki knew. If it is less, there is nothing I can do.'

Chembankunju began walking.

Pareekutty stood there for long, clutching the money. He was dazed and confused.

What did he need money for? What need for money for someone who lived off what he made every day? How much money had he lost? Just money? He had lost his very life itself. He had money for the day's food. So when life stretched ahead, wasn't this sizable sum of money a huge thing? An old debt was being paid back.

Pareekutty looked at his hand. He was clutching the money. The ends of the notes were fluttering in the breeze. What did he need the money for? Had he ever considered it would be his? So how could it be his? So whose was it then?

Hearing loud laughter, Pareekutty trembled and turned. A little away, the boat that Chembankunju had bought from Kandankoran was hauled up to rest on two logs on the sand. It had been there for several days now. For many many days now its stern was inclined upwards. As if the stern was staring at the sea, at something beyond the horizon. Something was beckoning it from there. The sea and the outer seas were old friends. Not just that, wasn't it too part of the ocean. Shouldn't it live on the ocean? It was built for the ocean. For days now, it has been longing to race into the sea. All it needed was one touch, and it would ride the waves, cutting and slicing through the water. And through currents and streams it would weave its way into the deep seas.

How long am I to sit on this shore? Look at me, my body is cracked and broken by the piercing rays of the sun. Won't you let me into the delightful depths of that brine? It seemed to say.

The wind that rose from the water might cool it a bit. That was Pallikunnath Kandankoran's boat. It was Chembankunju's boat. The boat with the biggest catch; an elegant boat; a boat that flew like a bird.

The other end of it was slanted into a heap as if to say it was going.

It was from that side of the boat that the piercing laughter had risen. It was a cold, mirthless laugh. Chembankunju was laughing.

The sisters embraced each other. Neither of them knew how long they stood there. The two of them were crying. Karuthamma had left defying her father and seeing her mother sink onto her deathbed. She had carried with her for a long distance the echoes of her little sister's plaintive 'e-che-chi!' That call had resounded in Karuthamma's ears many times again. Since then so much had happened. Amma had died. A stepmother had come ... and finally now the sisters met.

Panchami whose plans had collapsed had headed straight to Trikunnapuzha. Where else could she go? Panchami's arrival was unexpected. Palani stood gazing at the weeping sisters locked in an embrace. The baby in his arms gurgled and laughed. It was prattling. The baby seemed to be enjoying the sight too.

Palani asked, 'Who is this now? Panchami? How did you come here?'

Before Panchami could reply, Karuthamma took the baby. It leapt into Panchami's arms from hers. Karuthamma said, 'This is my baby's aunt!'

Panchami covered the baby with kisses. She had been dreaming of it all this while. Palani didn't ask anything about Neerkunnath. He had nothing to ask about that place. What ties did he have with it? Nothing at all.

Karuthamma had much to talk and discover about. And Panchami too had much to say. Palani didn't care about who or what Karuthamma was curious about; in fact he hated the very thought. He didn't even like the mention of 'Neerkunnath!'

Perhaps he didn't dislike Panchami. A simple little girl. Why should he dislike her? She was blameless. But where was she coming from? And whose news did she bring with her? Palani wasn't seeing the orphaned Panchami. What he saw was a black shadow enter his house that would turn Karuthamma's thoughts towards everything that was repugnant to him. What would Karuthamma remember when she saw Panchami who had come from Neerkunnath? What would she ask? Whom would she enquire about?

Palani wasn't enthusiastic. Once again a black shadow fell upon that house. There was an unhappiness. The baby's prattle alone lit up with an occasional flash the grey mass of gloom in that house. That baby never cried; it never had to. But now the baby began crying. Then Panchami would say, 'Echechi, don't make the baby cry!'

She would pick the baby up and try to comfort it. The baby liked this 'little mother'.

Nothing could be asked or spoken. Everyone seemed to be holding their breath. Everything had to be heard or said away from Palani's hearing. And that moment couldn't be found.

Palani was perhaps curious to know what she would ask about. It was quite possible. And if so, how could you blame Palani? He was a husband and a father. Karuthamma had sworn and made promises. Nevertheless, her heart had once been someone else's. What certainty did he have that the Muslim didn't live there even now in some secret place? Even if that wasn't the case, it was only natural that a husband, any committed husband, would suspect his wife. What would Karuthamma ask about Pareekutty?

Like never before Karuthamma was annoyed by just about everything. Palani too was irritable. They were always on the brink of a quarrel.

Something was stifling the two of them. The clutch of a discomfiture.

Once Panchami began hesitantly, 'You are a tough one…'

'Why do you say that?'

'You didn't ask about Achan once?'

Karuthamma said, 'Quiet! He'll hear us!'

Palani said he was leaving early that evening to put the fishing lines out. That was a relief. He baited the fishing lines. She cooked the meal early. At dusk, the mother and child watched him set out to sea in his boat. The little child lifted its little hand and waved. That was customary. The father sitting in the boat too would bid farewell with a wave of his arm. But that evening it didn't happen. The boat raced to the west. He was paddling it further and further away. The baby cried.

The sisters were alone at home.

Panchami began talking. The loving mother's death, how she was entrusted into Nallapennu's care, how Amma gave her permission to Achan to wed another woman – all of it was told.

'And echechi, one day Pareekutty boss came to see Ammachi.'

Karuthamma changed the subject. Her heart was thudding. Panchami asked, 'Why? Don't you want to hear what happened?'

Pretending not to hear that question, Karuthamma asked, 'Why wasn't I told when Ammachi died?'

'Everyone said we shouldn't.'

'Everyone?'

'Yes. Everyone said that echechi was bad! You were so hard-hearted. But then you never had much love; you are a hard woman!'

Then she talked about the stepmother. When that story came up, she had an important matter to disclose. 'Our boat and nets are all gone! It was mortgaged to Ousepachan. And that money stepmother gave her son.'

Then she recounted the rest of what had happened. Their boats and nets were lost! Karuthamma saw in her mind her father standing on the stern and the boat racing ahead through the waves like a bird. Her parents had worked all their lives for it. She had loved that boat too. Before Palani's boat, it had been the boat she had pointed out to and said, 'Our boat!' Now it was someone else's. She had nothing more to do with it. Again Karuthamma cried.

Karuthamma then asked, 'How will Achan manage now?'

'Who knows!'

It was Panchami's indifference that hurt the most. More than anything else, that stabbed and scored Karuthamma's heart. How their father would manage seemed of little consequence to Panchami.

Karuthamma forgot herself and said, 'What a hard creature you are!'

Panchami seized on that. 'Why do you say that?'

'You didn't wait to find out how Achan would manage. You just left. It wasn't as if they sent you away. Whom does Achan have now?'

'Oh! Let's not get into that. What about you? What did you do?'

That's true! Panchami was right in what she said. How could Panchami alone be blamed? But there was a difference. Karuthamma had no option but to forsake her parents. That wasn't how it was with Panchami.

Panchami said, 'If you hadn't left that day, none of this would have happened. Like Ammachi, you could have looked after our home.'

Karuthamma sat lost in thought. If that had been so, would everything have turned out right? That poor child! She didn't know a thing. So much would have happened! There wouldn't have been an echechi then to speak of. But she didn't know any of this. Panchami who had a vicious tongue continued, 'When a fisherman appeared, you forgot everything else and went after him!'

'No, that isn't it!' sprang to her tongue from an aching heart. However, it was more like a few incoherent syllables that slipped out. Shouldn't she have said that it was because she believed that as the loving wife of a fisherman she ought to do his bidding and it was her responsibility to follow him where he asked her to? She lived in Palani's home, ate the food he earned from his tireless toil in the sea. Shouldn't she have said that?

The poor man! He was out. In truth, she had fled the place. It wasn't because she loved her parents or because she was a loving responsible wife. And as Panchami claimed neither had she run after her fisherman.

Amidst all the news, Chembankunju's bout of madness also came up. Panchami described it. Gritting her teeth with barely concealed anger, she said, 'That fatty said that you were seduced by that Muslim and ruined the shore!'

With some pity she continued, 'Poor Achan! He went mad…'

Unable to respond, Karuthamma went numb. Her ears buzzed. Her eyes glazed. Panchami kept talking. So all of that was still a matter of gossip on that shore. It was still being discussed. And her proud father too had come to know about it. Would her father ever forgive her?

Again Panchami brought up the topic of Pareekutty. She narrated that young man's pathetic tale. She said, 'He has nothing, echechi. He's a pauper. And he keeps wandering on the shore. You'd think he's a mad man if you see him. It is really very sad!'

Karuthamma didn't say anything about whether Panchami ought to go on or stop. She was eager to know all about it. If circumstances had been different, she would have asked about Pareekutty herself.

She too was perhaps seeing in her mind the little boy dressed in a yellow shirt and trousers, wearing a cap, a handkerchief knotted around his neck and clinging to his father's hand. The shell that she had gifted him ... One by one each scene from that romance played itself out in front of her eyes.

A valuable life had been wrecked. It was falling apart. No, it had been destroyed. Unconsciously she asked Panchami, 'Does Little Boss still sit on the boat and sing?

Panchami responded, 'Ah ... sometimes he sings!'

Does Panchami know what the song was all about? It wasn't possible.

Karuthamma asked, 'Do you ever see him?'

'Sometimes!'

'Does he then ever ask you about echechi?' Karuthamma's voice quivered.

Panchami said, 'When he sees me, he smiles!'

'And sometimes he would ask about her!'

A voice that had never been heard before spoke up. Palani stood in front of them.

Panchami and Karuthamma leapt to their feet.

Karuthamma's secret was out.

Twenty

Karuthamma discovered a courage like she had never known before. A purpose. A hazy but definite plan began to formulate in her.

Life and circumstances had brought her to it. Until then she had been a timid woman. Afraid of everything and everyone, without a will or desires of her own. Perhaps she may have had dreams of her own. But none of it had been spoken about.

The change was sudden. Perhaps Panchami's arrival had something to do with it. She had a companion. When all her secrets had been flushed out, what was left to hide? What was left to fear? That life had to be kept safe had ceased to matter. But despite all the precariousness of her life, she wasn't alone. She had someone – Panchami.

She reiterated her promises to her husband. She opened her heart out to him. 'Apart from being your playmate, what was he to you?' Palani asked. The answer to that was she hadn't ever allowed herself to be anyone else's.

Palani didn't want to hear that. He asked, 'Were you in love with him?'

She saw in front of her eyes the Pareekutty that Panchami had described with pity – *A Pareekutty who had lost everything in life and now wandered through the shore like a mad man singing his* song. 'I will always sing this song; I will sing this song so it is heard at Trikunnapuzha' – the words pounded within her ears.

'When you have your boat and nets, will you sell us your fish?'

When Karuthamma took a long moment to answer, Palani repeated his question. Someone within her asked severely, 'What is left to hide? You are not at fault. Before you were married you were in love with someone. What's wrong with that?'

Karuthamma said, 'Yes I was in love!'

A deep dense silence filled the room. What sound could break through it? Palani's question ripped that silence. 'Did you bid farewell to him?'

She didn't reply.

One more question. 'When did you tell him that you would see him next?'

'I never said anything like that!'

The child woke up and cried. She picked the child up and suckled it. That day she didn't attempt to win his heart over. But again and again she sought to appeal to his intelligence with her vows of loyalty. A wife's vows. What other women pledged silently with the mere ritual of marriage she did with words uttered. It seemed as if she was asking what more he expected of her.

At the crack of dawn, Palani rose and went away without speaking a word. Panchami asked, 'Is he angry?'

Karuthamma said, 'The two of us don't have anyone.'

Panchami said, 'You have someone to cling to. I have no one!'

'No, my little sister. We are both in the same situation. We will live together!'

Karuthamma continued almost bitterly, 'The capable Chembankunju's children!'

That afternoon when Palani arrived, Karuthamma went to him with a request. 'I want to go to Neerkunnath once.'

He didn't speak.

She told him of Chembankunju's current state. 'My father has no one.'

He didn't reply to that either.

As was customary, on that day too he fixed the baits onto the rods. She served dinner. Palani walked ahead with the fishing rods and paddle and Karuthamma followed him to the shore with the dinner pail in one hand and the child in the other. That day too the child lifted its hand and waved. When Palani had gone a little into the sea, he looked back. The child was holding its hand aloft.

Karuthamma continued to stand there for a while. It was twilight. The western sky was like a curve of molten gold. What a deep colour it was! Where the blue seas and that dense swath of colour met, a black line had formed. Beyond that line was a secret land. Where the biggest secret of all rested.

Palani's boat fled through that eternal sea into the south. He was paddling standing on his feet. The boat bobbed up and down. A lot of water filled the boat.

It had been so long since he had stood in a boat rowing so vigorously. His dormant energies were awakened, kindled again. But the oar wasn't sturdy enough to handle his vigour. It was a flimsy paddle and the boat was small. Aiming for that black line in the horizon, he rowed on, unconscious of the water filling up his boat. The roar and growl of that rekindled force went unheard in that expanse. Palani's little boat flew through the skies.

What could have aroused that primeval force? And what power could tame and contain it? An uncontrollable force had been unleashed. He was leaving.

A school of dolphins gathered around the boat. One of them hoisted the end of the boat on its back and then shrugged it off. The boat rose off the water. Would it capsize? Sparks darted off Palani's eyes. He clenched his teeth and roared. No, it was a bellow. He rowed again. The boat was hoisted and thrown off the dolphin's back. All in a moment! The boat didn't turn over. The dolphin's back gave way and it sank. Palani was rowing again. To the west, deeper into the west … where was he going? Wasn't there an end to this west?

The child on the shore cried for no reason. Perhaps in its innocence it could perceive its father rowing away as if possessed by a madness. The child could be crying seeing its father go away to the endless western horizon. Palani didn't hear that cry. The wind was to the east. But the wind brought to shore his roar from that tussle with the dolphin. Did Karuthamma hear that? No, it wouldn't reach her ears. She wasn't chaste enough to hear that.

Palani was in pursuit of a secret. Palani saw the moon rise from the sea. He was entering a new world. A world where silver talismans had been scattered on a blue expanse. Suddenly he knew a fear. He was hemmed in by the horizon on all four sides. His universe had shrunk. He rowed again. He had to race ahead and break through that wall.

Sea snakes slithered into his boat. They were gliding over the silver talismans on the blue expanse. At the edge of the boat, they stood on their tails, dancing. And then they slithered back into the water again. Two snakes coiled around each other within the boat.

From the west, a giant wave that covered the horizon came rolling. He felt a great desire to cut through the heart of that wave and go across. But the wave took the little boat on its crest and tossed it over with a white laugh of spray. There weren't any waves there. Calm. But the sea was tinged with black. From the south-west, a long tongue seemed to snake its way under the surface of the sea. The calm was unlike anything before. It wouldn't come in the path of the boat. Instead it had a pull. There was a whirlpool somewhere. Caught in the current, the sludge of the sea floor too was moving.

No, he had to fight that tug. Palani's boat was being dragged away by that current. He rowed against it. In the distance, a light was spreading. Something entered it.

Seagulls rocked themselves on the small waves. They were sleeping. Suddenly they rose screaming for their lives. They were not frightened by the boat. In that sea, a commotion could be heard.

Shark! A seagull had been snapped by a shark.

Palani put out his fishing rod. Only an experienced and skilful fisherman would attempt it.

The sisters sat talking for a while. They were not discussing what had happened. There was nothing left to talk about their mother or Pareekutty. All those were events of the past. Chembankunju was a living problem. And the capable Chembankunju's ill-fated daughters were living problems too. And as they spoke to each other Panchami fell asleep abruptly.

Karuthamma couldn't sleep. A continuous wind blew. A wind with a song that had never been heard before. Karuthamma felt as if traces of Pareekutty's song had merged with that wind. She listened; she listened hard. And so she flowed into that part of her life entitled Pareekutty.

Her fisherman was at sea all by himself. He was putting out bait in the far seas. And so like that first fisherwoman, she too ought to stand on the shore praying for his safety. Instead, she thought of Pareekutty.

It wasn't done consciously. She wasn't asleep nor was she awake. Pareekutty was a nice man, a good man, a loving man. These were all definite facts. She couldn't forget Pareekutty in

this life. Ever. Nor would she do so. Pareekutty was hers; and
she was his.

No one was preventing her from within. No throbbing in
her heart either. In that trance she murmured: She was waiting.
Pareekutty would come; Pareekutty would call her. She would
heed his call.

Which was why she was awake.

'Karuthamma!'

Karuthamma woke up. Had someone called her?

'Karuthamma!'

She felt as if she had heard that call from the distance. Had
she imagined it, caught between a trance and the business of
life? Or, was it someone calling from the door?

Once again the call. 'Karuthamma!'

Only one man had ever called at that time of night at her
door. It was a call that came every night. Palani would call when
he came in from the sea. It was almost time for him to return.

'Karuthamma!'

Was it his voice? Who else it could be? She called out, 'Yes.
What?'

The voice didn't ask her to open the door. Usually he would
ask her to. But still she rose, opened the door and stepped out.
Unlike any other day a strong wind blew. A wind with a certain
savagery to it. A clear moonlight spread and flowed around.
There was no one out in the yard. She went towards the west of
the house. Towards the shore. To gaze at the sea. A man stood in
the moonlight. It was Pareekutty.

Karuthamma wasn't frightened; she didn't scream. She stood
as if she had stepped out in response to his call. He walked slowly
towards her. She looked at that figure carefully. This wasn't her
Bossman. He had become very thin.

When he came closer, wasn't she afraid? Wouldn't he stare

at her breasts and buttocks? No, she had no such fears … her breasts no longer rose up pertly pretty. A baby's tender lips had drunk deep of those breasts, turning them fuller, gentler. Nevertheless, when Palani was out at sea, should she be standing there at night speaking to a man? Karuthamma wasn't afraid. Hadn't she met him before in the solitude of night? And even otherwise, shouldn't she be offering that wrecked life the solace of a meeting even if it was only a brief one?

They stood looking at each other. She had ruined this man who stood before her. Deep in her soul Karuthamma knew that he loved her and would do so forever. No matter what happened to him, no matter when and how, he would always love her. And he would always forgive her. She could do him the worst harm. And he would bear it for her.

In that brief moment, Karuthamma forgot all the disappointments of her life. She was not a defeated woman. She had a great wealth. A wealth that no other woman had! As she had once thought that she was under the care of an able man; as she had once thought her life was secure. She was confident about life. She would never go hungry; she would never know what it would be to be troubled by the world. All of this had given her confidence. Her Palani was strong. And his spirit too was formidable. A man loved her. She would always be a beloved to him! And it was the one who loved her so standing before her.

She moved into his outstretched arms and laid herself against his chest. She raised her face to his. He whispered into her ears, 'My Karuthamma!'

'What, my dearest?'

His hands moved over those buttocks that once he, a Muslim, and the riff-raff of the shore had ogled at.

Pareekutty asked, 'Karuthamma!'

Once again in a trance-like state she responded, 'What?'

'Who am I to you?'

She cupped his face between her palms and with half-closed eyelids whispered, 'Who are you to me? Why, you are my pot of gold!'

Once again they were one. In rapture, she whispered sweet nothings into his ear. She wasn't able to break or move away from that embrace.

In the far seas, a shark bit the bait. A huge shark! Until then such a huge shark had never bitten anyone's bait! No fisherman had ever got such a big fish before. As soon as the fish had swallowed the bait, the big fish slapped its huge tail. The water churned and the spray rose sky-high. Then the fish leapt forward. Palani saw it rise above the water. The line trickled out of its mouth.

Palani had caught the biggest fish on that shore. In joy, Palani called out loudly. He had to make his mind up right now. Should he rein in the line and bring the fish in? Or should he let it swim and give it a chase till it succumbed? He had to decide now. If the hook had sunk deep into its throat, all that was needed was one firm tug to put an end to that grand creature. But it might flail around and break up the boat. If he left it to try and get away, the boat would have to chase it. But where and how far would it go?

Already the shore was not visible. In fact, he didn't even know in which direction the shore was. Holding the fishing line in one hand and steering the boat with the paddle in the other, Palani looked at the stars to navigate his way. The star he sought wasn't there. Clouds covered the skies here and there. But even then the boat furrowed ahead at an unbelievable speed. The boat cut through the water as it traced its course. There were no waves. The sea was calm. But the sea grew darker and denser and was acquiring a frightening dimension. If one looked carefully into the water to gauge the flow of the current, the direction of the shore could be found based on that. But no matter how hard Palani looked, he couldn't fathom it.

The shark dragged the boat at the speed of wind. Where was it going? How far had they gone?

Through clenched teeth, Palani growled again. 'Stop it! It isn't time yet for you to take me to the sea mother's palace!' He pulled at the line tightly. Suddenly the pace of the boat slackened. Palani laughed loudly. 'Ha … that's the way, my boy! Stop there!'

A little further away the shark flailed its tail about in the throes of pain. Excited, Palani tugged at the line again. The shark leapt and fell.

Even though the boat had come to a standstill, it was caught in a current and moved in a circle in the broad expanse of the sea. The current whirled in a circle. Palani looked again carefully. Was he caught in a whirlpool?

Again that circular sweep. But he still held onto the fishing line. He looked at the sky. Not even a star was visible. All his stars had disappeared. The clouds had covered them over.

Palani stood up in his boat and looked around. Until then he had seen the sea stretch. Water on all four sides! Now it wasn't so. He was surrounded by a ring of mountains. He and his boat were in a hollow. The helm of the boat was raised. The sea mother's palace was on the ocean floor deep in the sea. That was where the sea mother lived. Palani had heard descriptions of that palace. You reached there through a whirlpool. A whirlpool that churned up the entire ocean and tunnelled its vortex to knock at the doors of the sea mother's palace.

Palani felt as if the mountains on all four sides were looming more than ever. He slackened the line a bit. Once again the boat raced at an unbelievable speed. Had Palani escaped that whirlpool? Had he crossed over the mountain?

From somewhere a fierce roar could be heard. He had never heard such a sound before. A whirlwind.

Waves rose as high as hills. One by one the waves quickened and drew closer. He had never seen such waves before. These waves didn't come in lengthwise. Instead, they rolled in with ends meeting and gathered around him in a circle.

Palani understood this strange anger of the sea in a moment. He knew how to ride the crest of a wave. He had learnt how to battle whirlwinds. He had rowed through pitch darkness.

Lightning flashed. And the gigantic heave of thunder. Palani slackened the boat. If he reined in the line and the boat paused, the shark would break the boat into bits. Let the shark of the sea drag the boat at its own pace.

As the boat rode the crest, Palani used the paddle as a lever to throw himself up and so reduce the weight in the boat. And as the boat reached the crest, he would fling himself down. At that time the boat would almost be on its head. And there would be yet another wave waiting with gaping jaws to swallow him and his boat.

Roars resounded. The sea roared furiously at that wretched fisherman. The whirlwind tuned that roar up. The thunder beat a rhythm. What diabolic dance was this? He was a mere mortal. Did the sea mother have to unleash such powerful forces to vanquish him? How easily she could drag him to her depths!

Perhaps these waves might have rolled onto the shores. And flung itself over the tops of the houses there. Perhaps now venomous serpents were crawling on the shore. In the distance something high could be seen. Was it the crest of some strange wave? Or was it a sea monster rearing its head up and opening its cavern-like mouth?

Had that fisherman's indefatigable strength been broken? When a wave came, he threw himself up but couldn't rise. That wave with its open mouth washed over him and his boat. In one mighty flash of thunder and lightning, not just the clouds but the sky itself was shattered.

All the waters of the sea gathered in one place. The whirlwind screamed, wanting to wreck everything. The boat's helm could be seen atop a wave. When the wave had subsided, it was seen that the boat had capsized and Palani was clinging to it. He was grabbing at it so as not to lose his grasp. For one moment, he exhaled and screamed, 'Karuthamma!'

Palani's call triumphed over the whirlwind's roar. The call rose above all that.

Why was he calling for Karuthamma? Wasn't there a reason for that? The goddess who protects the fisherman at sea is his fisher wife at home. And so it was to her he was appealing for prayers as that first fisherwoman had prayed for the safe return of her husband. Didn't that first fisherman return despite being caught in a whirlwind storm? Only because of his wife's penance. Palani too believed he would return. He had a fisherwoman. And she would pray for him. Hadn't she promised him this that very day?

The fury of the storm grew. But Palani vanquished that as well. The storm aligned itself with the waves. Yet another wave came towering in! By the time his lips formed 'Karu...' the wave was on him. Nothing was visible. The winds, thunder and lightning all together vented themselves. It was a last big effort. All the forces were united in their fury. They were putting the final touches to that act of destruction.

The water rose sky-high and cascaded. The sea became a cave. The whirlwind became a tangible force. It could be seen.

Again the boat rose above a wave. Palani lay on his belly over it. He was still holding on. Would that head rise?

Was the merciless act of annihilation complete?

Caught in a cross-current, the boat stood erect like a pillar and then sank.

One star was visible. It was the star that fishermen navigated by. The fisherman's guiding light. But its radiance seemed to have dulled.

As if nothing had happened, the next morning the sea stirred itself at dawn. Some of the fishermen who had woken in the night said that there was a huge haul in the deep seas. The waves had come as far as the doorsteps of some houses. Some sea snakes were seen on the white sands.

On the shore, Panchami wept, holding the baby who was screaming for its parents. Her brother-in-law who had gone out to sea the night before hadn't returned. And Karuthamma who had gone to sleep with her was not there either. She wept and tried to console the baby at the same time.

Two days later, the dead bodies of a man and a woman locked in an embrace came to rest on the sands. Karuthamma and Pareekutty.

At Cheriazhikal, a dead shark with a line still attached was found on the shore.

P.S.

**Insights
Interviews
& More...**

The Story of My Chemmeen

Thakazi Sivasankara Pillai

I kept putting it off for a very long time. Perhaps it was best that it happened this way. The idea lay in my mind germinating. On and off these days, it occurs to me that if I had let the thought lie for a longer while, it would have ripened and burgeoned further...

For many days, I had talked at length about it. At times, the novel *Chemmeen* that I was planning to write sounded almost like a threat. Many of my friends assumed that it would deal with the lives of fishermen; that it would be about the coalition of fisher folk, and would stir up unrest and revolution in their minds. This included Mundasseri Master who was like a venerable older brother to me. It was quite natural for anyone who had observed my literary growth until then to think on those lines. It wasn't that all that I had written until then had to do with only the workers' union and unification of their forces; but that thread of thought was what bound them together. My friends, no matter how close they were to me, couldn't comprehend either the company I kept when not with them or my state of mind; neither did they have a proper understanding of the physical realities of the world we lived in, I presume.

It was a time when progressive literature was grappling with the Gordian knot of maintaining structural sanctity. No matter what Dev and I wrote, we were hemmed in by catcalls and howls of outrage. We couldn't even whisper a protest. Dev was unable to even sleep in his house in Pudupally. They wouldn't let him. In an insidious way and almost without his own knowledge, a land dispute had slowly led to his becoming part of the Congress party. Could there be any peace thereafter? Naturally, it put Dev's back up too. He claimed that the people of Pudupally disliked the fact that he had become a landowner.

At Thakazhi, I didn't have to endure the serious dislike that Dev had to suffer in Pudupally. The people of Thakazhi didn't form mobs to yell their displeasure. There were no raucous cries or declarations of disgust. No study classes were organized against me. It makes me want to laugh thinking of those days. The arguments in favour and against what I wrote ran a peculiar course. And there were enough protest groups who expressed their antipathy towards me.

It was a chaotic literary environment. However I continued to write. I couldn't but write. I remember a story from K. Balakrishnan's *Kaumudi*, 'Chendakotu' (The drum beat). Yes, writing like the drum beat has a purpose – to disrupt everyone.

The Thakazhi of then isn't the Thakazhi of now.

The Thiruvalla–Ambalapuzha road runs in front of my house. This is an important road. There is the constant whine of traffic. In those days, this road was a narrow canal. I kept two boats locked to the pier there. I brought the stone, lime, timber and gravel required to build my house in these boats. The gate that you see now was the pier from which I accessed the canal for my daily swim and bath. In those days what was unique and convenient about my house was its proximity to the canal. The land was 28 cents in all. Kaatha, our children and I lived in a two-roomed house with a lean-to. It was built of laterite stone with bamboo rafters and a coconut palm leaf thatch. Kaatha and I dreamt day and night of making this into a more solid and secure structure. Though I had written over seven novels and several stories, I was unable to build this dream house. Some of those novels had even been successful. Suddenly, I had two sources of inspiration: one, to provide a fitting retort to the drum beat of speculation around me; two, to roof our house with wood and tiles and make it into a light and airy home.

My intimacy with the seaside began when I was nine years old. I knew all the faces and moods of the sea goddess. My mind was flooded with thoughts of the sea goddess and the chakara. One morning, I stuffed a few shirts and mundus into a bag and walked to Ambalapuzha. I was on my way to Kottayam. In those days, to reach Kottayam, one had to go to Ambalapuzha and then catch a boat from there. If I set out from Thakazhi in the morning, by the time I had caught the connecting bus and boat, it would be 2.00 in the afternoon when I reached Kottayam. This wasn't the Kottayam as we know it now. But that's another story.

In what is today's private bus stand, there used to be a two-storeyed building with seven or eight rooms. A lodge. It was managed by one Mr Mathai. Mr Mathai ran a strictly vegetarian restaurant on the east road. The food there was cooked to very exacting standards and in the utmost of hygienic conditions. I don't mean to ridicule but the people of Kottayam referred to Mr Mathai as Mr Mathai Pottey.

The lodge that Mr Mathai ran was owned by the Karapuzha Arakkal family. In those days, DC, who was the sales manager of SPCS, handed me over to Mathai's care.

'That father of mine talks of buying a boat and nets...' I began writing. It was the dialect of the seaside that I had heard since I was nine.

Of the many people who visited the lodge every evening, or the Boat House Lodge as it was called, one person deserves a special mention. C.J. Thomas.

CJ's visits had a purpose. To read what I had written that day. He wouldn't speak a word; he would read and then leave. And so C.J. Thomas became the first person to read *Chemmeen*. In those days, CJ was a cover designer at Sahithya Pravarthaka Sahakarana Sangham.

D.C. Kizhakkemuri was also one of my regular visitors.

And thus by the eighth day, the story of *Chemmeen* fell in place. Only then did Mathai Pottey let me drink some beer.

It wasn't difficult thereafter to renovate our home in Sankaramangalam. *Chemmeen* sold very well. We made rafters of timber and laid tiles on it. We added a few more rooms. But how we added to the 28 cents land is yet another story.

Chemmeen was the first Malayalam novel to receive the then just announced Sahitya Akademi award. I received it from Jawaharlal Nehru. Radhakrishnan looked on and applauded. With that money, I bought 60 para of paddy fields at Kolathadi padam.

Chemmeen was translated into many languages. It was first translated into Czech. Kamil Zelabil was the translator. He was a Tamil scholar who later studied Malayalam. When he came to Madras, he heard about this Malayalam novel *Chemmeen*. And, he didn't think he would have trouble understanding or translating it. He also translated *Rand Edangazhi* (Two Measures) into Czech. Later, under the auspices of UNESCO, *Chemmeen* was translated into all European languages. In between, after the Czech translation, the Russian translation appeared. Among the Asian languages, *Chemmeen* was translated into Arab, Japanese, Vietnamese, Sinhala and Chinese.

Who would have thought the drum beat would have helped accomplish as much? Was it an act of triumph? It would be presumptuous of me to claim that. For only time will tell.

31 October 1995

In Peggy Mohan's novel, *Jahajin*, I stumble upon a phrase: *un coup de foudre*. An attack of madness.

She describes it as 'a swarming melee of manic energy seeking a focus'.

Chemmeen – the translation – was born of one such *coup de foudre*.

I was between novels. The writing of *Mistress* had filled my life so absolutely that suddenly I had a huge empty space when the novel was written. What was I going to do with myself?

And then came a thought: Unayi Warrier's *Nalacharitham*. I had fallen in love with Kathakali all over again on reading *Nalacharitham*. Surely the rest of the world ought to be able to draw pleasure from it as I had. Find the solace it offered in moments of abject darkness. It became a dream project that grew in my mind until one day I mentioned this grand obsession to Karthika at HarperCollins.

As all good editors and as all good friends, she counselled that I cut my translation teeth on something not as ambitious but just as magnificent.

Like what? I asked.

Chemmeen? she suggested.

From somewhere the strains of a song wafted in my head. The desolate Pareekutty singing his heart out on a moon-drenched seashore. The restless Karuthamma standing with her bosom heaving, wanting to escape everything and run to Pareekutty's side. The gleam in Chemankunju's eye when he spots Palani for the first time. Scenes from the film *Chemmeen* played out in my head.

Was chitchat turning into something of consequence? Was that how it happened? Was that how I took on *Chemmeen*? *Un coup de foudre*. What else?

I had no formal education in Malayalam. What I did have was an ability to understand and comprehend the nuances of the language. I was already enchanted by its wondrous innate lyricism where a butterfly has the magical wings of a 'chitrashalabam' and a weevil is a 'nikrishtanaya puzhu'.

During the writing of *Mistress* I had worked in a few translations of Kathakali attakathas into the narrative. But this wasn't going to be enough. A translation would require me to walk the way of another writer and see his landscape and characters through his eyes. Would I have the restraint to bridle the desire to tweak a thought here, add a dimension there? I am a writer of fiction first and it was going to be hard to keep myself out of Thakazhi's *Chemmeen*. To bring forth the beauty of a book without succumbing to the need to edit. To let the grammar of the region prevail without making it seem like an idiomatic translation … In contrast, the author has it easy. Write as your heart leads you and damn everything else…

And there was one other thing. I was going to have to summon great stamina. Each time a word flustered me, I would have to dive into a Malayalam Nigandu. (Dictionary is too sanitized and limited a word unlike the bottomless abyss of the Nigandu.) I would have to find my way through, inch by inch, word and word.

The very first line of the book had me in knots. *Chemmeen* is written in fishermen's dialect. This was unfamiliar territory and I put the pen down. What was I going to do?

From somewhere the mysterious voice of the God of translation spoke to me: Dialect – Ear – Hear it – and that became the key to this translation.

Over the course of the next fortnight, I roped in my secretary Mini Kuruvilla, a Malayali, to read out the book to me. I heard the novel read rather than read it myself. A certain familiarity with the cadence grew into a natural ease. I heard it read again and then one day I was ready.

Thakazhi wrote his *Chemmeen* in eight days. It took me two years and at least four rewrites before I was satisfied to let it go. Over the two years it took to complete the translation, words and phrases that weren't in Nigandu had to be deciphered. Help came from a friend in Trivandrum – V.S. Rajesh of Kerala Kaumudi. And then it was done.

It is ironic but most of the books that we consider to be the finest examples of contemporary writing are translations. Whether it is Marquez or Kundera, Grasse or Xingjian, what we have had access to are the translations of their works. Here is one more. A classic novel that no matter how many times you read it nudges your soul.

Chemmeen is a novel about forbidden love. It is also a novel that bares the seams of the mind of a fisherman who goes out into the sea. What brings him back to the shore? What causes him to lose his way? *Chemmeen* is about hopes and hopeless love. It is a story that lives long after the book is read. And reverberates in the mind just as the waves dash on the shore. Again and again.

The noble patriarch once said, 'That there is a language called Malayalam and that it has a literary tradition is universally known. It was with *Chemmeen* though that a Malayalam novel first found its place among many other languages of the world. In fact, *Chemmeen* can certainly claim that honour. However, nobody need assume it is because of this that I consider *Chemmeen* to be the best novel written in Malayalam. It was one of those strange and happy quirks of destiny! *Chemmeen* changed my financial position for the better. Instead of that ramshackle hovel, the house came in its place. And I acquired some paddy fields.'

Chemmeen – the novel that brought Thakazhi Sivasankara Pillai international acclaim and changed his life for good – was also the reason for much anguish in his later years. Like the end of that love story that was tainted by grief, the storyteller of Kuttanad who became the storyteller of the seashore too was haunted by sorrow.

'That father of mine talks of buying a boat and nets.'

'What a lucky girl you are, Karuthamma!'

Chemmeen began thus. Having forsaken Pareekutty and their love, Karuthamma marries Palani. And then when a completely devastated Pareekutty's cry of anguish echoes on the shore, Palani's wife, Karuthamma, goes seeking Pareekutty. The dead bodies of Pareekutty and Karuthamma locked in an embrace are found on the shore. The transgression of a fisherwoman invoked the wrath of the sea mother. The husband who went out into the sea to fish was taken away by the sea mother.

From a lodge organized by D.C. Kizhakkemuri in Kottayam, Thakazhi finished writing the novel in seven days, and in two weeks the first print run had been sold out. When it received the Central Sahitya Akademi award in 1958, *Chemmeen* became known nationally. It was thereafter translated into several languages including English, Spanish, Italian, French, German, Czech, Slav, Dutch, Polish, Hungarian, Russian, Arabic, Vietnamese, Japanese, Sinhala…

When *Chemmeen* was made into a film, it took Thakazhi and Malayalam into world limelight. Kanmani Babu optioned and acquired the film rights for *Chemmeen* through a Bombay production house. 'I don't remember precisely how much I was paid. Rs.25,000/- I think! It's with that money I bought ten acres of coconut grove in Thakazhi. Later I sold that,' Thakazi said.

In time, the financial benefits of *Chemmeen* dwindled. But the antagonism towards the premise of the novel continued. From his student days till the time he worked as a lawyer in Ambalapuzha, Thakazhi had come to understand the life on the Alapuzha shore stretching from Purakkad to Thykall. His love for that life and its tradition manifested as *Chemmeen*, but along with the novel came several protests. Some leaders of the fishermen community accused him of presenting their life and language in an ungainly fashion. And some progressives attacked what they claimed was a blatant build-up of superstition, namely the myth that the sea goddess would take away the husband of any fisherwoman who transgressed. The accusation and Thakazhi's routine explanations continued much after the novel was written and published.

Three years ago, Babykuttan adapted *Chemmeen* into a play for Kollam Thulika. Thakazhi had blessed this endeavour. When the play reached the stage, the protesters woke up once again. Thakazhi, incapacitated by old age, was threatened and tormented by them on the phone.

One other thing that caused him much grief was the idea of a sequel to the film *Chemmeen*. When the subject was broached, Kanmani Babu protested that there shouldn't be a sequel. Caught amidst this tussle, Thakazhi watched helplessly. Apart from a dakshina offered by the actor Suresh Gopi, he received nothing more, Thakazhi later said.

The film that later came out as *Thirakalkkappuram* was not even a patch on *Chemmeen*. In fact, the pointlessness of making a sequel to *Chemmeen* was pointed out by the screenplay writer of *Chemmeen*, S.L. Puram Sadanandan.

More recently when Ismail Merchant of the famous Merchant Ivory film-making duo was in Kochi, he expressed a desire to turn *Chemmeen* into a film. This was the final heartache that *Chemmeen* bestowed upon Thakazhi. Thakazhi, who read about Ismail Merchant's desire in the newspapers, waited eagerly for Merchant's arrival at Sankaramangalam.

It was an abject desire of that elderly mind to see his story that in his own words 'encompassed sorrow, pleasure, anxiety, love, anger, all in its purest form' make its presence on the international film arena. So he waited with much delight and expectation.

But when Kanmani Babu staked a claim that the right to make the film in any language was his alone, Thakazhi's hopes were once again dashed.

'From the day I wrote that first line, "That father of mine

talks of buying a boat and nets," I have had to endure much incrimination. Nothing has changed even now. When it comes to condemnation it's all reserved for me; as for the cash, that's all for someone else.' A quivering voice, moist eyes encapsulated this tedious and demoralizing situation.

Then he spoke of Karuthamma. 'If I go to the seashore of Neerkunnath, Purakkad and Ambalapuzha and call for my Karuthamma, she will heed my call. They will all emerge radiating love and devotion. Pareekutty, Palani, Chembankunju, Chakki, Panchami – all of them.'

It seemed that if the thought of all that *Chemmeen* brought his way lit up that wrinkled visage, it also cast its shadows by the grief it thrust on him.

11 April 1999

Chemmeen the novel anticipates a film as no other novel in Malayalam has ever done. The novel taps into cultural dimensions that are precisely the foundations of cinema as a mode of mass entertainment. Human drama as populist spectacle underlies the spirit of the novel as the film. The mise-en-scène of the film bears very close resemblances to the imaginary frames of the novel and this proves interesting in view of the fact that in nearly half a century of its history many Malayalis might have seen the movie first and then read the novel, raising interesting conjectures about the possibilities of the superimposition of subsequently accumulated star value of actors such as Sathyan, Sheela, Madhu and Kottarakkara on to the characters of the novel they portray and the ways in which it could affect both the interpretation and aura of the original.

Before the prolific appearance of new media or visual modes of mass diffusion, *Chemmeen* was a narrative pregnant with the cinematic, dexterously negotiating the Malayali's iconophobia and logophilia or the deep cultural prejudice against and stigmatization of the visual arts and media, probably also stemming from an over-valorization of the written word. What is often called the 'essentially pornographic' filmic image offers itself in the novel, demanding our scopic gaze both literally and figuratively. In the novel, for example, Karuthamma chastises Kochumuthali, begging him not to 'look' at her in 'that' manner. The 'look' and the ensuing 'bashful realization' of her breasts and single piece loincloth embody her in a fleshly materiality that is characteristic of the visceral pleasures of cinema. Conversely, one can find in the film the thematic and narrative persistence of the novel with an added novelty offered by the material variations due to the cinematic apparatus. The very first shot of Karuthamma in the film marks the meaning she bears – her body is constructed as the object of the male gaze. Thus the cinematic apparatus, always already compromised in the ideology of vision and sexual difference cannot but construct Karuthamma as image, spectacle, and the object of gaze. The taut body of Sheela's Karuthamma marks the transformation of the central female subject of a coastal community drama into an objectified erotic figure created on demand to the visual and erotic desires of Malayali audiences. Even the

Works Cited

Arayan, Velukutty V.V., *Thakazhiyude Chemmeen: Oru Nirupanam.* Thiruvananthapuram: Kalakeralam Publications, 1956.

Beeman, William O., 'The Use of Music in Popular Film: East and West', In *India International Centre Quarterly*, Special Issue 'Indian Popular Cinema: Myth, Meaning and Metaphor', Pradip Krishan (ed.) 8 (1), 1981.

Cowie, Elizabeth, *Representing the Woman: Cinema and Psychoanalysis*, London: Macmillian, 1997.

Crisp, Colin, *The Classic French Cinema, 1930–1960*, Bloomington: Indiana U.P., 1997.

Dhareshwar, Vivek, 'Caste and the Secular Self', *Journal of Arts and Ideas* 25/26 (1993): pp. 115-126.

Dissanayake, Wimal, 'Rethinking Indian Popular Cinema: Towards New Frames of Understanding', in Anthony Guneratne and Wimal Dissanayake (eds), *Rethinking Third Cinema*, New York: Routledge, 2003, pp. 202-225.

Eapen, Mridul and Praveena Kodoth, 'Family Structure, Women's Education and Work: Re-examining the High Status of Women in Kerala', in Swapna Mukhopadhyay and Ratna Sudarshan (eds), *Tracking Gender Equity under Economic Reforms*, New Delhi: Kali for Women, 2003.

Gabriel, Karen, *Melodrama and the Nation: Sexual Economies of Bombay Cinema, 1970–2000*, New Delhi: Women Unlimited, 2010.

big dark mole on the breast in the movie serves to accentuate active scopophilia. That both the novel and the film are fetishistic is beyond doubt. Nevertheless, the success of the film, its huge popular appeal is probably owing to the fact that it is able to tap much more into this fetishistic gratification using the image of 'chemmeen', or the catch from the sea, as a fetish for the woman, the 'catch' from the land. The film creates a narrative enigma which is not as prominent or pronounced in the novel. The question of whether Karuthamma loves Palani or Pareekutty, whether she does not forget or forgets Pareekutty creates a strategy of exchange and equivalence in the film. Often the fish or the 'catch', creating an 'insistent impression of display in the *mise en scene*, marks out a process of fetishistic substitution' (Cowie 276). It is Karuthamma who becomes fetishized in this process of substitution. Throughout the film, Karuthamma and the fish catch are in a 'circulation of substitution and exchange' where one can decipher 'the palpable over-investment in or excessive value on the visual within the image' (Cowie 268). Marcus Bartley's camera captures the fishing boats coming in again and again to create multiple connotations of objects circulated and exchanged.

For Thakazhi the writing of the novel was impelled by an acute monetary need – to make money for building a house for his wife and children. This act of consumption, so embedded in notions of the popular, gets translated into the lives of his characters like Chembankunju and Palani. The adaptation too can be seen as another massive investment, fiscal, emotional and psychic, accommodating and replicating this act of consumption within the representational form of cinema. *Chemmeen*, the catch from the sea, as the title suggests can also be thus seen as a palimpsest for the numerous acts of consumption that mark the trajectory of the novel from its writing to its popularity, its numerous translations into different languages; as also its immensely successful screen adaptation and the awards, accolades and the popular cult status of both novel and film.

The novel's realism is a visually pliable one that happily yields to the film's complex conventions of portrayal and also to the cultural expectations of Malayali and pan-Indian audiences alike. Thus, the film's opening pan and long-shots fix the locale and present the life of its fisher folk characters in the most innocently 'realistic' manner. Yet the novel is Thakazhi's attempt to shrug off the ideological burdens of the

Jameson, Feredric, 'Third World Literature in an Era of Multinational Capitalism', in *Social Text* No.15 (Autumn 1986), pp. 65-88.

Kodoth, Praveena, 'Property Legislation in Kerala: Gender Aspects and Policy Challenges', *eSocialSciences* 31 August 2005, 20 July 2011, <http://www.eSocialSciences.com/data/articles/Document13182005150.493252.doc>

Mukhopadhyay, Swapna, 'Understanding the Enigma of Women's Status in Kerala: Does High Literacy Necessarily Translate into High Status', in Swapna Mukhopadhyay (ed.), *The Enigma of the Kerala Women: A Failed Promise of Literacy*, New Delhi: Social Sciences Press, 2007.

Vasudevan, Ravi, *Making Meaning in Indian Cinema*, Delhi: Oxford University Press, 2000.

realist tradition of the Progressive Writers' Movement. The novel's rather superfluous realism, which is in contrast to Thakazhi's earlier social realist mode of writing, offers itself to the regiming of representational realism that the film seeks to achieve. It is the brilliance of Ramu Kariat's direction and the lucidity of S.L. Puram Sadanandan's screenplay that create the aura of social realism and humanism in the film. Thus it has to be emphasized that what is fabricated by the narratives of both film and fiction as the real, authentic life of the Araya community is actually a logbook of the ideologies and ideological contradictions of the Kerala society coming to terms with the idea of the conjugal family and attempting to contain the subversive potential of that social unit. Both Chembankunju and Palani, at the heart of the bourgeois family, face social and emotional isolation signifying the crisis of masculinity trapped in a domestic interiority and struggling with new cultural codes appropriate to the male providers of the new family ideal. It is noteworthy that the split between the public space of production and the private, domestic, emotional space of reproduction is much more cutting in the film. The iconography of the film, its editing, and its visual vocabulary emphasize this divide very powerfully with the waves which act as a metaphor for the dichotomization of the interior and exterior, private and public, sea and shore. Yet the film latches on to only those conventions which register as 'realistic' with the Malayali viewing subject. Therefore Sheela as Karuthamma, though most unlike in physical features to real fisherwomen (generating innumerable 'academic' critiques on Sheela as 'Veluthamma' referring to her fair skin), caters to popular audience expectations on how the heroine of a melodrama can plausibly be constructed on celluloid according the aesthetic conventions of cinema, in the process becoming popularly accepted as realistic. As Colin Crisp points out: 'Emphasis on plausibility and credibility can lead even the most extreme fantasy texts being deemed realistic if they conform to existing social conventions of representation and/or to the operative generic conventions of representation' (242). It is the film's conformity to the conventions of representation and its reproduction of dominant ideological perceptions of the audience that makes it realistic in effect, for these again erase the materiality of the processes of its representation.

The film's construction of the private space of marriage and its attempts to map conjugal happiness on to this space is at slight variance from the novel. Karuthamma in the film is more preoccupied with the 'idea' of a home and fashions herself in the aesthetics of this imagination. However, it is interesting that the novel apparently tries to critique the politics of this self-fashioning, given the gendered compromise of modernity it affects in the climatic episodes of the story.

A significant point is that in the 1950s when the public sphere in Kerala was registering a more popular and wider support for liberal, socialist, egalitarian values as a result of the social reforms and the communist movements, helping more women to step out into the paid labour force, the novel seeks to entice women back home through the domestic ideal. One has to remember the Araya socio-political activist Velukutty Arayan's polemic pamphlet critiquing Thakazhi's myth of Kadalamma as investing dangerous ideological dimensions, especially compromising the liberty of Araya women, on what he calls mere poetic speech and figurative language of the community. It is indeed important to analyse how both fiction and film set the practice of imagining the modern family sans attempts to modernize gender relations. Thus the casting of chastity as the defining virtue of women and materially grounding this in the women of the Araya community, where large numbers of women work in the public sphere, selling, curing or processing fish, illustrates the gender blindness of modernity in Kerala. 'An informed reading of the history of social reforms in the state from a feminist perspective suggests that while all social reformers have emphasized the importance of literacy, the proposed "emancipation" of women has invariably been looked upon as an instrument that is to be used for the benefits of the family and society, not for the benefit of the woman as an individual in her own right. Literacy may even have been an instrument facilitating the process of internalization of that message. The message has clearly gone very deep in Kerala society, for in terms of gender-related issues in public life, Malayalee society continues to be very conservative' (Mukhopadhyay 15). The novel even goes to the extent of portraying Karuthamma's feeling of 'conjugal bliss' when forbidden by Palani to venture out of her home to sell fish. Moreover, it validates Palani's reiterated demand for Karuthamma's chastity in return for the economic and social security he provides her with as a husband, with Karuthamma herself calling this demand if not a woman's 'need', her 'right as a wife' and a tangible proof of the husband's love. It is the marked absence of the discourse of social reform which so clearly marks the social history of Kerala in the mid twentieth century that makes *Chemmeen* so much more of a moral fable or myth. If the novel attempts at creating a mystique around the conjugal imaginary that would nevertheless provide obstacles in the path of real Malayali women to access education and employment, the film is much more curt and ends the issue with a cryptic, matter-of-fact order from Palani forbidding Karuthamma's work forays into the public sphere which seems most natural in the circumstances. Yet one can read into the text and recognize the beginning of the process of shaping the hegemonic masculine that would become the hallmark of popular Malayalam cinema at a later period in history.

Cinematography by the Anglo-Indian Marcus Bartley, music by the Bengali Salil Choudhary, another Bengali Hrishikesh Mukherjee's editing and Manna Dey singing the famous '*Manasa maine varu*' – one sees how a pan-Indian imagination strengthens the sign of the 'modern' in the film. Thus the film's crew re-narrativizes the regional from a renewed sense of the national where parochial/caste identities have to be refashioned in the new moulds of a national 'secular' self. The transition from the traditional to the modern is best effected through the imagining of the modern family and reallocation of new roles and models especially for women to emulate within the confines of this ideal. It is significant in this context to note how both the novel and the film valorize women's social/national importance as keepers of eternal transcendental values. Both the novel and the film, as discourses of modernity, capitulate to the project of constantly pondering over the woman question and in the process regulating female sexuality.

It is also significant that the film is more discreet over the issue of caste, conveniently doing away with Karuthamma's more protracted agonizing over Pareekutty's Muslim identity in the novel, the film apparently offering a safer habitus of secular modernity untainted in any significant or alarming manner by caste. In tune to the popular paradigm the film displays a delicately poised ambivalence in affirming either traditional or modern assumptions of caste, erasing the unease and embarrassment of caste by what Vivek Dhareshwar calls 'freezing' it as a social institution, by 'disavowing it publicly and politically' (116).

The novel as a popular bestseller and the film as a popular classic, fall in the representational genre of melodrama, typical of mass and popular cultural entertainment, focusing on intensely emotional moments in a family drama and seeking to evoke similar powerful emotions in the audience. The movie adds on to the novel's melodramatic narrative by using melodramatic techniques like lighting, colour and music (one of the first colour movies in Malayalam) which gave a startling effect to the cinematic mise-en-scène and contributed to its box-office success. The intense emotionality as well as the interpellation of the audience as subjects of popular sentimental and moral codes – replicating the hegemonic and thus involving the viewer in the material and moral dilemmas of the protagonists in a highly dramatic fashion – imbue the film with its hugely successful melodramatic sensibility. From the earlier social realist mode *Chemmeen* marks a shift in Malayalam cinema to the melodramatic, consolidating its characteristic features as a focus on the family as a microcosmic site reflecting larger social crises, anxieties over the ideal of femininity and the endless deferral of modernity especially with regard to gender. As Karen Gabriel points out, 'It cannot be stressed enough that a melodramatic displacement of narratives of the social is not merely onto the familial and the domestic, but more crucially into the more nebulous realms of gender and sexuality' (70). However, it is to be credited that one significant difference between *Chemmeen* and the classic Indian melodrama is that it radically topples the trope of the 'sacrificing mother', offering a moment of subversion when Karuthamma's sexuality and desire triumphs over her motherhood. Yet in the last run this theme is made complicit with the dominant ideology, marking her desire as transgressive and traumatic.

That the melodramatic sensibility of Malayali audiences and readers had to be imbued in an 'air' of social realism provides interesting insights into the socio-cultural contexts of reception in Kerala. Thus Thakzahi's *Chemmeen* while laying claims to the social realist oeuvre of the writer undermines it in favour of the metaphysical dimensions of the ethical, moral and sexual anxieties of the protagonists as well as the heightened emotional 'effect' that could be drawn out of this conflict, while the film melds all these into a spectacle. The film more than the novel, borrows the melodramatic genre's characteristic ambiguity towards marriage, simultaneously representing it as liberatory and repressive.

The movie owes a large part of its popularity to its songs which formed its best advertising and marketing material too. The song and dance in popular cinemas in India, unlike that in Hollywood musicals where it cleared a representational space in which both characters and audience could indulge in flights of fancy, were and are used as 'natural and logical articulations of situations and feelings emanating from the dynamics of day to day life' (Dissanayake 209). In *Chemmeen* the spectacle of the songs appear as obvious and natural, punctuating the emotional statements in the story and inhabiting almost the same continuous narrative space. Thus the song interludes signify neither fantasies nor memories, neither pretending to access an inner psyche nor creating temporal or spatial ellipsis. What they do most powerfully, both visually and verbally, is to eroticize the sea and the quests/journeys on the sea in a manner as never before or after in popular Indian narrative language. The ambiguity of the quest, the metaphorical implications that a journey on the sea has, would be best epitomized in the 'Gulf Boom' of the 1970s in Kerala, a moment that the narrative of the song *'Kadalinakkare ponore kana ponninu ponore, poyi varumbol enthu konduvarum'* (O you who travel across the seas, what will you bring on your journey back?) presupposes. The sea 'imagined' in the songs becomes an archetype of the innumerable journeys that would mark the social, cultural and economic history of Kerala in the years to follow. Thus the journey into the outer sea captured in frame after frame in the songs signify a foundational aspect of the Malayali imaginary and functions as a popular trope that would equip the Malayali to reckon with the experience of migration, within and outside the state as also beyond the nation, in both its personal and collective significance. It is the sea that maps the Malayali self and becomes a central metaphor in all modern attempts at cartographing this self on to national as well as global narratives. The huge popularity of the songs even in the subsequent decades after the release of the movie is partly due to this rather popular hermeneutics of the sea as a metaphor for Malayali migrations.

One must also take into consideration the interrelated tropes of *kanaponnu* (hidden gold), *ponvala* (golden nets) and *chakara* that offer paradigms of the rarest of rare catches and treasures the migrant would bring back home, interpellating both actual and aspiring non-resident Malayalis as subjects in discourses of desire and home. Thus the narrative of the songs while simultaneously drawing on pre-modern atavistic associations and spiritual connections with the sea also attempt to construct it as a modern epic imaginary of contemporary struggles for labour, survival and subsistence. These songs have also played a crucial role as 'migration narratives' of Malayalis, buttressing claims for female chastity as men sail away to far-off shores to amass economic resources for the family. Three of the choric songs track back and forth to the constant setting out and movement of boats into the outer sea, symbolically linking Kerala to the commodity chains of a global trade in human resources that would become the hallmark of its economy.

All the songs in the film are diegetic, directly invoking the sea which adds to the power of its mythopoeia. It is interesting that the novel keeps on referring to the songs, both Parekutty's mellifluous rendering of his love as well as the folk songs sung on the shores of Neerkunnam, which we actually get to hear only in the movie. The novel's understanding of the inseparableness of music from Malayali narrative traditions and the way it grounds itself on a clear notion of the semiotic function of music in this tradition contribute significantly to the film's use of music as an integral narrative agent, contributing to the creation of not only its mood or emotion but to its very mythopoesis. That the novel can foresee and invest in the mythical unconscious of the filmic audience speaks volumes about the folk base of the popular in India and the vast repertoire of oral traditions from which both novel and film draw their sustenance. Music thus having the 'expressive equivalence to speech' (Vasudevan 9), Indian audiences do not feel the 'artificial break' which might be felt by audiences in the West when an actor bursts into song (Beeman 83). Borrowing from the folk tradition it is interesting to note how singing is constructed as part of the daily life of the fishing community where instead of the protagonists, it is the ordinary, apparently sidelined characters who are fore-grounded and singing, where the 'sing along' nature of the songs constitutes a community and instills the film with its folk motif. The mesmerizing allure of the lyrics of Vayalar Ramavarma, by far the most popular lyricist poet in Malayalam, rests on the imagination of a mythic land of moonlight where *nisagandhi* blooms and mermaids frolic on the waves of the ocean of milk (*palazhi*), a land where beautiful women with shapely eyes like the pearlspot fish (*karimeen kannal*) take vows of chastity to ensure the safe passage back of their men from the turbulent seas. The folk idiom is set to pan-Indian folk tunes by the magic of Salil Choudhary, thus literally making the songs acceptable to mass audiences as folk songs in tone, theme and tenor. The only song that stands out at a more individual level in contrast to the songs of the community is '*Manasa maine varu*', but even there one can see the pervasive aura of the mythic seascape where the incessant waves become tropes of the untrammeled desires of the human heart.

But the evergreen popularity and appeal of *Chemmeen*, the film as also the novel, is in construction of a 'Keralan' mythology, using indigenous symbols from this coastal strip of a state to imagine a 'Malayaliness' that finds an echo in the hearts of Malayali readers/audiences. The golden beaches, the swaying green palms, and in the background the rich and poignant beauty of the enigmatic ocean offering a symbolically lush landscape to the agonies and ecstasies of the romantic hearts on shore. In a land which according to popular myth arose from the sea, the sea is also mythologized as 'Kadalamma'. Kadalamma is not only a benevolent goddess but also the terrifying mother who threatens symbolically to devour the fishermen if female chastity is not ensured at home, posing the threat of physical and psychic annihilation. Karuthamma like Kadalamma is linked to the primal fear of obliteration and loss of identity, of being swallowed up by the feminine. One of the shots in the film that cannot be found in the novel is the morning after the wedding night when a fisherman asks whether Karuthamma has swallowed Palani – a prophetic statement of what is to follow. Palani is devoured by Kadalamma in death as he is devoured by Karuthamma in life. Once again one can see here the anxieties of a society shifting from matrilineal to a patrifocal residency, the exigencies of strengthening the notion of the conjugal family and the fine tuning of the nature of relationship between the husband and wife hinging on notions of 'security' from man and 'chastity' from the woman. In the context of this shift it was considered a humiliating practice for a man to stay on in his wife's natal home which is why Palani's refusal to stay in Karuthamma's house is considered natural in the circumstances. The logic of the patrifocal nucleated family can be found in the motives for writing the novel. Thakazhi in a prefatory note titled 'The Story of My *Chemmeen*' in the twentieth edition of the novel states that he wrote the novel at a time when he was living in a thatched makeshift house with Katha and his children. Day and night Katha and he dreamt of transforming the house into a 'strong', 'solid' one. Though he had written quite a few novels and stories by then, he had been unable to build a house. Therefore, the writing of *Chemmeen* had two causative factors 'a reply to the drumbeats of criticism raging around him; as also an airy, bright-lit house built with wooden rafters and tiled roof'. Towards the end of the note he says he wrote the novel in eight days and with its publication he had no difficulty in building the house 'Sankaramangalam'. '*Chemmeen* was in high demand. Rafters were made with wood. The home had a tiled roof and three or four additional rooms were also attached.' In imagining and consolidating this relatively new social unit of the modern family, tradition and myth had to be necessarily invoked especially for mapping the dynamics of gender and representing/containing sexualities.

However, Karuthamma is not entirely without agency and in the novel is bold enough to contemplate even conversion to Islam (the discourse on dress in this context is highly significant), silently critiquing the chastity myth and seeking to validate female desire as normal and ubiquitous, both temporally and spatially. She pesters Chakki to steal from Chembankunju, and mother and daughter try to pay back Pareekutty's debt partly and covertly. These female-action oriented scenes are entirely absent in the movie which represents her as more detached, her self-conscious ambivalence towards patriarchal mores poignantly brought out by Sheela in a supreme performance. The complete disdain towards the system is brought out in the utter contempt with which she finally acknowledges her love for Pareekutty to Palani. This is so contrary to her reactions and body language in the rest of the movie that a feminist interpreter would not be able to resist attributing an extra-auteristic impulse (given the commodified representations of the feminine in Kariat's oeuvre), the *manodharma* of the actor as per Indian performance traditions, a free play of imagination which helps her to triumph as 'woman' over the aesthetic and ideological perspective of the director. However, her answer (that she loves Pareekutty) in the present tense as opposed to the past tense in the novel, inscribing the bold continuity of her love, asserts an apotheosis of the more gendered and revisionist readings of the novel in the nine years following its publication and before its adaptation.

Thus while both the novel and the film exhibit a 'non-synchronism' characterized by disjunctures in the temporal and psychic, where the mythic might cohabit with the rational and the pre-modern with the modern, it is much more pronounced in the ending of the film where Karuthamma suddenly awakens from her mythic maidenhood to a 'modern', 'individualistic', 'feminist' sensibility. Palani's raised hands to strike his wife is lowered as his gaze shifts to his child but the question is reiterated in another form as 'Is this child his?' This anxiety over paternity is a modern anxiety in contrast to Palani's own uncertainty of legitimate lineage. This question has to be contextualized in the relative flexibility of conjugality in Kerala in an earlier matrilineal tradition which was in a sense compromised for the fixity of the patriarchal institution of the modern family in the twentieth century. Thus the rights of the father started being privileged over that of the mother with a patrilineal shift in ownership of property, presupposing an over investment in conjugal fidelity and chastity and leading to a new centering of the father with the marginalizing and sentimentalizing of the mothers and daughters.

This question of anxiety over paternity is significantly absent in the novel and pushes the argument of the non-synchronic nature of the film farther as we see in it the fuelling of 'older' anxieties by the more 'modern' impulses of women's emancipation and sexual liberation, which have to be contained in the interests of the modern conjugal family and the transfer of paternal property to 'legitimate' children. It has been fairly proven that leftist development initiatives and social reforms have in effect augmented female seclusion in the state. Gender difference was at the very heart of modern caste identities in Kerala, a legacy of the early-twentieth-century social reform movements which projected patrifocal marriage as the natural and pre-eminent site of material relations in the private realm (Eapen and Kodoth, 2003). Conjugality as the predominant marker of a woman's identity is fraught with change from Chakki to Karuthamma as also from novel to film, as a further and further shrinking of the private space of women. This shift from the 1950s to the 1960s in Kerala's social fabric could probably be accounted for by the further transitions in the structure of the family from a broad-based production unit to an intensely private domestic unit primarily of consumption and reproduction (Kodoth 2005).

The novel can also be read as a Nehruvian national allegory where State 'Planning' and economy had to ideally take stock of and preserve spiritual traditions embedded in the more private spheres of social life. It also embodies the rise of new economic individualism and private enterprise in a post-independence India which are at odds with the older ideals of democratic socialism with its 'central' planning, solidarity economy and social cohesion. Thus the private libidinal dynamics of Pareekutty, Karuthamma, Chembankunju and Palani might 'necessarily project a political dimension in the form of national allegory' where 'the story of the private individual destiny is always an allegory of the embattled situation of the public third world culture and society' (Jameson 69). Such a reading would also pose numerous questions as far as the translations of *Chemmeen* are concerned, critiquing the notion of an unproblematic accessing of the 'national', always already complicated by caste, gender and class as also their regional ramifications. Thus one cannot read either novel or its adaptation without taking into consideration the national and historic contexts, the linguistic constitution of the regional and the necessities of imagining that sub-national identity, the anxieties over what was the nascent state of Kerala, the crisis of agrarian and indigenous modes of livelihood facing the modernization project of the nation, the persistence of feudal and neo-colonial forces in a postcolonial history, as also the dichotomization of the private and public and the processes of gendering the nation, all begging for more nuanced political readings instead of overly psychological ones.

It is popular history parading as populist myth that one encounters in both novel and film. Yet from all the other elements in the novel it is the myth and the mystification of women through this mythogenesis that is at the core of the filmic adaptation, offering a heady cocktail of visual and narrative pleasure combining the popular, the mythical and the musical in a mise-en-scène that is heavily coded and throbbing with severely repressed passions, and in the last run hybridizing these with the market and mass culture. That the first Sahitya Akademy Award for Malayalam novel and the first National Award for Malayalam cinema came at the cost of re-presenting many Karuthammas of Kerala as compromised signs in the gendered commodified systems of exchange that popular 'canonical' literature and popular cinema often become, gives us important clues to reading the popular.

Novels

Thyagathinu Prathiphalam	1934
Pathitha Pankajam	1935
Susheelan	1938
Vilpanakari	1941
Paramardhangal	1945
Thalayodu	1947
Tottiyude Makan	1947
Randidangazhi	1949
Thendi Vargam	1950
Avante Smaranakal	1955
Chemmeen	1956
Verilla Katha	1956
Ousephinte Makkal	1959
Anchu Pennungal	1961
Jeevitham Sundaramanu Pakshe	1961
Enippadikal	1964
Dharmaneethiyo? Alla: Jeevitham	1965
Pappyammayum Makkalum	1965
Mamsathinte Villi	1966
Akasham	1967
Anubhavangal Palichakal	1967
Chukku	1967
Nellum Thengayum	1969
Pennu	1969
Vyakulamathavu	1969
Nurayum Pathayum	1970
Pennayi Piranal	1970

Short Stories

Oru Kuttanadan Kadha	1992
Jeevithathinte Oru Edu	1993
Katha	2000
Vellapokavum Mattukpradhana Kadhakalum	2003
Thakazhiyude Pranaya Kadhakal	2004

Auto-biography/Memoirs

Ente Vakkeel Jeevitham	1961
Ente Balyakalakadha	1967
Kure Kadhapatrangal	1980
Ormayude Theerangalil	1985

Other Works

Thottila (Drama)	1946
Kaalpadukal	–
Indulekha	1962
American Thirasheela	1966
Ente Ullile Kadal	2000

Accha, Achan: Father

Ammachi, Amma: Mother

Arayan: a caste among fishermen

Chakara: The big catch; occurrence of mud-banks and appearance of plenty of fish for a short period at some places along the Kerala coast during the monsoon.

Chedathi: sister, but used as a term to denote respect to an older person (woman)

Chettan/Chetta: brother, but used as a term to denote respect to an older person (man)

Ichechi, Chechi: elder sister

Kambavala: strong net

Kasavu/Zari: fine threads of gold or silver used in embroidery

Kuruchi: a kind of sea fish

Mannarshala Ayilyam: the main festival conducted in Mannarasala Sree Nagaraja Temple, located at Mannarasala in Alappuzha District. The festival is celebrated on the Ayilyam asterism, which comes in the Malayalam month of Kanni (September/October). During the festival days thousands of people assemble at the temple to worship and propitiate the serpent gods.

Marakkan: a caste among fishermen

Muhurtham: auspicious time

Mukkavan: a caste among fishermen

Mundu/ Mul mul mundu: a sarong made of white cotton cloth

Neriyathu: cloth with fine (thin) texture

Para: a large measure especially for measuring paddy (according to the ancient scale of measuring prevalent in Kerala, 4 Uzhakkus equal 1 Nazhi, 4 Nazhis equal 1 Itangazhi and 10 Itangazhis equal 1 Para). The size of paddy holdings were based on how many such measures of seed could be sown in those fields.

Podava: wedding cloth or saree

Pottey: a Brahmin caste name

Pottu: a decorative mark on the forehead

Theeyal: a kind of coconut-based vegetable curry with tamarind

Uruli: Shallow vessel made of bell-metal

Valakkaran: a caste among fishermen

Vaapa: father (term used by Malabar Muslims)